THE Flight OF THE CROW

A NISEI IN WWII AND BEYOND

CHRISTINE SUSUMI

BLUE FORGE PRESS

Port Orchard ✪ Washington

Blue Forge Press is the print division of the volunteer-run, federal 501(c)3 nonprofit company, Blue Forge Group, founded in 1989 and dedicated to bringing light to the shadows and voice to the silence. We strive to empower storytellers across all walks of life with our four divisions: Blue Forge Press, Blue Forge Films, Blue Forge Gaming, and Blue Forge Records. Find out more at www.BlueForgeGroup.org

Blue Forge Press
7419 Ebbert Drive Southeast
Port Orchard, Washington 98367
blueforgepress@gmail.com
360-550-2071 ph.txt

For my parents

"History doesn't repeat itself,
but it does rhyme."

—Mark Twain

ACKNOWLEDGMENTS

My heartfelt thanks to Bob Schumacher and the Silverdale Writers Group, which include Pat Ryan, Joy and Jake DeVore, Donna Hamilton, David Snapper, Becky Bauer, Kerry Stevens, Aiona Hartley, and Bryce Easton. Without their guidance and encouragement, I could never have written this novel.

Also, my deep gratitude to Mrs. Joanne Turpin, Bill Smith, Donna Kelleher, Kristin Von Kriesler, Ken Mochizuki, and Katherine Lindsey for their editorial help.

Thank you to Stuart Hirai for his generous help on the accuracy of the history of the 442nd and their battles.

Thank you to my cousin, Monique Broux, for taking me on walking tours of the pertinent sites in Écueillé as well as introducing me to Mr. Luke Morin. He spent hours sharing his experiences up to and around the battle of Écueillé which he survived, but where his mother was killed. He gave me references for books which helped my research on the local Resistance and Maquis.

Thank you to Fernande's son, Guy Laroche, for taking me to the locations of the Tivoli Bar, my mother's apartment, and the tobacco factory, as well as to visit La Martinerie.

I'm very grateful to Blue Forge Press for their support and guidance in publishing my novel.

Eternal thanks to my family and friends for their faith and inspiration even when I had lost both.

And thank you to my husband, Jay, for his continual support over the years.

the Flight

of the Crow

A NISEI IN WWII AND BEYOND

CHRISTINE SUSUMI

1

CHATEAUROUX, FRANCE
1951

December 7th was the day Art's life unraveled. Little had gone according to his youthful dreams since Roosevelt's famous "a date-that-lives-in-infamy" speech. The atrocities of that one fateful day in Pearl Harbor had affected him like a bomb hitting its target. Art was Japanese American.

So much had changed since that day. Starting from the shame of false accusations to being corralled into camps. He volunteered to fight in WWII, hoping it would prove his loyalty to the U.S. but the racism continued. Since the end of the war, he had continued searching to find himself, to no avail. Now, ten years later, he was back in France. How would he find his rightful place in life, when everything he knew and loved was in Seattle?

He hesitated before pulling open the door to the Tivoli bar, wondering if tonight would be any different. In central France, there was little entertainment to fill the nights. So he chose another night, dancing with clumsy drunk women instead of playing cards with the other soldiers on base. Maybe good fortune would shine on him and he'd meet someone of interest.

Art gave the creaky door a good tug and paused,

letting his eyes grow accustomed to the dimly lit dance hall. A film of smoke floated through the room, carrying lingering odors of cheap perfume and sweat. It was one of the few places in town to dance and how he loved to dance. There was even a live band at the far end of the room, or rather one man playing the accordion. The portly musician jostled a harmonica around his neck while using his foot to beat a drum set in front of him. His stout body tucked beneath his gear, with a round belly peeking out that jiggled with each drum beat. Somehow he delivered a decent array of waltzes and foxtrots.

"Welcome, Art. It's good to see you. How are you?" the owner of the bar asked, grasping him to plant a kiss on each cheek.

Being American, it was awkward the first time a man had embraced him. But the camaraderie it formed was refreshing, and he found himself often initiating the greetings.

"Doing well and you?" Art replied in stilted French.

A warm sensation filled him from the acceptance by the French people, compared to the treatment by many Americans. Knowing his race or appearance seemed to go unnoticed here was refreshing. Somehow, he fit in. This might explain why many American black artists brought their talents to France, like Josephine Baker. Her unusual dance style wasn't to his taste, but her character was unsurpassed as she rose from poverty in St. Louis to become an important figure in the French Resistance. It was disheartening to witness America; the land founded on welcoming all, be such an unwelcoming place for some.

The one-man band sounded good to him, though Art wasn't very picky. He never had the luxury of dancing to the popular big bands in the United States.

Wooden tables with mismatched chairs were

scattered around the room's periphery. Scanning a group gathered around a makeshift bar, his eyes landed on a blonde. Her hair tumbled around her face in soft curls, her thin lips pursed together. Her eyes peered in his direction, but he wasn't sure if there was contempt or interest in them. He walked to the bar, ordered a whiskey, then found an empty table and lit a cigarette. He wondered if he should venture over and ask the blonde to dance.

He sat for a spell, lonely in a sea of inebriated women and soldiers. A few attractive women looking a bit too eager, draped across American soldiers, pressing legs and bosoms on the receptive men. It was hard not to blame them, as the war had been devastating to the French. The Nazis had raped and pillaged their land, killed citizens for speaking out or looking defiant, and provided ration cards with no food to buy. The people had suffered through so many years of misery. There still wasn't much available in the country. The invaders left behind roads, fields, and buildings in ruin and the recovery process was slow. Now the French had the chance to relax, drop their defenses and let it all hang out, in a manner of speaking. But he kept being drawn back to the blonde. There she stood, in a slim fitting skirt and a blouse buttoned almost to her chin. What harm would it do to just ask her for a dance?

The music started back up. This was his cue. He extinguished his cigarette and straightened his shoulders to make his 5'4" appear taller. Crossing between tables, he thwarted a redhead's advances to stand in front of the blonde.

"*Voulez-vous danser avec moi?*" Art asked, extending his hand, glad to find he was a few inches taller than she was. Her eyes sparkled green, reminiscent of raindrops glistening in the Pacific Northwest forests back home.

Could she understand his heavy accent? Even if not,

his intention seemed clear. With a hint of a smile, she nodded her head.

The band had started a foxtrot, one of his favorites. He lifted her right hand and swept his other hand around her petite waist. There was an instant connection as they moved across the floor, her feet following his as if they had danced together many times. With only a gentle touch on her back, she changed with the desired response. Her body knew when to hesitate, turn, or dip, as if she was reading his mind. Their bodies melded to one. The vibrations from the accordion moved through her body into his own. He pulled her closer, not wanting to lose the sensation. Was she feeling the connection as well? He'd never had a dance partner with such similar sensibilities.

His thoughts flashed back to the Minidoka incarceration camp, where he'd had quite a selection of dance partners, especially his two favorites, Mitzi and Butch. The dusty wood floors of the camp cafeteria weren't much different from the old floors in this bar. Similar uneven boards caught their steps in the same way. Since everyone in the camps had taken lessons together, they danced identically. Couples swept across the room, turning and dipping in perfect harmony, never bumping into one another. Not the same here—with every few turns, murmurs of, "*Excusez-moi,*" were uttered. Minidoka was long ago and far away. He wondered what Mitzi and Butch were doing now and what they would think of his new blonde dance partner. Not much, he suspected, but it wasn't like there were any Japanese women in these parts. In fact, he wasn't sure there were any Orientals at all.

Concentrating on his dance partner, he wondered the best way to keep her around. If he left her side, she might get snatched up, seeing she was an excellent dancer. His heart was racing more than the dancing could explain. Each time he brought his face close to her neck, he picked up the sweet aromas of jasmine. Or was it rose? It sent a warm rush through him.

"Would you like to go outside for some fresh air?" Art asked after the "band" had placed down his accordion for a break. He pointed to the door and pulled his collar away from his neck.

She agreed. "*Oui, merci.*"

Once outside, he continued the conversation with his amateur French.

"*Je m'appelle Art, et vous?*" *My name is Art, and you?*

"*Venez-vous ici beaucoup?*" *Do you come here often? Geez, did that sound stupid.*

"*Voulez-vous une cigarette?*" *Would you like a cigarette?*

At least that's what he hoped he had said. He tried using his hands, a habit he had picked up when speaking with Italian locals during the war. But he had studied French. Why wasn't it easier? He needed to learn more and remembered a sign posted at the Air Force base advertising French lessons. He would call tomorrow. Then he could impress her the next time, but would there be a next time? She said she came here on occasion. Should he kiss her? No, he didn't want more than a dance partner. After all, his assignment here was for a limited time. Soon enough, he would return to Seattle, to his Japanese community, where he belonged. Though something was alluring and different about her. Thoughts were flying through his head, like a nervous sparrow, jumping from tree branch to branch. He didn't know what it was, but hoped something would come from this chance meeting with his new blonde dance partner.

2

The tin bounced down the sidewalk into the adjacent wooded area. Art never passed up a good game of 'kick the can.' Crunching over some maple leaves, he circled the towering Douglas tree to retrieve the tin. Inhaling the fresh scent of fir, he nodded at the thick ridges of bark sticking out of the tree trunk. It was as if a friendly hand was being extended. He grabbed hold of it.

"Hello Mr. Douglas Fir, how do you do?"

From above, a resident squirrel chattered an aggressive scolding, his tail flicking to and fro, warning the unwelcome intruder.

"Don't worry, I won't get into your nut stash," Art said, smiling at the perturbed resident. Nothing restored his soul like walking among the trees and its fauna.

His West Seattle neighborhood had a continental feel. There was a mix of Swedes, Norwegians, Greeks, and Yugoslavs, plus a sprinkling of Japanese living in brick and clapboard homes. Most Japanese lived closer to downtown in Japantown, along 12th and South Main. But his family had settled at the base of West Seattle on Spokane Street, in an area called Youngstown. Their shop, Highway Florists, also served as their home. It was owned by Bethlehem Steel, whose factory loomed above the shop. The steel company transported coal to the waterfront docks on tracks that ran over the small wood-framed building. Each time they transported their cargo over, it caused their shop and home to tremble. When the earthquake of 1939 occurred, the family assumed at first that it was a coal delivery.

Art was in his final year at West Seattle High School, doing his best to fit in with the other students. Sure, he had been called "slanty eyes" or "Chinaman" but over the years he learned to avoid such hateful or judgmental people. Instead of being conscientious about his looks, he focused on embracing the differences between everyone. Each person had something unique to offer to their community. By standing proud, he hoped to convince others of the same.

The week had finished on a high note. His classes were going better than ever. The math, he was having a hard time grasping, had become easier, just as his father had said.

"Perseverance, my son. Keep working and a light will switch on in your head, then everything will fall into place."

He'd had his doubts, but once again, his father was right. After months of laborious hours pondering over the math, the light did come on, illuminating the solutions. He wondered how his father could know such things, not having had any formal schooling in Japan.

Art's hours dedicated to gymnastics were paying off as well, mastering his tumbling routine. Flipping backward was scary at first, wondering if his hands could or would land midway to catapult him back to standing. Again, his father helped him develop the courage to do the back spring.

"Trust in yourself. You may miss a few times, but your body will develop memory and you'll succeed."

They practiced on the grassy area next to their home.

His father's outstretched arm under his back gave him the security and support he needed until his hands found solid ground.

He was proud of his routine, combining a backhand spring followed by a twist, then a backward somersault finished by a round off. He had even perfected an aerial cartwheel today. His coach said their team might make the state championship.

Art fantasized how impressed Sharon would be, who sat in the bleachers, cheering the team during practices. She never missed a competition and seemed to pay particular attention to his performances. Maybe it was his imagination, but his teammates noticed as well.

"She's sweet on you, Art. She can't take her eyes off of you."

He wasn't used to that kind of attention. Few girls looked his way as Sharon did. Short in stature, and sporting wire-rimmed glasses, he didn't fit the image of the athlete that attracted many girls. His stocky physique was muscular enough, but he envied how whirls of hair peeked out from his teammates' tank tops. Like Cary Grant and Burt Lancaster—they had hair on *their* chests. If he could find a nice Japanese girl, he bet she would prefer his smooth legs and torso. That would please his parents as well. It went unspoken, but was clear that they preferred he stayed within the race.

When Sharon smiled his way, her blue eyes twinkled like stars in the early morning sky and her cocoa brown hair bounced in perfect curls on her shoulders. They sat together daily in homeroom. Now he needed to collect his courage and ask to carry her books home. He would do that Monday. Everything was going great. His senior year at West Seattle High couldn't be more perfect.

December 7, 1941, started like any other Sunday. Tea

was brewing, and the radio was playing Tommy Dorsey's "All the Things You Are." Art's mother sat on a three-legged stool, trimming and arranging the bundles of flowers she would sell at the Pike Place Market.

She picked various flowers from small buckets containing roses, carnations, and baby's breath. Then she'd place white pine branches throughout before wrapping the bouquet in paper. Stepping back, she might shake her head, rearrange the branches and add a few sprigs of baby's breath. When she was content, she'd place the wrapped arrangement carefully in a cardboard box and start on the next one. The sale of these flowers supplemented the small income from the grocery his father tended. In the shadows, he could make out his father stocking items on the store shelves. It wasn't much–tobacco, sugar, flour, rice, candy–but they had loyal customers. The family's cramped yet comfortable quarters behind the tiny storefront were the only home he'd ever known.

Similar versions of Sunday mornings played out across the country in many American homes. The homes of immigrants, those seeking a better life and a new chance in America. Where all people are created equal with unalienable rights, including life, liberty, and the pursuit of happiness. His father had been carving out a niche and future for his family over the past thirty years, his faith unwavering in this American pledge.

When Commodore Matthew C. Perry entered the Bay of Yedo in 1854, not only did he open Japan to American commerce but also to Japanese immigration, especially after the Chinese Exclusion Act in 1882.

Art's father, Itaro, had immigrated in late 1914, boarding a ship in Yokohama and never looking back. He found his wife, Yuzo, as a picture bride and she joined him in

1921. After many years of working odd jobs, they saved enough money to open a small grocery in West Seattle. The Immigration Act of 1924 restricted any further Asian immigration into the U.S. and banned *Issei* from becoming U.S. citizens, owning land, or obtaining business licenses. This didn't dissuade him from having confidence in his newfound country.

"Honesty and hard work will give you recognition as an upstanding member of society," he declared. "Then you'll reap the benefits available in this great country."

His father also held tight to his faith in Buddha, which gave him a sense of home and grounded him in an otherwise foreign land.

Art was the eldest, the firstborn son. His sister Lillian came two years after him. It was another seven years before his sister Grace arrived. Art called her *Chibi*, meaning Little One in Japanese. He felt especially protective of her and a little jealous. Since Grace was the youngest, his parents indulged her. They expected Art and Lillian to be serious and perform at the top in everything, while they gave Chibi more freedom. If she talked out of turn, Art's father would smile and allow her to continue. If Art ever tried that, he would get a swift eagle-eye glance, reminding him he was speaking without being asked. Art understood though, since his heart melted when she smiled, and it was hard not to laugh at one of her mischievous expressions.

An announcer's voice interrupted the music. Art's mother stopped working and cast a puzzled look his way, as her English was poor. When she saw his expression, she dropped her flowers and joined him at the radio.

"Father, come listen, he says Japan has bombed us, somewhere called Hawaii?"

"Hawaii? That's a U.S. territory in the Pacific," his

father rushed into the room, stumbling over the footstool. "Japan has already invaded Korea, Taiwan, the Philippines—my God, where are they going to stop?"

They stood around the radio and stared at it in dismay. Dread filled the room.

"The White House announces Japan has made war on the United States without declaring it. Warplanes have attacked the great Pearl Harbor Naval base on the island of O'ahu in the Hawaiian Islands," the announcer said.

For the rest of the day, Art's mind was numb. He was as American as the next guy and no one aligned him with Japan. Or did they? He understood and spoke enough Japanese to communicate with his parents, but English was his first language. It was the one he used in school and with his friends. His parent's culture brought from their homeland was pervasive. The lunches his mother packed embarrassed him. He hid the rice balls and fish from the other students. His face was different, his glasses were thicker, and he was shorter than the average Joe. Otherwise, he fit in with his schoolmates, even if he was quieter. Did they think of him as Japanese or American? He didn't think he stood out much.

At dinner, his father barely touched his food, fumbling with his napkin, folding it up, then unfolding it, over and over.

"We must be careful," his father said. "Japan has made a grave error in attacking the United States and I worry we'll suffer the consequences."

Art was sure his father had no reason for concern. They were living in the U.S. and had no ties to Japan. Besides, Art and his sisters were American citizens, having been born here. His father got up from the table, leaving his napkin carefully folded in the shape of a crane. He walked into the living room and began leafing through his traditional Japanese record collection. Art had never seen him look so confused and despondent.

Glancing up at the poster across from their kitchen table, Art read the creed of the Japanese American Citizens League.

"This is how I feel about the United States, which has given us so many opportunities," his father had said with pride as he nailed it to the wall, just a few months ago.

The JACL was founded in 1929 and its mission was to protect the civil and human rights of Japanese Americans and to help preserve their heritage. This seemed like the perfect time for them to speak up. Art scanned the poster and uncertainty crept over him.

I am proud that I am an American citizen of Japanese ancestry, for my very background makes me appreciate more fully the wonderful advantages of this Nation. I believe in her institutions, ideals, and traditions... she has permitted me to be a free man equal to every other man.

Art stared at the words, would he be considered equal to every other man? He read on.

Although some individuals may discriminate against me, I shall never become bitter or lose faith. I pledge myself to do honor to her at all times and in all places; to support her constitution; to obey her laws; to respect her flag; to defend her against all enemies, foreign or domestic; to actively assume my duties and obligations as a citizen, cheerfully and without any reservations whatsoever, in the hope that I may become a better American in a greater America.

A fortitude filled him. Yes, he had faith in this great nation. It wouldn't let him down.

By 7:00 pm that evening, darkness had fallen, and the radio station, KIRO, announced that the states along the west coast had to enforce a blackout.

"All lights must be out," the newscaster said. "What if

those *Japs* are heading back? Seattle would be their next target. Don't forget what the Germans did to London during the Blitz."

The thought of Seattle being attacked sent a chill up Art's spine. Dwelling on what that could mean, he didn't hear his father.

"Son, are you alright? I need help adding extra cover to our windows. Our drapes are too thin and light can pass through," he said. "Cars can't use their headlights and even cigarettes can't be lit outdoors."

This added to the toll weighing on Art, but his father stressed the importance of following rules given by the government. The golden rule in their home was that, above all, they should never question authority. The curfew would start at 11:00 pm and implementation of blackouts was immediate. Likewise, civilian radio stations went off the air, since enemy aircraft could use radio waves to locate cities. This left many people confused when radios went silent on the night of December 7.

Art helped his father with the windows, taping up dark butcher paper his mother used in her flower arrangements. As the night approached, the house fell silent. He wasn't sure why, but everyone whispered as if it would keep their voices locked in the house with the lights. His father called for the family to gather around the table. "I've heard they are setting up volunteers to watch the Japanese in the LA and San Francisco Japantowns. There's concern there may be spies or saboteurs waiting to take action."

"Father, what if people become afraid of us? What if we can't live our lives as usual?" Art's voice rose in pitch. "How can this be happening?"

"*Shikata ga nai,*" his father said. Some things can't be helped.

Art had heard this phrase enough times that it had become a part of him. He hung his head, the phrase not bringing much solace.

That evening, Art's mother prepared the bath. They had a *furo* or traditional Japanese bath in the back of the home. She filled the metal tub with water before starting the fire beneath.

"It will calm everyone to bathe, *ne?*" his mother said.

Art's father first washed himself, the act of *kakeyu*, before sinking into the hot water with a deep sigh. Art's mother joined him and they took turns rubbing each other's backs. Once they finished, it was Art's turn. The tension of the day floated away with each ripple passing across the water. It wasn't long before his sisters started nagging.

"That's long enough. Mama, make him get out," Lillian said.

"Yeah, I always go last," Chibi added. "That's not fair."

"Chibi, you'll learn soon enough that life isn't fair," her father said.

Art feared she would learn the lesson too soon in her young life.

The next day, Art entered his first classroom, thankful no one seemed to pay much attention to him. He glanced over at Sharon, who had moved to a different table. It looked as if she didn't want to sit with him any longer. What a fool he'd been to think something special existed between them. He blinked hard to hold back the wall of water building behind his eyes. Sitting in his usual place, he slumped down in his chair, wishing he looked different than he did. Of course, the only topic of the day was the bombing of Pearl Harbor.

"As you know by now, Japan attacked Hawaii yesterday. It was just a matter of time after the U.S. sanctions, which only aggravated them. Japan signed the tripartite pact last year with Germany and Italy. Now it seems they want to take on the world," the teacher said.

Art sank further, wishing to slide right off and slink out the door. *Why did I come today? I don't have any reason, but I can't help feeling like I'm to blame.*

He was sitting next to his buddy, Tom, who was also Japanese American.

"Is your dad still at home?" Tom asked, his face pale and his eyes ringed with red.

"Yeah, why do you ask?"

"Well, two tall white men came to our house yesterday afternoon and took my dad away. We don't know where he is or when he'll be back. My mom's terrified. I was worried about leaving her home alone today. We don't understand, my dad just tends to his little radio repair business."

Dread crept over Art. What if those men go to their house while he's at school? His mother wouldn't know what to do.

He didn't learn until much later that in the early 1930s, after Japan invaded China and Korea, federal agents began surveillance of Japanese American communities. In conclusion, they decided the community posed little threat to the U.S. They had made a list of Japanese who were suspect— Japanese language teachers, judo instructors, and priests at Buddhist temples. These "detention" lists, called the ABC lists, provided names for the local authorities to arrest if the need arose.

Art was sure everyone's eyes were on him while the teacher continued discussing the attack. Warmth crept over his face and the back of his neck and his palms began to sweat, followed by a wave of nausea. Did his classmates think he was guilty?

After the school bell, he went straight home without hanging around the gym. All his hopes to walk Sharon home vanished. Besides, she wouldn't even look his way. This was so unfair. Why did Japan do such a stupid thing? And why had Sharon turned on him?

"No, I'm an American. Just because I'm Japanese, it shouldn't change anything," he muttered as he hurried home.

When he entered the back room, his mother was cradling a wailing Chibi. A couple of boys had thrown rocks at her.

"'Go back to Japan!' one of them yelled at me. They called out *Jap*, what's that? And why would I go to Japan? I don't even know where it is! Why do they want me to leave my friends and my home?" Her little face was red, her eyes puffy from crying.

Art's heart ached for his little sister, not able to protect her since even he didn't understand what was happening. He saw his dad behind the house, breaking those vinyl records he'd been sorting through the night before, tears streaming down his face.

"Father, why would you do such a thing? You love those records."

"These are traditional Japanese Enka records. I love listening to the strings and bamboo flutes, but I must destroy them. We can't have anything to aggravate the officials. No ties to Japan."

His father's face was drawn and blanched. His usual sparkling eyes were dark, and his slightly rounded cheeks, deflated. He had never looked so somber.

"President Roosevelt has declared war on Japan."

3

CENTRAL FRANCE
1940

It was June 12th. France's surrender to the Germans had sent shock waves through the country. Yvette's parents hunched over their little radio tuned to the banned BBC station listening to General de Gaulle. Yvette strained to hear what he had to say.

"The French Government, after requesting the armistice, has now full knowledge of the conditions dictated by the enemy. As a result, the French Army, Naval and Air Forces will be completely discharged, our weapons laid down, the French territory occupied and the French Government under the control of Germany and Italy.

One can say that this armistice will not only result in capitulation but also in slavery.

However, a large number of French people do not accept the capitulation or the enslavement for reasons that are called honor, common sense and the higher interest of the Nation.

I am talking about honor! Indeed, France is committed to not laying down its weapons unless its allies agree to do so. As long as its allies continue fighting, our government does not have the right to capitulate. The Polish Government, the

Norwegian Government, the Belgian Government, the Dutch Government, as well as the Government of Luxembourg, although evicted from their own countries, have understood their duty.

It is absurd to consider the struggle as lost. I call upon all Frenchmen who want to remain free to listen to my voice and follow me. I, General de Gaulle, am undertaking this national task here in England. Whatever happens, the flame of French resistance must not and shall not die."

"You see, we must not give up," Yvette's father, Maurice said, hammering his fist on the kitchen table.

Yvette remained crouched on the stone steps of the stairway, eavesdropping on her parents, trying to comprehend the gravity of the situation. She was familiar with the stories of the last war and had seen its toll on her parents' generation. She was fourteen and mature for her years, having to carry her weight in chores and responsibilities. Each of the family's five children had a set of daily tasks. Hers were caring for the animals where her heart lay. She loved milking the cow and goats early in the morning, then watching them head out to the pasture. The goats always ran, head butting each other along the way while the cow, Clara, would plod out to the nearest green spot of grass. Her last task was to brush down Belle, their plow horse, whose gentle demeanor was as immense as her size.

Yvette's heart overflowed with the excitement of a bright future. Would she find a boyfriend, marry, travel to a larger town, maybe even see Paris? She often wondered what lay outside of her tiny village of Écueillé.

Listening to her parents whispering about the recent German invasion of their country alarmed her. Would she ever realize her dreams? France had fallen to the Germans with an ease that surprised everyone. In six short weeks, the German blitzkrieg defeated France to add yet another country to their conquest. After the last war, the French had reinforced the Maginot Line with additional fortifications to repel any further German invasions. The massive concrete wall ran along their fragile eastern border from the impregnable (or so they thought) Ardennes forest to Switzerland. Yet the Germans bypassed it altogether, storming directly through the Ardennes and taking the nation by surprise.

The Germans had penetrated the massive Ardennes forest with their Luftwaffe and Panzer tanks, overwhelming France then continuing northwest toward Calais. By May 24th, they had cornered the British forces against the sea at Dunkirk. The British had little choice but to evacuate back to England. Then the Reich did the unimaginable and took Paris on June 10. On June 14th, the swastika replaced the *tricolor* on the Hotel de Ville. France was left broken and distraught.

The surrender of France took little effort. Turmoil existed in their government, the Third Republic. General Marshal Pétain, the famous hero of the Great War, swiftly commanded leadership of France and agreed to an armistice with Germany.

"France has been conquered, soon to be followed by Britain," Pétain said. "Our only sensible course is an armistice. We don't want to end up like Poland, under military rule. Instead, we can preserve our government and live peacefully under the New European Order of the German Reich."

The weary populace fell in line, believing lives would be spared and another war avoided.

When France signed the surrender documents, Yvette's father broke down in anguish.

"How did this happen? Our men put up a tremendous fight, but the military made strategic errors not preparing defenses in the Ardennes. No, we must regroup and continue this fight. Giving up is too dangerous for our country."

"Please keep your voice down," Yvette's mother, Juliette, replied in a hushed voice. "The Germans have a tremendous force this time, and we lost so much from the last war. Why can't we just be at peace?" Seated at the kitchen table, she dropped her head in her hands.

"We can't be at peace as long as *they're* here. Remember what General de Gaulle said, after what that coward Pétain did." her father's face was flushed red and his large farm hands balled into tight fists. "We must continue to fight."

So tonight Yvette listened from the safety of the stairwell, trying to comprehend the gravity of the situation.

"Pétain shouldn't have the right to hand our country over to those *Boche* Nazis," her father said.

"Germany could succeed this time," her mother surmised. "And by joining them, we'll have a more secure position in the future. Maybe it will save lives."

"Don't even think such a thing. Germany will never win this war. Maybe this battle, but never this war. Now they've invaded all four corners of our country, ruling it with a cruel hand. This so-called unoccupied area's governed by Pétain in Vichy and they may be worse than the Germans, who knows? He's changed our motto from *Liberté, égalité, fraternité* (Freedom, equality, fraternity) to *Travail, famille, patrie* (Work, family, country). They're undermining our democracy with their fascist ideals," Yvette's father spat out the words.

The French capital had moved from Paris to Vichy, only about 140 miles to the southeast of Écueillé, but it might as well have been on another planet. Yvette had never traveled outside of her tiny village, except in her dreams.

"Pétain has become a dictator," thundered her father.

"This government is a farce. Pétain might have helped defeat the Germans in the last war, but now he's in bed with the Nazis. We can't trust any information coming out of this new government. Everything's controlled by the Nazis. We need to listen to General de Gaulle. Don't forget, he's also a war hero."

The children, unnoticed, had worked their way into the kitchen. Yvette moved to the side as they snuck behind their parents: first her oldest sister, Reneé, then Madeleine, the next oldest, leading her younger sister Mauricette and little Robert by the hand. Each crept into a chair around the table, somber expressions on their faces.

"Please Papa, don't say these things in front of the children," Yvette's mother pleaded. "What if they repeat these words at school or to their friends?"

"They must understand what's happening. Look at me, children. You must never, I repeat, never, share any of these anti-Nazi ideas with anyone." Maurice glared at them, causing each to fall back against their chairs. They nodded in unison, too frightened to cry or even utter a word.

How this De Gaulle was going to make a difference perplexed Yvette, but the look of determination in her father's steel-gray eyes inspired her.

"Meanwhile, these Nazis are taking our resources," her father said. "And they've deported over one and a half million of our soldiers to Germany. We're lucky to be in the countryside with a few animals and a garden. Those in the cities are starving."

"What if the Nazis work their way down here?" asked her mother, pacing the room. "How will we protect ourselves and our children? We're vulnerable out here."

"More reason to rally our men for defense, we must collect weapons."

The occupation started cordially with German soldiers

cooing over French babies in strollers and giving their seats to women on the subway and buses. Then, as the occupation progressed, food, materials, and people began to disappear while the Nazis filled themselves at the restaurants. Fascists were increasing in Italy under Mussolini, Spain under Franco, and the Nazis—right here in France spreading the notion of the supremacy of the Aryan race, in one all-powerful leader. It was an authoritative and dictatorial form of government the French loathed.

Thousands started heading south, from as far as Belgium and Holland, attempting to evade Nazi persecution. By the time they made it as far as Écueillé, the lines of people had thinned to the most hardy. They passed through her village with vacant stares from sunken, dark-ringed eyes, their gaunt bodies, and tattered clothes telling the tales of the journey. They were too weak even to ask for food or help, continuing on, perhaps in hopes a relative further south would welcome them. Yvette and her family set out bread and water for the passersby that stopped on their trek. A few with savings stayed in the Hotel de Ville in the center of Écueillé.

They came with accounts of life in Paris. There was little to no food. Jews were made to wear yellow stars, and had lost their businesses, jobs, and their pride. Then the worst began to happen, something unimaginable. The Nazis had lists. Lists given to them by fellow Frenchman. Lists with names of those who had spoken against the Nazis, who were helping or even suspected of helping Jews. French turning in their own neighbors. Homosexuals, Jehovah's Witnesses, Freemasons—types of people Yvette hadn't heard of. But the longest list was of Jews. At first, it was only the foreign-born, but soon it included French citizens and their children. Vans would screech up to residences and heavy, black-booted soldiers would storm into homes and apartments. And it was happening in Écueillé, the jealous glance if you had eggs or a piece of meat, whispers behind your back that your father was baking bread using white wheat and not the required bran. The local police were collecting names as well.

So the lines of people heading south continued in search of a safe place. Where was it safe, and for how long?

Yvette's father was aware of the rumors his townspeople were spreading.

"We must be very careful not to trust anyone. The Nazis are aware of unrest here. After all, Britain hasn't fallen like France, so questions are spreading. Why did we agree to this arrangement that's only benefiting the Germans? Day-to-day survival's becoming more difficult. The ration cards only cover meager amounts of sugar, lard, and grains. We're going to fight and we're going to win."

"In fact, more people are joining the fight. Germany invaded the Soviet Union after having taken Czechoslovakia, Poland, Denmark, Norway, Belgium, Holland, and Luxembourg. Britain is holding strong but for how long?" Yvette's father thrust his fingers up as he counted off the countries. "Resistance groups are sprouting up in corner bars from Paris to the tiniest villages, even Écueillé. Flyers are being distributed with genuine news, not this false propaganda being printed by the Vichy and Nazis."

A few weeks later, a news flash came in a flyer from a distant Resistance group. Yvette's father flew into the kitchen, waving the paper in his hand.

"I got this at the café. Let me tell you what our friendly occupiers did in Paris. They executed a young man, a twenty-eight year old engineer, because his friend bumped into a Nazi soldier. His friend had a few words with the soldier, but they killed his companion, Jacques Bonsergent. He was just a bystander to someone who had bumped into a Nazi. So much for these 'correct' occupiers. There's a young resister named Jean Moulin who stood up to the Nazis, refusing to collaborate with them. Thrown into prison and tortured, he somehow escaped and made his way to London to join the Free French under General De Gaulle. This fight has just begun," her father declared.

"I don't want any of you speaking of this. This isn't a game, far from it—they're taking people away for the smallest of offenses. Some people are drawing the symbol 'V' for Victory and the BBC starts its reports with 'Ratata-taa', the Morse code for V, which is also the opening to Beethoven's Fifth Symphony. This will show the Nazis there're more of us than they can imagine," he concluded.

Yvette's head reeled as her father's defiant acts against the Nazis battled against her mother's common sense within her. The dilemma was tearing her apart as she tried to choose between her parent's beliefs. She knew her mother's approach to avoid conflict would be the easiest way to sit out this situation. But her father's ideas inspired and caused her heart to soar believing they could beat these invaders. Confused, she went out to bring the animals in from the pasture. Brushing down Belle, she explained the situation to the stoic animal. This would help straighten out her thoughts.

"Mother's cautionary approach makes sense. Living under German rule could save lives and may not be that bad, right?"

Belle turned her head and gave Yvette a firm nudge with her muzzle.

"What? So you think father's right? His ideas do sit better here," she said as she pressed her fist to her chest. "After all, we're French and always will be. I believe you're right. We must stand and fight for what's right, no matter the consequences." She wrapped her arms around the horse's massive neck with a new found confidence.

Yvette had seen V's in the strangest of places: over crosswalks, carved into the bark of trees, even drawn in the salt bin at the grocers. She resolved to add a few V's of her own.

4

People Art thought were his friends were shunning him. The one that hurt the most was Sharon. She had made a 180-degree turn away so fast he could feel the blow as if she'd slapped him across the face. Now an invisible wall of guilt was forming around him, locking shame behind its imaginary walls. He didn't know why. It replaced his confident demeanor.

"It's safer to stay within our group," he mumbled to himself. "We understand each other and trust one another. They think of us as outsiders and don't accept us, no matter how they act to our face."

Wasn't he as American as the next guy? The other students in his school never treated him *that* differently. And it seemed a relationship was starting with Sharon, at least until December 7th.

He'd met discrimination before when trying to find work after school. Employers wouldn't hire Japanese. They weren't racist, they claimed, but their customers or other employees would object. After the initial shock, frustration sank in, knowing his race prevented someone from giving him a fair chance. His father always said to look to the core of a person, where the true self existed. His words echoed in Art's mind.

"It's a delusion to think we're separate or better than others. That's the heart of racism. Clinging to these ideas leads to paranoia. It can't be us against them—that weakens everyone."

Art became hardened to the refusals until he found the National Youth Administration in downtown Seattle. They provided him with job training in clerical work—learning to type and file. Then a lucky break and he was moved to the machine shop. There he learned to use his hands to build things. Art gained confidence upon seeing his final results. He would saw wood at specific angles then finesse the pieces together to form shelves or boxes. On the lathe, he learned to drill holes in glass and made a lamp for his mother out of an old whiskey bottle. It didn't pay much, but the education would help him get a good job someday, and America was the one place providing him this opportunity. Was the war going to steal away all his dreams?

At school, he spent most of his time commiserating with Tom.

"It's like they've thrown me into another country where I don't belong. But if we complain, they may oust us all out of here." Tom said, keeping his voice low.

"I helped my parents re-register as aliens and we applied for travel permits, in case we need to go outside the city. I even turned in my camera. The newspaper said we might take pictures to send to Japan. Can you imagine that? Pictures of my gym classes or my mom's flower arrangements? And who would I send them to? Geez, I'm going to miss taking pictures. Anyway, I'm trying to do my part."

"I wish there was something to get my dad back. We haven't heard a thing about him," Tom's voice sagged under the strain of not knowing where they had taken his dad or for how long.

"Yeah, that's tough," Art said. He didn't know what else to say to help buoy his friend's spirits.

Nobody had questioned Art's loyalty to the U.S. before and there was no reason why they should now. America had given birth to him, fed, clothed, and educated him, so logically, he pledged his allegiance to America. He didn't go around with a flag in his hand and the national anthem on his lips, but he displayed his loyalty in more sincere ways.

But what could he do about the newspaper's depictions of him? That Japanese Americans were spying enemies. And the caricatures were revolting, pictures of buck-toothed faces with thick spectacles. Why would anyone laugh at such cruel drawings? Other students were avoiding him and whispering to one another as he passed by. Walking down the hall corridors, he felt like an outsider in his own school. Around the next corner, would there be a friendly face or a scowl with fingers pointed at him. Did he belong here and could he ever trust these people again?

More articles started to appear in the papers. Talk of sending American-born Japanese as well as nationals to the interior of the country for the duration of the war.

"We need to get these people away from the coasts. They're engaged in fifth-column espionage and sabotage. They're plotting to destroy blood plasma, are blocking roads and sending coded messages to Japan. All this, plus gathering information to help the Japanese attack again!" Such slander gathered momentum.

Art knew that none of this was true. The elders had left their homeland to start a new life in America, which offered everything not found in Japan. They wanted what any other immigrant wanted—a chance at a good life for their family and an opportunity for their children to succeed.

These accusations terrified him and he began to second guess every move he made. He felt his rights being stripped away one by one for no reason except that he resembled the enemy. Suspicion in the air enshrouded him and he saw it in the eyes of those passing by. It was alarming and he wasn't sure what to expect next.

Early one evening, there was a knock at the door. Art opened it to find two white men in dark suits. His mind flashed to Tom's father who had been taken away. Dazed, he blinked at the men. Were they here to take away his father?

"We're with the FBI and need to come in to check a few things," the taller man said, shoving past Art.

"Come in, we've nothing to hide," Art said, gripping the door to regain his balance.

He swallowed the urge to yell out. How could they barge into someone's home? Didn't they need a warrant or something? He ran to catch up with them, his nose burning from a strong odor, was it Old Spice?

One man started rifling through the books on the shelves, while the other examined the bottom of the dishes. He hesitated when finding the mark 'Made in Japan' on the bottom of the teapot, then replaced it on the counter. He grabbed Chibi's favorite doll, a gift from Art's father, a perfect replica of a Japanese woman dressed in a silk kimono. Chibi loved to comb the black hair, saying how she wished she had long hair. Mama preferred to keep hers cut right at chin level. On seeing the man take her doll, Chibi screamed and started to cry. The man showed no feeling: in fact, he looked smug. He glanced at the JACL poster on the wall that stated the Japanese American faith and dedication to the U.S. Again, his expression didn't change. If anything, he looked more smug. They left with the doll, a butcher knife, a book on Buddhist sutras, and the radio.

"Please don't take my Philco. I saved for months to buy that." Frantic, Art couldn't imagine losing his radio. It was his source of music, news, his way of staying current with everything. *They couldn't take it.*

"Ha! Young man, this radio has short-wave potential. You may be contacting Japan with it," one of the white men said.

"Why would I do that? I don't know anyone in Japan and wouldn't even know how to do it with such a simple radio."

"You look quite clever. I bet you know how." The men marched out the door, leaving behind the musky scent of their aftershave.

Art watched in horror as his precious radio left. He looked back at his parents - their mouths agape, trying to comprehend what had happened. The two men were in and out of the house within a few minutes.

"Isn't there something we can do? They stole our radio."

"There's nothing we can do, son. It's the FBI and we're now considered the enemy," his father replied.

"Enemy? What have we done besides tend to a little grocery?"

"Don't worry, we'll get another radio, one without short-wave potential."

"Really, is that all you have to say?" Art stared at his father in dismay, but at least he was still with them. He dropped his head in deference.

"I'm sorry, Father. You're right, of course."

Chibi was curled up on the floor with her arms around Prince, their mixed collie dog. He always comforted her when she was upset. She rocked him back and forth, burying her runny nose into his thick fur. He licked her hands as she fell asleep against him. He wouldn't move until she woke up.

Over the next few months, things settled down a bit. After the FBI arrested those Japanese they considered suspicious, a relative calm fell over the nation. People felt this would prevent any fifth-column activity or sabotage.

"Our Buddhist temple has been closed. I've read that some temples are being vandalized or set on fire. They've arrested most Buddhist and all Shinto priests and taken them away," Art's father announced.

"Why would anyone be afraid of those priests?" Art asked. "Wasn't America founded on religious tolerance or has fear replaced this tolerance?"

"I'm not sure, son. Sometimes people feel threatened by things they don't understand."

Art's mother's retail florist business plummeted as the wholesaler refused to sell to her, claiming she was the enemy. About 50% of the farmers working at the Pike Place Market were Japanese, so the effect was widespread. One owner of the market's arcades promised to fire not only the Japanese working the stalls, but those in wholesale and working on the farms. Hateful sentiments spread like wildfire.

Their grocery store income dropped to a fraction of the usual amount. It was getting more difficult for them to make ends meet. Art's parents spent their evenings, heads bowed over the table counting coins and pushing bills from one side to the other. Things were going from bad to worse.

Art and his sisters continued at school, but an awkward tension existed between them and the non-Japanese students. Classmates would repeat things in school they had heard their parents say.

"Once a *Jap*, always a *Jap*," or "You can't trust those shifty eyes."

Art existed alone among a sea of white faces, faces that once had been his friends. Did he even belong with these people? His father preached feeling superior to someone was wrong, that it stemmed from an underlying fear of the unknown. Were these people judging him indeed fearful of what they didn't understand? And how could he show them they weren't that different from one another? Art kept searching for the reasons people didn't trust them. It was enough to break one's spirit.

5

ÉCUEILLÉ, FRANCE
APRIL 1943

It had been close to three years since France had surrendered to Germany. Its people appeared subdued and disheartened, but under the cloak of gloom smoldered a powerful spirit. The spirit of a people wanting to be free, to be able to work for themselves, to share meals around a table, and to drink champagne again without worrying about being killed. What appeared to the Nazis as a beaten nation was clawing its way back up from the ruins. General Charles De Gaulle's nightly speeches on the BBC invigorated and rallied throngs of men and women.

The Nazis were killing innocent citizens in retribution for Resistance activity, believing this would curtail any further violence against their regime. Instead, it had the opposite effect, leading to greater support for the Resistance and stoking further aggression towards the Nazis. Thus perpetuating a cycle of attacks, reprisals, counter-attacks, and counter-reprisals.

Then Operation Torch in North Africa triggered an about face in Hitler's trust in the French Vichy, who he had left to defend the area. The ease by which the Allies conquered the region convinced Hitler he could no longer depend on the

Vichy to uphold his orders. He eliminated the non-occupied zone in France currently under Vichy control and placed the entire nation under his rule. Nazi soldiers spread everywhere, including Yvette's small village. Things were going from bad to worse.

Yvette helped her mother to hide their few belongings. It wasn't much—a set of Limoges plates and cups, a few silver utensils, and the gold Napoleon coin that had belonged to her grandmother. They wrapped everything in old linen towels then gingerly packed them into wood boxes so as not to crack the fragile china. Her father dug a hole behind the house where surrounding blackberry bushes hid the freshly turned soil.

Yvette wiped the dirt from her hands on her apron, admiring their work.

"That will protect our things from the prying hands of those Nazis."

Another stronghold move by the Nazis was replacing Pétain with the heavier-handed Pierre Laval.

"Laval says the Germans are winning this war and we must collaborate or suffer the consequences," Yvette's father said. "We'll show them what they're up against."

The next day, Yvette headed home following a long day of queuing in lines. The wait at the store had taken over three hours with more than a dozen people in front of her, trying to get a bit of sugar or a few grams of lard. The ration cards covered so little, leaving much debate as each person strived to get whatever was available.

"I don't have any rations left for sugar. My little boy will be so disappointed when I can't make his favorite cake. He turns ten tomorrow!" Madame Richard said.

Yvette looked at the coupons she had left- three for the month. Madame Richard's son was in Robert's class and turning ten was such an important event. She handed her the coupons.

"Madame, will these be enough for the cake?"

"Oh, you're my savior. My little Francis won't be heartbroken after all. Bless you!"

Madame Richard collected the sugar and hurried out the door, but not before giving Yvette a big hug.

"That was kind of you, Yvette. What may I get for you?" asked the woman behind the counter.

"May I have ten grams of salt and 100 grams of lard, please?"

"We have salt, but no lard today. We've been out for days."

This was the only store in the small village of Écueillé selling general supplies. And since the war had started, the shelves were often bare. Yvette was glad there was salt which would help give a little flavor to the bread they baked at home. The mandated National Loaf of 85% bran resulted in loaves so heavy and flat that they dropped like bricks onto the tables. The Nazis, thinking they were clever, called it "wheatmeal" but it disgusted the French. They loved the baguettes with soft, white interior dough. Yvette missed cracking off the end of the warm loaf to pull out its airy center, letting it melt into her mouth. Since the war started, only dreams of those traditional baguettes remained.

Yvette walked down the cobblestone road towards the center of town, familiar with each home along the way. She had spent all sixteen years of her life in this small village, along the edge of a small river, the Touraine, situated in the district of Berry. Almost 2000 people lived in Écueillé, calling themselves *les Berrichons*. She often imagined what life might be like outside of her small enclave where everyone knew the goings-on of everyone else. Here, a story could ricochet between neighbors like a petanque ball. A statement would become so distorted by the time it came back around, it would have little resemblance to the original if it ever indeed had been a fact. For instance, a rumor started involving Mrs. Lillet, the baker's wife, and Mr. Moret, the plumber. By the time it made it back to Mr. Lillet, the rumor had morphed into Mrs. Lillet having multiple affairs with the school principal, the town doctor, and the local veterinarian omitting the original man, Mr. Moret. She thought it would be lovely to live someplace where people didn't snoop into everyone else's personal affairs. But on the other hand, if anyone was in need, that would spread quickly as well. People would come offering food or anything else that might help. Maybe gossip was a small price to pay for the close-knit fabric small towns provided.

She smiled as she passed the bakery of Mr. and Mrs. Lillet on the edge of the town square. Despite the rumor, they were a happy couple and ran the best bakery in town, in her opinion. But her smile disappeared on seeing the near bare display window. What a change from before the invasion. Now the bakeries were void of the fruit and cream-filled pastries, croissants, and the rows of assorted sizes of French breads.

Around the corner, she passed the two bars on either side of the hair salon. Each bar had seating on outdoor terraces facing the town center. As in every town, a fountain marked the center square. The one in Écueillé contained a statue of a young girl kneeling with water encircling her legs. Most bar patrons were found outside if the weather permitted, though there was always an older gentleman or two saddled up to the counter enjoying a snifter of cognac or a Pernod. Whether it was 8 am or 8 pm, you could count on one being there.

She continued through the parking area where the outdoor market took place every Wednesday. Merchants came from neighboring villages to set up small canopies and sell fish, fresh produce, and those delicious honey toffees Yvette loved.

Once in a while, someone would come from one of the larger towns or on occasion, even from Paris. They might stop in for a drink at one of the bars or get a meal at the Lion d'Or restaurant attached to a hotel of the same name. Then gypsies came in their horse-drawn caravans every summer, setting up camp by the river adjacent to the church. Most of the villagers didn't trust them.

"You'll get enticed to have your fortune told, while another will be pilfering your sack or stealing your husband," townsfolk would say.

Yet Yvette enjoyed visiting with them to hear about their adventures. She would sit by their fires, listening to the men play guitars while the women sang and danced. Yvette found the women beautiful. Their flamboyant jewelry sparkled in the firelight as their skirts twirled to the music. The spicy aromas of these women were earthy and sultry, nothing like the usual perfumes of French women. They stopped coming once the Nazis arrived. People said the Nazis "eliminated" them.

She walked past the closed-up jewelry store on the far edge of the square, disappointed to see the empty window cases instead of the beautiful pieces of jewelry previously displayed. Gone were the ancient French coins encircled by gold bands as well as the earrings and rings which glimmered in every direction. The jeweler had abandoned the store to move south to join her daughter.

Passing the shop, she noticed a young German soldier standing in a doorway on the corner of the road. He wasn't but a few years older than she, his face the color of a porcelain plate with strong features, as if chiseled in a Limoges factory. As she passed by, his hardened blue eyes softened. Yvette straightened her shoulders and tried to look purposeful as she continued home, wondering if he had noticed her lower lip tremble. His footsteps began to follow hers, so she quickened her pace, only to have his follow suit. She fought the urge to break into a run; others had been shot for such a thing. Her whole body quivered. What did he want? She was only going about her own business, picking up a few groceries. Her mind went into a frenzy. Did she have anything contraband on her? Did she have any of her father's bread that wasn't 85% bran? Looking for an escape, she hadn't noticed two other German soldiers who stepped in front of her yelling, "Halt!" They looked much more menacing than the other young soldier and now they had her trapped. They moved close to her, the odor of sweat mixed with stale tobacco and alcohol burning her eyes. One began sneering and reached to grab her around the waist. He jumped back when the first young soldier came up from behind, barking a few words and stepping between them. It was clear he was in command and the other two soldiers parted for her to pass. Yvette wanted to thank the young soldier, but was too afraid to even glance at him. She felt fortunate *this* time, but there would be others. Her little village was no longer the safe haven she had once known.

The final kilometer home was quiet. There were few homes along the way, desolate enough that German soldiers seldom came this far. Her breathing returned to normal and her shaken nerves calmed. A few steps from her house, she heard rustling in the grass under her favorite oak tree, where she loved to take naps. She followed the sounds from tree to tree, parting the grass to get a view. Every few feet, there was a glint of light reflecting off a blue/black background. It finally came to a stop just short of a clearing. Kneeling to investigate, she saw a young crow with crystal blue eyes and a beak that was still pink and soft in the corners. He gaped his mouth open, fearful this would be his end. Scooping him into her arms, she hoped he wouldn't die from the shock of being taken captive, sympathizing after her experience with the soldiers.

"What have you found this time?" asked her mother. Yvette was always the one to find an injured animal.

"Oh, Maman, it's an injured crow. It looks like his wing's hurt, but he can walk. I'll care for him until he can fly again. I've named him Arthur."

"Did you know it's a good sign to find a crow? The crow is one of the most strong-spirited animals. He'll bring you luck and protect you. Crows are always on the lookout for danger."

Yvette smiled, her mother still held to the superstitious beliefs of the elders. Regardless of old notions, this little crow gave her hope in a world that had become hopeless to a young woman. She headed off in search of a few worms near the creek alongside their home.

6

SEATTLE, WA
SPRING 1942

The family was seated at the table and Art's mouth watered in anticipation. His mother had prepared his favorite meal, *sukiyaki*—thin slices of beef with vegetables served over rice. She set the sizzling pan on the table, wafting aromas of soy and onion toward him.

"Scramble an egg to pour over the dinner, Papa." Art loved having a raw egg over the meat. It added a tasty flavor along with the sauce. Out of the corner of his eye, he saw Lillian scrunch up her nose. He smiled at her, no one else in the family appreciated this culinary delight.

"You know how to make a good *sukiyaki*, Mama," his father said. Art's mother's face beamed with pleasure, serving herself last.

It was a peaceful evening. Soft music flowed from the RCA radio, accompanying the tapping of chopsticks against plates. There was the occasional slurp made by Art's father as he enjoyed his *shirataki* or yam noodles. Prince lay under the table, softly snoring, as Chibi rubbed her stocking feet along his back. It was a symphony to Art, soothing his nerves that were on edge since the visit from the FBI and the events at school.

A loud voice broke into the smooth sounds of Glenn Miller. Everyone froze in place to hear what had interrupted their tranquil evening. It was hard not to fear the worst.

"President Roosevelt has issued Executive Order 9066 giving the U.S. armed forces the authority to declare any region of the United States a military area. Lieutenant General DeWitt has established Military Areas No. 1 and 2, which will encompass all of California and the western halves of Arizona, Oregon, and Washington. All persons of Japanese descent, U. S. citizens included, will be removed from these areas."

"What did he say? This can't be right. They can't remove us," Art said.

"Shh, tell us what else he's saying," his father said.

The report continued saying Seattle was in the new "military" region and all Japanese Americans would be classified 4C, enemy aliens. They were now a threat to national security.

"Enemy aliens," Art repeated, the words reverberating in his head.

His thoughts left his delicious dinner and he began to wonder how the government could do such a thing. He had studied about the writ of habeas corpus, the Fifth Amendment, and the Bill of Rights. Didn't that ensure due process? Or did that only apply to Caucasians? They hadn't done anything wrong, why was this happening? It must be a mistake. He wasn't an enemy alien. He was an American citizen. His head throbbed as the questions built up, one atop the next. He tried to focus on his family sitting around the table, but they looked like a blur, fading into the wallpaper. He dropped his head and closed his eyes. Maybe when he opened them, it would have all been a bad dream. They would be eating sukiyaki and everything would be as before. That's it, just a bad dream. Then Chibi placed her hand on his.

"Are you okay? What does 'alien' mean?"

Alien... It's not a dream. He glanced at his little sister's face, afraid anything he'd say would shatter her innocence.

"Papa, if I'm an enemy alien, do I even belong to a country?" he asked. The thought of not being an American any longer terrified him. What would become of them?

"Son, I don't know the answer," he replied.

But you always know the answer, Art thought. He tried to hide his anguish.

"Will we have to move away and where will we go? We have our businesses here, our only means of livelihood," his mother said.

"We'll have to put our faith in our nation. I'm sure they have only the best intentions."

"Really, Papa? Do you think they care about us? You're not even allowed to become a citizen or own any property. White immigrants don't have those restrictions. I've read people are lashing out at us across the country, not just on the West Coast. There's a minister in Colorado who wants the country to clean up 'the Japagerms' but their governor, Ralph Carr is speaking out."

"Look here," Art said as he spread the newspaper out. "The governor sent an appeal to the Colorado public. He reminds them America is the great melting pot of the modern world. That all Americans have their origins beyond our borders and we must work together for the continuation of universal brotherhood. See, not everyone's against us."

As the days passed, their worst suspicions came to fruition, in spite of support from some officials.

On March 18th, President Roosevelt created the War Relocation Authority. It was given the responsibility to develop a program to evacuate the Japanese population. Once the West Coast was divided into military zones, a curfew order was implemented. No Japanese was allowed to leave his or her residence between 8:00 PM to 6:00 AM, it forbade them to possess firearms, explosives, cameras, radio transmitters, or shortwave sets and barred any travel outside of five miles.

It didn't take long—by the end of March, all the Japanese living on Bainbridge Island were evicted from their homes. This news shocked Art and his family. Would this happen to other Japanese families? And when?

The wait was excruciating. Then on April 24, the posters went up in Seattle. Art saw a number of people grouped around a telephone pole as he was heading back home from the National Youth Administration office. He pushed in between the others to see what it said.

INSTRUCTIONS
TO ALL PERSONS OF
JAPANESE
ANCESTRY
LIVING IN THE FOLLOWING AREA

All that portion of the City of Seattle, State of Washington, within that boundary beginning at the point at which the northerly limits of said city meet Shilshole Bay; thence easterly and following the northerly limits of said city to Roosevelt Way; thence southerly and following Roosevelt Way, Eastlake Avenue, Fairview Avenue, Virginia Street, and Westlake Avenue to Fifth Avenue; thence southeasterly on Fifth Avenue to Yesler Way; thence easterly on Yesler Way to Maynard Avenue; then southerly on Maynard Avenue to Jackson Street; thence westerly on Jackson Street to Elliott Bay; thence northwesterly and northerly, and following the westerly limits of the City of Seattle, to the point of beginning.

Pursuant to the provisions of Civilian Exclusion Order No.

18, this Headquarters, dated April 24, 1942, all persons of Japanese ancestry, both alien and non-alien, will be evacuated from the above area by 12 o'clock noon, P.W.T., Friday, May 1, 1942.

The following instructions must be observed:

1.   A responsible member of each family will report to the Civil Control Station to receive further instructions. This must be done between 8:00 a.m. and 5:00 p.m. on Saturday, April 25, 1942, or between 8:00 a.m. and 5:00 p.m. Sunday, April 26, 1942.

2.   Evacuees must carry with them on departure for the Assembly Center, the following property:

 (a) Bedding and linens (no mattress) for each member of the family;

(b) Toilet articles for each member of the family;

(c) Extra clothing for each member of the family;

(d) Sufficient knives, forks, spoons, plates, bowls and cups for each member of the family;

(e) Essential personal effects for each member of the family.

All items must be securely packaged and tied and limited to that which the individual can carry.

3.   No pets of any kind will be permitted

No personal items and no household goods will be shipped to the Assembly Center.

All instructions pertaining to the movement to the Assembly Center will be obtained at the Civil Control Station.

Go to the Civil Control Station to receive further instructions.

J.L. DeWitt
Lieutenant General, U.S. Army
Commanding

"An Assembly Center? What's that?" an older man asked, perplexed, pushing his cap back to scratch his head.

"Maybe it's where we'll get more information, then be able to return to our homes," another said.

Art squeezed forward between the people to read the rest. The instructions were vague— only bring what each person could carry. They were given less than a week to pack up everything to leave and it didn't sound like they would be coming home any time soon.

Everyone stood in quiet dismay, unsure of what to say or do. Indeed, the entire west coast was being sent somewhere, away from the only home Art had ever known. He hurried back to tell his parents.

"But where are we going and for how long?" Mama's voice rose to a shrill Art had never heard before. "How can we possibly be ready to leave in just a week? What will we do with all the grocery store items, our home, and furnishings? And on top of it, we must pack up all of our personal belongings. How do we choose what to take?" She paced the living room muttering to herself, her hands waving from one item to the next, as if they could answer which one of them should be taken.

Art's father tried to calm things.

"I'm sure it won't be for long. They may need to move us to a secure location until things settle down a bit, the best interests of the few sometimes must be sacrificed for the good of the many."

Chibi, wanting to be helpful, started to pack up Prince's leash and bowl. "Mama, how many days of Prince's food should I bring?" Chibi asked, her dark eyes wide with concern.

Art exchanged a glance with his father. Neither wanted to break the news that pets weren't allowed to go.

His father took her hand and lifted her onto his lap.

"Chibi-chan, We aren't allowed to bring Prince. But don't worry, we'll find him a safe place until we can get home."

Her face went from a blank stare to sheer defiance. Bursting into tears, she dropped off his lap, and ran to Prince. "I won't go, I won't go—I can't leave him. He's my best friend!"

Mama went over, stroked her hair, and murmured it would be okay, some things can't be helped. "*Shikataganai,*" she repeated, hoping to calm not only her young child but herself as well.

Chibi's head buried in Prince's fur, convulsed as she sobbed. Her mother kept repeating things would be okay, that they'd be back so soon Prince would think he had been on a little vacation.

"No, no, no" Chibi cried, "I won't leave him behind!"

The next few days flew by. They couldn't find anyone to take Prince so Papa tried his last resort and sent Art to the veterinary clinic on Rainier Ave So. The veterinarian had always been good to them. Chibi didn't want to go.

"No, I can't. He'll think I've deserted him. If I stay here, he'll know I'm waiting for him." She wrapped her little arms around his neck one last time, her eyes almost swollen shut from the constant crying. Art didn't think so many tears and snot could come out of such a small child.

He headed out the door to the clinic, a long trip by bus. Prince sat like a statue by Art's side while he caressed his head, becoming lost in thought. Something was mesmerizing about petting a dog. The soft fur running between the fingers, the warmth emanating from the crown of the head, the rhythmic inhalation and exhalation of the dog's breath. Art became so relaxed, he almost missed his stop, jumping up to pull the cord. As he and Prince descended the steps, he looked across the street to the hospital.

A line of Japanese weaved halfway down the block, holding either a dog—some big, some small, and a few cats. Many were weeping, not wanting to leave their beloved pets behind. He joined the line behind Mr. Uyeno, who was clutching an orange tabby cat.

"Do you think he'll be able to help us? There are so many people here," Art asked.

"I know he will if he can. He's Jewish and understands the challenges of immigrants. He escaped from Krivoy Rog, Ukraine during its Revolution. They suffered pogroms, being attacked or killed, just for being Jewish. He's worked hard to get this far and has always been kind to me. I hope he can care for Mikan until we get back. My little Mikan is very shy, only coming out when I'm alone. He loves to sit in my lap and purr while we listen to the radio together. Who'll take care of him? What will become of my sweet Mikan?" Mr. Uyeno peered up at Art, his dark eyes ringed by swollen and red lids.

"I hope he can help you too." Art knew Mr. Uyeno was widowed. He looked so lost and forlorn, holding his cat to his chest and kissing the kitty's forehead. It made his problems seem small. At least he had his family for support. Why couldn't they bring their pets? *Doesn't the government have any heart? Or do they think we don't?*

The veterinarian, "Doc" as everyone called him, stood in the doorway, speaking to each person, giving them hugs as they turned their pets over to his assistant. Everyone appeared overwhelmed by the situation.

As Art approached the head of the line, he saw that the kind doctor was out of ideas. "I have a large kennel area where I can board your pet for as long as possible," Art overheard him telling each of the distraught pet owners.

When Art got up to him, he handed over Prince's leash. Doc looked into his eyes with a kindly but sorrowful gaze, his face drawn tight from the emotions of the day. "Will we get to see Prince again? My sister's so worried."

The doctor put his hand on Art's shoulder, heavy with the burden of how to care for all these pets. "I'll do my very best." His eyes were sincere but his voice was doubtful.

Would this be the last time they'd see Prince?

7

ÉCUEILLÉ, FRANCE
SPRING 1943

Yvette's father, Maurice, was spending less time around the farm. Instead, she saw glimpses of him in the local town café, the Café des Sports. The owner, René, was known for resistance activity, gathering men in the back of the café, rather than on the terrace facing the town square.

"Mama, what is Papa doing with René at the café?"

"Don't pay any mind to him. He's all worked up about the Nazis and what's happening around Paris. As if there isn't enough to worry about with the mill and farm. I've warned him, neighbors are looking for anything to report to these Vichy police."

Yvette furrowed her brow. The Vichy had already taken away several men in their town. What would happen to them if Papa disappeared? They needed him to help run the farm and mill—they would be forced to abandon it.

His visits to town became more frequent and lasted longer, sometimes well into the evening. Yvette was certain he was involved with the Resistance, and she heard what people were saying around town.

"Stay away from the café during evening hours. Meetings are going on there that are endangering the whole town," Yvette overheard a woman in the bakery say one day.

She worried more about her father and the risks he was taking endangering the entire family. She had seen strange men in the early morning hours, cleaning up by their creek, speaking languages she didn't recognize.

"Don't concern yourself with them. They're only passing through, in need of a place to rest, the less you know the better," Yvette's father warned his family. Her mother only turned her head away, looking disheartened.

Her father was a miller by trade, running the small mill at their home. A wooden wheel attached to the side of the house was powered by the current of a creek running parallel to the north side of the house. It mesmerized her watching the water tumble into each paddle which powered the massive wheel. This drove an upper stone to grind against a lower, crushing grain between its grooves. The flour would tumble into the attached bin, like sand into an hourglass. The neighboring farmers brought their wheat and other grains for her father to grind, but business had shrunk since the start of the war. The Germans confiscated most of the grain to feed their troops and population.

It happened a few weeks later. Her father called a family meeting to make an announcement.

"The Nazis have taken over our entire country, wreaking havoc. They're eliminating people they find undesirable or not supportive of their regime. Some Jews have been hiding in the Lion D'Or hotel, but it's no longer safe with Nazis patrolling our town. We will shelter one of those couples."

Yvette's mother opened her mouth to protest, but he raised his hand to cease any further discussion.

"It's a big risk, but we have no choice. They'll move into Madeleine's room since it's upstairs and will give them some privacy."

"Where will I sleep? I can't share with them," Madeleine protested.

"Of course, you won't share with them. You'll move in with Mauricette. Her bed's big enough for the both of you."

"Umph, that's a terrible idea," she complained. Mauricette smiled and said she would love to share with her sister. Yvette was relieved to still have her room.

Many refugees were migrating from Holland and Belgium to evade the Nazis, leaving behind their homes, their belongings, and their livelihood in search of safety. Caravans of people trailed through and past Écueillé, heading south of the Loire River, which had marked the separation between the occupied and unoccupied regions of France. But since November 1942, the Nazis had spread throughout the country, sending people scrambling to find safe houses for the Jews and others being persecuted.

Yvette overheard her parents arguing.

"We'll be risking the safety of our children," her mother said.

"We must help. They've nowhere to go and if the Nazis catch them, they'll be sent to those camps to be tortured, perhaps even killed."

It was agreed and the next day a couple arrived, the Wolffs. They were a quiet pair whose daughter was separated from them as they were fleeing Holland two years earlier. Since then, they hadn't received news of her. They were grateful to have a room for themselves where they spent most of their time, except for when it was safe enough to join the family for meals. At any sign of someone coming, they would hide. No one could be trusted. The Germans weren't occupying their village in large numbers, but French citizens were reporting their neighbors and friends, often without any proof. They would get compensated with extra ration tickets or cash, but at what cost? How someone could turn on their own and support such a treacherous regime was unfathomable. One had to be careful, as even a trusted neighbor might decide to turn on you.

The Wolffs were from Holland yet spoke French well, especially Mrs. Wolff. She talked often about their daughter, Anna. She described combing her brown hair, never being able to tame the curls that she would have to tie back with a ribbon.

"I told her—don't hide your pretty face behind all that hair. See, it's better pulled back." Mrs. Wolff's eyes filled with tears as she smiled, unable to hide her sorrow.

How lost and afraid they must be and to be separated from their daughter only added to their plight. Yvette tossed and turned at night, having visions of this sweet little girl with tumbles of curls around her face, wondering what had become of her. How anyone could condemn a group of people based on a particular belief or even appearance. She thought of George, the young man living in the home for disabled people. He frightened her at first, but as she grew to know him, she learned his abrupt movements and loud outcries weren't menacing. *Au contraire*, she saw how insightful and gentle he was with the stray cats living nearby. He seemed to have a unique rapport, drawing even the most timid cat to him. How wrong she had been to judge so quickly, based on only an unknown fear.

Flopping onto her back, she knew her father was right to harbor this couple, even if it meant risking the family. If caught, it would mean sure death, probably preceded by torture. There were stories of mangled bodies of people who had aided refugees hanging in trees or on the sides of buildings. Everyone would have to be vigilant so as not to arouse suspicion. Rolling back to her side, she dropped into slumber.

It had been almost six months since the Wolffs had joined the family. Mrs. Wolff was a robust woman with full cheeks and bosom, in contrast to her husband, who was thin, almost frail in appearance. When the nights were cold last winter, he caught his pants on fire as he sat too close to the wood-burning stove in their upstairs room. He didn't hurt himself, and it did make everyone laugh a bit, especially him.

"If you would move about more, you wouldn't be so cold," Mrs. Wolff lectured him.

"Yes, dear. I shall start doing laps around the room next time I get cold."

Since spring, they would sneak outside after dark to enjoy the fresh air in the hills behind the house, where Yvette and her mother had hidden their few precious belongings. There they were safe from any prying neighbors.

They fit in with the family well, and it wasn't much work to prepare extra food for them. Life had new demands with rationing and the strain of finding limited supplies but their family was much better off than those in the cities. They had the farm with their cow, Clara, and two goats, Brigitte and Nellie, who provided milk to make cheese. There were half a dozen chickens for eggs, and even rabbits for the occasional meat. And Belle, their draft horse, was a true blessing as she helped plow the fields where they grew vegetables and a small crop of wheat. Nonetheless, there was a nagging worry in Yvette's head, fearing when the Nazis patrolled by their house that they would decide to take one of the animals. It was common for them to steal farm animals to feed their troops. Their family was attached to all the animals, especially Yvette, they were like members of the family. It would be heartbreaking to see one of them grabbed by those barbarians.

Yvette always volunteered to go to town for supplies. She loved traveling the familiar roads, past the open fields where she daydreamed of days past. Sometimes, she would jump on her bicycle and pedal into town. The encounter with the young Nazi had shaken her, but most soldiers had left town now. She was young enough not to be suspect, but just a week ago, a young man was arrested on suspicion of transporting black market goods. No one had seen him since. Word was they sent him to a work camp in Germany. Just the thought of being taken away made her shudder.

To add to her concerns, her father left late at night, only to return in the early morning hours. Then other nights there would be a knock on the door, followed by a series of more knocks, some type of code. Her father would take these men to the cellar where there were hidden stashes of arms. Yvette overheard her mother whispering with exasperation to him.

"How can you take such chances putting our children in danger?"

"This is bigger than all of us. We can't allow those fascist Nazis to overtake our country. Remember what General de Gaulle said at the start of all this."

Yvette thought back on the speech given over the BBC airwaves. It was illegal to listen to the station and the Nazis would consider them enemies of the regime. The unthinkable happened to anyone caught, but they took their chances. Listening was the only way to know what was truly happening in their country.

General De Gaulle had moved to Algiers where he was proving himself a powerful leader of an independent France. He was bringing together other French territories as well, such as St Pierre and Miquelon off Canada, Dakar,

Madagascar, Syria, and Lebanon. He was becoming synonymous with all resisters, and Yvette's father followed his every word.

Yvette just wished things would return to the way they had been before all this crazy business started.

"Yvette, we need a few items in town. Can you hop on your bicycle to pick them up?" her mother asked. "See if you can get sugar. I'd like to make a milk cake."

Yvette's thoughts snapped back to the present. "Of course," she said. This was one of her favorite cakes. Her mother used the cream from the top of the milk, making a delightfully rich and moist cake.

She meandered the back roads through the countryside to enjoy the beautiful day. Newly emerged flowers flanked either side of the road—lily of the valley, yarrow, and bright yellow daffodils. The daffodils were her favorite, always making her smile with their cheery appearance, announcing spring had arrived. The smells were intoxicating as they fanned across her face. She entered the town a few blocks west of the square, parking her bicycle at the *epicerie*, the local grocery. Only a few women stood in line, which was fortunate since she often had a long wait to find the meager supplies had run out. She smiled at Mrs. Denis and her daughter, Marie, who was about her age. They smiled back tentatively. Everyone was on edge since the Germans had taken over.

She purchased the allotted sugar with her ration cards. Since she had her bicycle, she rode around town before heading home, pedaling across the square. She took the second road to the right, then headed down to see if the third bakery was still open. The shutters were closed tight and there was a note on the door stating they had closed as of last Sunday. Yvette gave a sigh of disappointment, not only for the loss of a good bakery but for seeing yet another business shut down in the face of all these challenges.

When Yvette arrived home, her mother had started dinner, milk soup again with a bit of salad on the side. She loved soups, even if it was only seasoned milk with chunks of bread. Somehow, her mother managed to make such simple ingredients taste delicious. No one complained, knowing they were lucky to have any food.

Tonight, Mr. and Mrs. Wolff joined the family around the dinner table. They were a friendly couple, though they always seemed melancholy. Her brother, Robert, described a funny incident that happened at school.

"One of my classmates, Thomas, brought a frog in his pocket. It was croaking, and the teacher kept looking around. All the kids knew about it, so they kept taking turns making similar sounds. The poor teacher wandered around until the frog finally gave Thomas away!"

Everyone laughed, even the Wolffs joined in. Then, as quickly as they had started, the Wolffs stopped. How cruel it was for them, unsure about their daughter. What she was going through, where she might be, or if she were even still alive. She was about the same age as Robert, and it could have been their daughter telling a cute story about her school if only things were different. They switched the topic, each person wiped the smile from their face and finished dinner under a somber cloud. Yvette and her sisters cleared the table and began washing the dishes. Her mother started preparing the barley drink, a sad replacement for their traditional after supper coffee.

A knock at the door startled everyone. It was rare for anyone to come visit, especially after the dinner hour. The Wolffs jumped to their feet and ran up the stairs. The Nazis were known to make surprise visits. Yvette's eyes scanned the dinner table to make sure any extra glasses or settings were cleared. The curtains were always drawn, in case a snoopy neighbor might peer in. Her mother opened the door a crack to find Pierre, the son of a neighbor.

"Can Renée come out for a walk?" Pierre asked sheepishly, not looking around the room. His gangly build amused Yvette, but Renée seemed quite taken by him.

Yvette wondered if he had heard the footsteps running up the stairs. Mrs. Wolff wasn't very light on her feet. Renée scurried out the door, tugging him by the arm, and they headed down towards the creek for a stroll, arm-in-arm. Anxiety eased and everyone exchanged smiles. Pierre had been calling on Yvette's older sister for several months. There would be more than strolling going on by the creek.

The rest of the family remained grouped around the table, while Madeleine brought the Wolffs back down, assuring them everything was fine. Everyone settled back to discuss the event, sipping the bland barley brew.

"That was a good rehearsal for us. We must make sure there aren't any signs of extra people here. Clearing all the dishes is vital," her father warned. A look of grave concern washed over his face as he shook his head, rubbing his fingers through his auburn hair, not able to hold back a groan of exasperation. Yvette's racing heart slowed, watching him finish his cup and leave the house. Everyone's eyes followed him, waiting to see what they should do next.

Though it was approaching bedtime, Yvette went out to find her father. First, she headed to the barn, thinking he was brushing down Belle, or ensuring the cow had enough straw. She found them standing in their stalls, alone. Belle was half asleep, her lower lip drooping down and the cow quietly chewing her cud. The serene setting soothed her frazzled nerves. The knock on the door had jolted her more than she expected. She left the barn and headed to the cellar in the far outbuilding.

Descending the rocky stairs, the drop in temperature and humidity added a chill to the night air, and she entered the darkened room. The dank odor of the cellar was tinged with the scents of vegetables and wine. She flipped on the switch to illuminate the single bulb hanging in the center of the room. Around her were shelves holding her mother's canned preserves, a few wine bottles, and potatoes and turnips from the garden. There was a noise from the adjoining partition. The shelves that normally blocked the entrance were moved to the side, allowing a dim light to filter through the opening. Certain her father was there, Yvette entered cautiously. She eyed a few rifles, some handguns, and what looked like small metal balls, perhaps grenades. Her father's face flashed up from the shadows when she appeared.

"What are you doing in here? Get back outside. This is no place for you," he barked.

"Papa, I know what you're doing, and I think I can help. I could deliver things in my bicycle bags. No one would suspect me." Yvette knew about flyers being distributed around the town.

Her papa's eyes pierced hers, making her fall back a few steps. "I don't want to hear you talk such nonsense. These things are much too dangerous."

She was cautious in her next move. Her father was very strict with his children, so she feared he would chase her out, even threaten a smacking.

But his eyes softened as she edged closer to him. He wrapped his arms around her shoulders, pulling her close. "I don't want you to get involved, *ma mignette*. It's much too risky." When he was in a good mood, he liked to call her "*ma mignette*," the endearing term for a loved one.

Yvette straightened up to look taller. "I want to help."

"You're busy helping Mama around the farm and with the Wolffs. Don't think about getting involved in these affairs."

Yvette scanned the cellar room, noting the organized piles of guns and ammunition. If she could figure out what he might need or where his next delivery would be, then she could find a way to help and prove herself to him.

"Go back to the house. It's late."

Yvette sulked back upstairs, thinking she would ask around town for ways to help. Her father would be watching her, so she would have to be clever.

A few weeks passed, and she asked nothing more of her father, wanting to convince him she had moved on. Her little crow, Arthur, had mended well and was now free to fly away. He wasn't about to leave, believing that Yvette was his partner, or at least his source of food. Everything seemed under control, just as her father liked it.

Some evenings, the Wolffs lingered around the kitchen table, keeping the children mesmerized with stories of Holland. None of the family had ever left the village and their eyes widened in wonder at hearing about the canals and intricate waterways of Holland. The Wolffs described the windmills used to pump water out of the lowlands.

"Since most of the Netherlands are below sea level, we must continually pump the water out to keep our feet dry!" Mrs. Wolff explained with a big grin, producing a raucous laugh from everyone.

"Similar to your water mill grinding grain, these use the wind to turn wheels and cogs to move the water. They were built in the 1500s and many are still scattered throughout our country," she continued to explain.

"Anna, our little girl, loved watching the mills turn in

the wind," Mrs. Wolff said, misty-eyed. Mr. Wolff reached for her hand, rubbing it between his two palms.

Yvette turned her head down to hide her sorrow, her sleepless nights were becoming a common occurrence. These were two of the kindest people. Why was this happening to them? She looked at her youngest sister, Mauricette. These innocent faces shouldn't have to experience such hard times. The war was causing anguish and despair to everything it touched.

"We'll find her again. We can't lose hope," Mr. Wolff said. His wife nodded as she dried her eyes with the tissue she kept tucked in her sleeve.

Yvette smiled in agreement. The war would end, and everything would fall back into place. Then she might travel from her small village to see other parts of the world. She needed to keep this dream close to her heart.

8

SEATTLE, WA
APRIL 1942

A rt and his family whittled their belongings to fit into the incredulous limit of one suitcase per person. Do they bring their winter coats and boots? It wasn't even summer yet. How could anyone imagine adding those bulky items to the already full satchels?

"I don't think we need winter clothes. We can't be gone for *that* long," Art said.

"I wouldn't be sure. You'd better take your brown overcoat." He heard his father's voice straining under the pressure as he spoke.

"I can't fit another thing in this suitcase. We're only allowed one and mine's half full of books. How will I pass the time if I can't read? Why can't I bring enough clothes and some books? What harm could that do?" It outraged Art that he had to make such ridiculous choices.

They had met in the living room, each squatting over their respective suitcases, fussing to squeeze as much as possible into each nook and cranny.

"I can't decide what to bring. We don't know where we're going, for how long, or what our living situation will be," his mother lamented. She twisted her hair with her fingers, leading to a bedraggled appearance. Now her tidy chignon toppled onto her shoulders in disarray.

"That's enough! Stop your bickering and complaining. It's not helping the situation. We have to do the best we can and that's that!" his father commanded.

Lillian ran over to console her little sister, stroking her hair.

"Now you've got Chibi crying. Please don't yell at us," Lillian pleaded, her face streaked from previous tears shed in private. Art worried she was keeping her emotions locked inside. He didn't know how to reach out to her, concerned about the toll this would take on a young girl.

"I'm sorry, but we have three days left to prepare. We can put the rest of our belongings in the shed of Mr. Suyama's neighbor." Art's father walked into the next room, mumbling to himself.

Art wondered if other families were going through the same breakdowns.

They picked and chose what to take, what to store, and what to give away. There wasn't time to sell anything. They stored Mama's favorite sideboard and sewing machine, plus most of their clothing. Chibi insisted on adding Prince's bowl and favorite toys, hoping he would get to use them again soon. Art tried to be optimistic by leaving his winter garments behind. Out of the corner of his eye, he saw Papa, the practical one, stash his brown overcoat in his bag. They were so exhausted that by the end of the week, everyone collapsed in a daze.

On April 30th, Art's dad got up at 4:30 am to prepare for their departure. The weather added to the gloom of the day—misty and gray. His mother made one last pot of tea. Then she meticulously washed and dried the pot before placing it between clothes in her suitcase. The family gathered together to wait. Silence fell over them like the dark, ominous clouds outdoors. The only sound was the ticking of the clock. Tick, tock, tick, tock, then the slurp of Art's father as he finished his tea.

It was 6:30 am.

"Look, Mr. Suyama has arrived. His neighbor is driving that grand station wagon," Art said.

The sight of the station wagon used to thrill him. Whenever he visited Tom, he admired how the wood side panels contrasted with the blue body. It looked classy to him. Today, the sight of the car filled him with dread. Tom's dad stepped out to help load the bags while the family squeezed into the overloaded vehicle. Art ran his hand over the smooth brown wood trim one last time before getting in. This should have been a treat for them, to cruise around in that car, listening to the motor's deep roar as it made its way over the West Seattle bridge. But everyone sat in silence, staring out the windows, numb with misery. The car hummed up to Beacon Hill and took a left to their destination at Jefferson Park.

Intermittent rain showers punctuated the agony of waiting. Hundreds of Japanese milled about, sitting on their bags or pacing up and down the sidewalk. Children ran, splashing in the puddles while their parents chased them.

"You'll ruin your shoes. Get out of the water right now!" a mother screamed. "We don't have other nice clothes for her. They had to be left behind. We don't have enough to even care properly for our child. How can we function like this?" The woman slumped into her husband's arms.

"Don't worry, look, she didn't get soiled, just a little wet. We can dry her off once we get on the bus," he said to console her.

"What's taking so long? Why did we have to be here so early? To sit in the rain?" a young man complained.

After three long hours, someone yelled out, "I see an entire line of buses heading our way!"

Sure enough, buses began lining up, old and dilapidated, adding to the embarrassment everyone was experiencing. A hushed quiet engulfed them while soldiers with guns at the ready, unsettled then angered Art. They labeled each person with a number and attached a corresponding one to their solitary bag. Art watched as his bag was tossed in the undercarriage of the bus, landing with a thud from the weight of the books. The soldier pointed his rifle at him, directing him to the bus to take them to Camp Harmony.

"That sounds like a nice place," said Chibi, clutching Prince's favorite stuffed rabbit.

"Yeah, right. I bet it's a great place," Art replied with a sarcastic tone. A wave of guilt swept over him when he saw her little face look up, shocked.

He overheard a man mumble *warui hito* under his breath, which meant bad man in Japanese. The soldier didn't change his grim expression. Either he didn't hear or more likely, didn't understand.

"How can you be calm when we had to leave our home? What have we done to deserve this?" Art asked his dad, slowly mounting each step in his small act of resistance.

"Some things aren't clear right now, but I'm sure our government must have a reason for this. We may be safer under their guidance. *Gaman*, we must endure and have patience, some things can't be helped," said his father. Did he note a slight rolling of his mother's eyes?

Once loaded, the buses left for the journey to an unknown location. The buses seemed to crawl south to the destination.

After two hours, it entered a gate, then started

bouncing along muddy roads toward a long line of buildings. Where the bus stopped astonished everyone.

"This is the end of the line—Camp Harmony," announced the driver.

"Is this our *Camp Harmony*?" someone on the bus asked in dismay. "This is the Washington State Fairgrounds. Why, there are only animal stables and arenas here!"

Art stepped down from the bus and sank into a few inches of mud. He tried to help his mother and sisters, but he couldn't prevent them from submerging in as well, soiling their best Sunday shoes and white bobby socks. Lillian tried stepping forward, screeching out,

"My shoe's stuck in the mud and now my bare stocking foot's in this horrible goo. I want to go home"

"Papa, take us home," Chibi joined in with her sister.

Art grabbed both his sister's hands, pulling them up and dragging them forward. Mama trailed behind, picking up Lillian's shoe.

They marched through the mud to a group of tables where they waited, again. Art flipped his collar up, but the rain trickled down his neck. Looking around, he didn't complain—everyone was miserable. One thing he could say about the Japanese, they were a quiet, law-abiding lot. His father said this was a strength of their race. Now Art wondered if they should have put up more of a fight and maybe this wouldn't have happened.

"It comes from centuries of tradition, my son. Our race takes pride in unity and never standing out. An old saying goes, *the nail that sticks out gets hammered down.* My father told me over and over the importance of humbleness, to always respect our elders and anyone in authority. We must stay honorable to being Japanese, as well as American."

Art led his two sisters and parents to their

"apartment" 80, in section 4. The room was about eighteen feet by twenty feet, with a door in the center of the street wall, and directly opposite, a solitary window. The walls were of single-thickness plywood, with cracks and knotholes. These formed an intricate design of lines and holes providing peek-a-boo areas. Separating their one-room 'apartment' from their neighbors were walls touching only one side of the sloping roof. The other end left a gap of about four feet between the apartments. Art looked around the room in despair, noting one light bulb hanging from the center and a small wood-burning stove. Their room already had five cots with thin cotton pads for mattresses, leaving a few feet of free space to arrange their meager belongings.

"It smells musty and there's mold in the corners of these cots! I can't sleep here—it's filthy," Lillian said, scrunching up her nose as she lifted an end of the cot.

Art threw down his bag. "I've got to go look around. This can't be it!"

He left his stunned family standing around the stove, still holding their suitcases as if they had somewhere else to go. He trudged through the mud to join a few other young men. They compared stories that were more or less the same for each person. There were eight rooms or "apartments" in each barrack that had these shed-type roofs, six barracks in each row, and twenty-four rows in the camp. A barbed-wire fence surrounded the entire complex, with sentry towers posted evenly around. The buildings were made of the cheapest lumber imaginable. But at least they were new, compared to others who had old stalls that housed livestock during the fairs.

"We're expected to live in an old horse stall. I can smell the manure and we don't even have mattresses. They pointed to empty sacks and told us to stuff them with straw.

No one can sleep on straw—there are bugs and the ends are sharp. Every time we move, we'll get jabbed by a piece of straw," a fellow incarceree moaned.

"And do you know what my father said? That a lot of good things grow from horse manure. Now, doesn't that take the cake!"

"I had a nice home with my own bedroom. Now I'm forced to live like a prisoner. My God, I was studying to be a doctor."

"What have we done to deserve this? Why are we being singled out?"

Art didn't know what to say—they didn't deserve this, yet here they were. And it had happened so fast.

He returned to their room to find everyone sitting on a cot, staring down at their feet. Except for Lillian, who was trying to brush her mattress off outside.

"I'm getting the dirt out of mine, then I'll do the others after."

Chibi was sliding her shoes back and forth, making tracks in the dirt covering the floor. It was mealtime. Art and his family joined the long line of bodies, hunched over under the sheets of rain. Once in the cafeteria, there were no available seats together. Art sat alone beside an older man who wouldn't even glance up to look at him. Was it shame, hatred, or perhaps fear, but Art felt the same, as he poked at the round pile of mush on his plate. Was it potatoes or soggy bread? The old man pushed the plate away in disgust.

"What do you think this is?" Art asked.

"No good, I eat rice and meat with shoyu. I will die on this food."

Art looked at the slumped figure of the man. *This is too much for a man of his age, having to stay here, eating such slop.* He looked at the sheer number of people, people of every age wearing expressions as fatigued as the worn wooden benches and tables they were stooped over.

His mind reeled—what did all these people do to deserve this type of treatment? Was this just the first stop on a long line of stops? How much worse would it get? Were they going to be held responsible for the attack on Pearl Harbor? The rumination was going from bad to worse. Maybe the next step would be to separate the women and children from the men. Could they do that? What would stop them? Most of the country seemed to back the government's actions. It was impossible to not worry.

No one seemed to get much sleep that night. He heard every stirring in the other "apartments"—people coughing, whispering. Then Chibi started crying for Prince.

"If only I could hold him, then I'd know everything would be okay," she said, gasping between sobs.

It was a fitful night, one to be followed by many more of the same.

Weeks passed, and most tried to make the best of the situation. A few groups developed. Those who believed it was their duty to support the war effort vs. those who felt guilty, believing they must have done something wrong. Why else had they been taken away and treated like prisoners? Then there was a small group believing their constitutional rights had been denied, one tearing themselves apart from the rest, causing trouble, according to the others.

Art and his family belonged to the first group. His father had complete faith in his new nation.

"I'm sure they had no choice, and it won't be for long." His father managed to keep up his spirits, though Art didn't understand how.

"Before I left Japan, I was told to stand as strong as Mt. Fuji," Art's mother said. "They said I would meet obstacles in America. When I fear I'm weakening, I remember the majestic mountain and it fills my spirit."

Art tried to think of Mt. Rainier, the equivalent mountain near his home in Seattle. He could even catch glimpses of it on a clear day from the camp. It filled him with hope their time would be short here. He would try to stay strong.

Following the other inmates, as they liked to call each other, he found scraps of wood to fashion a small table and amend what he could of their little abode. He put up a little shelf by the side of his bed and bought a small radio after his nicer one had been taken. The radio provided company in an otherwise lonely situation.

Then one sunny afternoon, Art was summoned to the front gate. Standing behind the wire fence was his good buddy, Bob, who was sticking his hands through the fence to greet him. Art not only felt like a criminal but he looked like one, trapped behind the barbed wire, like a tiger in a zoo, too dangerous to be free. It was hard for him to look Bob straight in the eye.

"Oh man, Art. I had to come down to see you. We're all with you, you know that, right?"

"Yeah, I know. It's been tough, cut off from all of you." He forced an awkward smile and saw Bob wince. The whole situation was impossible.

"Why are there guards? This is unbelievable. You're not any different than me. I have German blood, but I'm not locked away."

"I don't know why there are guards. I keep wondering what we've done wrong, but there's nothing. We're bound to be released soon, right?"

Bob just shook his head, looking down as he kicked at the dirt.

"Well, keep a stiff upper lip. You'll be out in no time, I'm sure."

"Thanks for coming to visit. It means a lot, say hi to the guys for me."

As Bob turned away, Art wished he could jump in the car with him—to go see a show or get a soda at the fountain on California Ave. It was great to see Bob, but now he felt worse than before the visit.

He missed his buddies in West Seattle and hoped to hear from them, as they had promised. It was depressing knowing life was continuing as usual without him, and he was missing out on it all. He wondered what Sharon was doing. Was she still visiting the gymnastics team, maybe eyeing one of his other teammates? What a fool he'd been.

Most of them accepted the government regulations as the directives appeared. They said it was for the good of the nation. Art knew too much idle time would depress him further. Finding work would give him a sense of purpose and get his mind off all those worries ruminating in his head. He found a part-time job at the hospital doing menial tasks— helping nurses care for patients and doing some basic cleaning. The hospital was on the far side of camp in section D and their apartment was in A and no one was free to move between the areas. They gave him an inter-area pass he had to carry with him at all times. He worried what might happen if he didn't have it, the guards were quite stern.

He tried to adjust to this penned-up life, but the tormenting thoughts kept invading his mind. *First, I couldn't stay in my home in Seattle, and now I'm not trusted to walk from one side of this barbed wire camp to the other. Do we really need armed guards? Would they shoot me? What do they think I would do? And where could I go? What's happening to our country?*

9

ÉCUEILLÉ, FRANCE
1943

Yvette's home was situated outside the town proper and having a large family made it an ideal safe house, or at least that's what her father believed. He stood his ground whenever her mother complained about the dangers he was taking.

"Even if the Nazis come this way, they won't find anything. I've stashed everything behind your conserves in the cellar. "

"What about those men who pass through here? They look like resisters. What if they're seen by our neighbors?" Yvette's mother asked.

"None of our neighbors can see our home. No, I'm sure it's as safe as it can be."

"It takes one accidental slip of the tongue among the children and the consequences would be disastrous."

"I understand... I think the children do too. They know how dangerous the Nazis are and the risks we're taking. The war has forced them to grow up too fast," her father said.

Yvette kept wondering how she could help—it was impossible to be complacent, knowing her father was fighting for the cause. It was time to try a different approach. She'd continue helping her mama with the cooking and other chores. Then on her next trip to town, she would do a little investigating. The owner of the café, Le Café des Sports, was involved in the local resistance. It was time to take the next step. After collecting her courage, she walked in to speak to the owner, Mr. René Couet.

"I'm Yvette, my father's Maurice. I understand he's a colleague of sorts and I was hoping there may be some way I could be of help?"

Mr. Couet looked around before guiding Yvette past the bar to the back room. The man at the counter was too busy nursing his cognac to pay them any mind. His traditional blue attire suggested he was a paysan or farmer, with more worries on his mind than what Mr. Couet was up to.

"I know your father well. He's of great help to us. Why isn't he here with you?"

Yvette felt comfortable with him from the start. His bushy mustache bounced as he spoke and his jovial, round face could disarm the angriest of persons. She cleared her throat.

"I've tried to talk to him but he's adamant I not get involved, but I can't sit doing nothing when so much needs to be done!"

Standing next to him was a young man, Didier. He voiced his opinion on the matter.

"She's young enough to make an excellent bicycle courier."

"What about her father," Mr. Couet argued. "Think of the consequences—we can't afford to lose his help."

They discussed it for a few minutes, Yvette suddenly self-conscious, alone in the darkened room.

"It's true the Nazis don't believe women are in the fight. We can take advantage of their foolishness."

René put his arm over Didier's shoulder as they gave her the news. Everyone looked pleased with the decision, especially Didier. His eyes sparkled even more than before, and she wasn't sure anyone's smile could be larger.

Yvette's first assignment was to distribute leaflets throughout the town and surrounding farms. She would pretend to be out for a ride in case anyone questioned her. Her contact would be Didier. They were to meet in the morning to discuss logistics, risks, and responsibilities.

Yvette rode out to the café the following morning. Didier was waiting, looking nonchalant, leaning against a chair. As their eyes locked, he knocked over the chair, falling onto the table. So much for being discreet. She warmed at the thought he might be nervous. Even though she was only sixteen, she was beginning to like this attention from the opposite sex. Maybe it was her natural blond hair, which wasn't so natural since she had found that bottle of peroxide. Whatever it was, it thrilled Yvette that Didier might have some interest in her. But she needed to concentrate on the task at hand.

Didier recovered from his maladroit maneuver and nodded at her. They rendezvoused around the corner, a few steps from the main town square, tucking into a narrow doorway belonging to the Richards, who were at work, making it a safe place to talk.

"We have papers arriving tonight with information on what's really happening in our country. The truth about the Nazis and our fight. We need to let people know there's hope, to not give up. Let's meet at the stade tomorrow."

Yvette knew the stade or fairgrounds well. Besides being the place for sports, it was a popular spot for young lovers to meet, in need of some quiet time. She was delighted to be of help, even if it was only a little.

The next morning, Didier was waiting on a bench as if they might be one of those young couples. She wondered how she had never noticed him before. His dark brown hair framed his face, accentuating strong cheekbones. A firm chin added to the determination he carried in his chestnut eyes. It was hard to hide her attraction and contain her enthusiasm as she pulled her bike up. She bent over to give him a quick *bise* or air kiss across the cheeks and he slipped her the bundle of leaflets. Tucking them in the bag behind her bicycle seat, she tried to calm her nerves while pedaling down the street to the farmhouses. She was familiar with each one — Mrs. St. Martin who made the delicious pyramid goat cheese, Mrs. Dubois whose specialty was the very best honey candies in the region, and Mr. Barrat who owned the horse meat store.

It was mid-day when most people were at work or out running errands. Still, she took care before slipping a leaflet into each home's paper box. The only home she ran into trouble was Madame Augustin who was tending her garden. Yvette was getting off her bicycle when the woman popped her head up from behind her rose bushes.

"Why Yvette, what are you doing out here? Are you looking for Claude?"

"Ahem, yes. I was wondering if he was here."

"He's helping his father at the garage. He'll be happy to know you came calling."

"Sure, thank you, Madame."

Madame Augustin's expression was skeptical as Yvette left to deliver the rest of the leaflets. She hurried home, stored her bicycle in the shed, then headed to the house, passing Mauricette kneeling in the garden.

"I'm picking lettuce for dinner tonight. You can help Mama chop the potatoes."

"I'm heading right in."

Yvette joined alongside her mother, cutting the potatoes into chunks while Madeleine whisked mustard with vinegar for the salad dressing.

Yvette smiled at her little brother, Robert, who was pushing a box around the kitchen making the sounds of a tractor. Her oldest sister, Renee, was likely out with Pierre. Everything seemed quiet. It was a relief to be back home.

The following day Yvette finished her morning chores and then jumped on her bicycle. Something was drawing her back to Didier, a desire she had never experienced before. Hoping to catch a glimpse of him, she peddled around the fairgrounds, the town square, then up and down a few side streets. Her heart sank when he wasn't anywhere to be found. It would be a long wait until their next planned rendezvous at the stade. She headed down the path homeward when a dark figure circled overhead. The familiar calling, "caw, caw" greeted her. Arthur, her crow, had mended well, ready and able to take off on his own. Yet he seemed content to stay near the family farm. Yvette enjoyed having him around to watch his silly antics, strutting about the farm, jumping through the grass in search of anything edible. In the air he was graceful, but on the ground, he looked clownish, which always made her laugh and forget her day-to-day miseries with the war.

Her father stayed busy milling the few grains neighboring farmers collected or doing the never-ending repairs on the farm equipment. But at night he was often gone. What else was he involved in? Yvette had heard about the bombing of a bridge and thought of the small grenades in the cellar. And the other morning, she saw two men washing themselves in the creek alongside the house. They weren't speaking French. Her mother said it was Polish and warned her not to talk with them.

"Stay out of your father's affairs. There's too much at risk with the Wolffs and our family. We mustn't draw any attention to ourselves."

Yvette mulled those warnings over. She didn't want any harm coming to her family, but something deep inside kept drawing her to a greater purpose.

The week crawled by until it was time to meet with Didier. She hurried to finish her chores—a quick brush for Belle before releasing her out to pasture, then she cleaned the stall before bounding on her bicycle. Riding past the café, she dashed up the street to the cement park benches at the far end of the fairgrounds. There was a bench tucked between a small stand of poplar trees and bushes. It would be an ideal spot for a private conversation. She leaned her bicycle against the bench, then slid herself down. The stone was cool on her bare legs beneath the cotton sheath of her skirt. Looking around, she reminisced about past parades. Every summer, there was a tribute to those who had lost their lives in the war of 1914. The town's band would lead the soldiers who had made it back. They were a mixed group of men—one missing an arm, another a leg, or sometimes both. Others had parts of their face missing, an ear or an eye. But they always walked with pride, as France had won that war. The band would play the Marseillaise to an audience of smiling faces, moist from memories relived. How Germany thought another attempt was a good idea was beyond belief. What scared her was it looked like this time, they might succeed. And that couldn't happen.

The world seemed peaceful from this bench. Sparrows flitted from branch to branch in the pine trees, and a squirrel cried a warning from above. Lost in thought, she didn't hear Didier walk up from the other side of the trees and jumped when he placed his hand on her shoulder. They greeted each other with the traditional *bises*, three times which was common in Écueillé but could range from two to four depending on the region.

He had a small leather bag slung over his shoulder. After he sat down, they exchanged the usual pleasantries.

"The weather is warm for this time of year," she commented.

"The crops could use some rain, but there isn't a cloud in the sky," he replied.

As they spoke, he opened his bag while looking around to ensure no one saw the exchange. He slid an envelope to her, then looking as casual as possible; she slipped it into her bag. At the same moment, a woman started crossing the field toward them. Didier grasped her hand in his left, then with his right, started to stroke her cheek. He ran his fingers through her hair, pulled her close to him, and gave her a long kiss. His embrace was firm yet tender. Yvette melted into him as the woman cut over to the other side of the field to give them privacy. Yvette was enjoying the kiss and hoped the woman would return. As soon as she had passed, Didier stopped and apologized for the sudden amorous maneuver.

"I'm sorry. I thought an embrace would be a good cover for us."

Yvette still felt his fingers caressing her hair and those lips, oh, those lips that pressed so confidently against hers. She was light-headed. Was he speaking to her? Had he enjoyed that, or was he only trying to cover for them? Her cheeks felt flushed, and she hoped she didn't smell too much like horses. The woman had departed only moments after they started kissing. He cleared his voice and released her hand.

"So those are new flyers to distribute to the homes, but don't let anyone see you. You never know whom you can trust."

Yvette, still dizzy, tried to gather herself. That had been her first kiss and what a kiss. She couldn't wait for another. Was anyone else coming by? Her eyes darted around, but everything was quiet and calm. A sigh of disappointment slipped out, which she hoped didn't sound like disinterest.

"Oh yes, don't worry. I'll be very careful. When shall we meet again?"

Soon, I hope, she thought. And perhaps at a busier time, closer to when the schoolchildren get out.

10

CAMP HARMONY, WA
JUNE 1942

A rt sat down to write a letter to Bob, expressing his gratitude for making the trip. It had been hard for Art to even look Bob in the eye. Standing behind the wire fence added a sense of guilt to the pressures enveloping him, like a vice gripping him tighter each day. How could he release the constraint keeping him from even thinking straight? Maybe a letter would help him work through it.

Dear Bob,

Thanks again for visiting me in my 'home away from home.' I will attempt to describe life here at Camp Harmony. Everyone complains about something or another. My chief worry at present is what the situation will be when the war is over. Will I be able to find a job? Or will the government be forced to annul our citizenship to prevent us from suing for losses incurred in the evacuation? I don't think I would sue; I want only a chance to work and live peacefully with the white Americans that I've been living with.

I've been working at the hospital helping where I can, taking pulses and temperatures. Miss Toshiko Takao, the head nurse of the men's section of the hospital, taught me how. We call her "Butch" and only a mild-tempered girl like her could stand the teasing we boys give her. Anyway, she's so good looking that she's bound to attract a lot of attention. She told me she used to work by Fauntleroy in West Seattle at the Laurelhurst Sanatorium.

Art paused as he dipped his pen in the inkwell, daydreaming of Butch. He teased her, but deep down; he had quite a crush on her. He wondered if she would ever take him seriously. With a sigh, he lifted the pen to start another line.

For recreation, we have ping-pong, chess, pinochle, dancing, basketball, indoor concerts, and judo. I go to every dance. We have a PA system that plays the records, and the dance committee bought wax for the floors. We don't need wax; we need a new floor. Our dance hall is Mess #4, and the floor is warped shiplap, so dancing is difficult. We have a basketball court with a dirt floor, but it's outside.

Art sat back for a moment to think about the dirt that was everywhere. He looked around the small room his family shared. His mother had made some curtains from fabric someone had sent to the camp. She had picked out blue and white gingham, but the white was already dingy gray from the grime floating everywhere. The window had a thin coating of dust, giving it a dream-like appearance as he gazed out.

Life around here is more or less degrading. Everyone wastes their time, and there's plenty to waste. I'm concerned for our elders—the Wonder bread and peanut butter are so foreign to them, they are barely eating. I've seen cases of diabetes and heart disease develop with the sudden change in diet. The stress isn't helping either.

Thanks again for the visit. It was great seeing you.

—Art

And so life continued at a mundane pace for everyone in Camp Harmony. With time, Art began making friends, realizing how special it was to share culture and traditions with other Japanese his age. There was his best friend from West Seattle High, Tom, and now another new buddy, Frank.

Frank and his family lived in the barrack next to his. Being from central Seattle, he had been raised with many other Japanese. Art was envious hearing about the delicious meals to be had in *Nihonmachi* or Japantown and going to a Japanese language school. These friends understood the stern discipline from parents. To only talk if spoken to first, to always respect your elders, and to never question their authority. Not standing up for one's individual rights stemmed from the culture their parents had brought from the old country. It was arrogant to draw attention to oneself. Instead, as a group they supported one another to form a strong community and did what the authorities said was the best for them.

Time crawled by for the three months Art and his family were in the Puyallup assembly center. His buddy Bob came to visit one more time, again only allowed to visit through the wire fencing which was awkward for both of them.

"This is unbelievable! You are the most American guy I know and here they have you locked up and under guard like a convict."

Art felt ashamed. Standing on the wrong side of the fence was humiliating. It must have shown in his face—Bob never came back to visit.

Everyone in the camp grew closer to each other, sharing in the day-to-day drudgery of incarceration living, but patience was wearing thin. How much longer were they to be detained?

The answer came in August. The entire center was being moved again, now to the Minidoka Relocation Center in

Hunt, Idaho. Where is that? Art wondered. He asked around and found that Hunt was in the far south of Idaho, about fifteen miles from Twin Falls.

So they were uprooted again. Down came the gingham curtains and Art stuffed the radio into his bag. Chibi hugged Prince's stuffed rabbit in one arm and held Art's hand in the other, and Lillian dragged herself behind them as they headed for not a bus, but a train. The Nazis had invaded Stalingrad, and the Americans were fighting the Japanese at Guadalcanal. The entire world was at war and they were getting dragged to another camp. Art felt the world spinning out of control, and he was trapped in the vortex.

The trains were re-commissioned ancient passenger cars that were old, dirty, and slow. The windows were sealed shut and covered. There was no ventilation whatsoever.

"We're being treated like felons being taken to God knows where. I'm still not sure why," one young man complained. "Have they found any of us guilty of anything?"

Art looked around at the other passengers sitting on the hard benches in the dark. Surrounding him were many old people and children and women who looked completely harmless to anyone.

Art stayed with his family to support his sisters. They were both so different—Lillian, the quiet one, staring down the train aisle, looking away anytime someone passed by. Chibi, on the other hand, was more engaging, smiling often. She still brought up Prince, asking if anyone knew if they were returning pets to their rightful owners. But that was getting less frequent. Art tried to convince himself that the vet had found him a new home.

The train crawled along at a snail's pace. It would chug onward, then almost stop, yet never cease moving, as if searching for the right route to take. Would they ever arrive or just travel around until the end of the war? At least they were being fed decent food with a dessert after each meal. They had chocolate pudding once, which was the cat's meow to Art.

The train ride seemed to take an eternity, creeping forward to who knows where.

By the first nightfall, Art pried one window open. The rest of the evening, he gazed out, watching the scenery change from mountains to barren sand dunes. A cool breeze blew across his face as he looked skyward at more stars than he'd ever seen. He dozed off for only a few hours before the sun blasted its heat into the train car.

"When are they going to stop? Can't we get out to stretch our legs or get some fresh air? I feel like a condemned criminal," the man behind Art said. Art turned, giving a sympathetic nod as they exchanged commiserating glances.

Finally, the train stopped, making no effort to start back up. Everyone looked around, even Lillian made eye contact with the strangers nearby.

"Everyone off the trains. We've arrived in Eden, Idaho."

Art blinked his eyes against the brightness. It looked as if they had landed on another planet. There were tumbleweeds and dirt spinning in circles as far as he could see. It didn't look like any Eden to him. He had never seen anything like this before. The armed guards directed them to follow the line of people headed to buses. Again, more buses. As they clambered in, people started coughing from the dust floating up in plumes. Covering their mouths was futile as the handkerchiefs became covered in grime within minutes. It was as if they had entered the Dust Bowl of the Great Plains.

The buses didn't travel for long, perhaps thirty minutes. Art stared out the window, becoming more depressed as the flat, arid land spread out for miles and miles. He had hoped to see a few trees as they took each corner, but none appeared.

The buses passed through gates surrounded by tall wire fences topped with barbed wire. More barbed wire and sentry lookout towers every 50 ft or so with guards, and long barracks lined up one after another. His heart fell at the thought of this being their destination. At least in Puyallup, he was near Seattle. Now they were far away, in a hot, dry climate that made it hard to breathe. Living in Seattle, everyone was acclimated to the moist, clean sea air. How long could they survive in a place like this?

They waited in line... patiently... again. They received their barracks number. Art's family was in Area 2, Block 28, Barrack 1-C. This time, instead of tromping through mud, dust covered not only their shoes but their entire body. Art felt the grit between his teeth, scratching under his eyelids and even creeping into his underclothes. They found their Block, which contained twelve barracks. Each barrack was divided into six rooms with one family assigned to live together in one room. The rooms looked much like the detention center in Puyallup, with one lightbulb and one coal-burning stove.

"Are we expected to live like this again? All of us crammed in one room and for how long *this* time?" a young woman cried out. Art suspected it would be longer since the last place was a temporary holding area and it had lasted three months.

"I guess we might be here for the rest of the war and maybe even longer," he replied.

His mother went looking for a broom and a few things to help clean up the place. There was dust everywhere, the heat sweltering.

"Why couldn't they have found a place near Seattle?"

Art asked.

"I suspect this was the only area large enough for so many of us," his father said.

"Out of the entire state of Washington, they couldn't find anything?"

"That's enough. Help me move these cots around while your mother sweeps."

It was time to curb his tongue. *Don't talk back to your parents.*

Minidoka was bedlam. From the first, everything seemed wrong. It was a rush job, and the contractors hadn't completed the work before the government started sending in the incarcerees. The plumbing facilities weren't ready, so outhouses had to be used, wooden planks with holes. There were no partitions for even a spattering of privacy, adding to the overall humiliation. No one had ever lived like this.

"My mother is so uncomfortable with the lack of privacy, she's avoided going to the toilet. Now she's all blocked up and needs treatment," one man said.

"We had a nice home. How can we live like this? It's a prison, but what have we done?" another asked. It was becoming the question of the year.

Most everyone had come from middle-class America, living in single-family homes. Sharing facilities with untold numbers of strangers created many anxieties. The horrors of showering and exposing their naked bodies among so many unfamiliar faces added to the dread.

To make matters worse, wiring in some barracks was incomplete. Candles served as a poor substitute, making it near impossible to read or do anything once night fell. The only source of heat was a pot-bellied stove and the one blanket provided to each person was thin. Sears & Roebuck catalogs became the hot item for the essential supplies.

Rumors spread that winters were frigid here and the nights were indeed already cold.

"Can you believe how poor these barracks are made? Look at these gaps where the planks don't meet. And now the green wood is drying and shrinking, I can fit my finger through this hole," Art said.

"I tried stuffing some paper between but the wind blew it right out. All this dust and even bugs are crawling in," Lillian said.

Their mother just shook her head as she grabbed the broom to sweep again. It was a never ending task she had adopted since their arrival.

Being philosophical people, almost everyone took things as they came and made the best of the situation. The elders kept repeating, "*Shikataganai*, it can't be helped, nothing can be done about it." Someone had said aptly that mass incarceration would have not been possible with the Irish—one day of camp life and they would have knocked down the fences and moved out!

Some incarcerees continued their usual craft. Their new neighbor in the adjacent room, Mrs. Fujita, had brought her watercolors with her. She was an unassuming older woman who kept to herself most of the time. Art never heard either her or her husband utter a negative word about the incarceration or the conditions in the camp, but the pictures she drew spoke volumes about her inner suffering. She had given one of her paintings to Art's mother. It was in tones of gray depicting the barracks surrounded by the fence. A guard was in a tower, gun at the ready, gazing down at a young girl. The only color to be found was a plant of purple heather near the base of the tower.

Days turned into weeks, then months. At first, Art found work at the mess hall preparing the tables for the meals. Thanks to contacts he had made in Puyallup, he found a better job in the hospital cafeteria where he would see Butch. She, too, was in Minidoka, and was a nurse in the hospital. She was becoming quite friendly to both his buddy, Tom and himself. A few years older, she acted more like a big sister. However, either of them would have preferred to be considered suitors. Anyway, the job paid $9.00/month, and it helped pass the time.

Being a waiter, Art had a white jacket, a white shirt with a tie, and an apron. He thought it made him look pretty sharp. He had the choice to eat first or last, but sometimes he did both. His job was to set the tables with salad, eating utensils, and to serve drinks. The meals usually were some type of overcooked meat alongside mashed potatoes with gray, sticky gravy, served cafeteria style. The elders missed rice and fish, which was plentiful at home. Many became weak and sick from the lack of vegetables or protein and the children failed to grow well since the much needed milk to support their bones was rare. And it was hard to eat much when it was so unappetizing.

"I know it's not very good but there is a war going on. We all need to do our best, things could be worse," Art tried to sound convincing. But even he had a hard time accepting the situation and felt his mood sink.

At least there were dances nearly every weekend. After a shower, he would dress in his best slacks and shirt, then cross the camp, hoping the dust wouldn't spoil his clean look. The almost constant grit between his teeth no longer bothered him, he'd wash it down with the soda at the dance. They only had records for the dances—the good oldies which were perfect for waltzes, foxtrots, and the like. The cafeterias became the dance halls once the tables got pushed to the edges of the rooms. They had the best floors for dancing, which wasn't saying much. Art's shoes would catch on the uneven planks, causing him to roll off and lose his balance. But he would laugh it off. As long as he was dancing, he wasn't going to complain.

It was the weekend, and as Art entered the dance room; he smiled to himself. Each couple moved around the floor in perfect unison, as if choreographed, the result of having the same instructors and dance classes. Each step, each turn, and each spin was the same. The couples moved in perfect harmony, never bumping into one another nor needing to look out for another couple. Art loved dancing more than anything at the camp and seldom missed an opportunity. He was becoming known as one of the better dancers. He noticed many women making eyes at him when he walked by. And his buddies teased him incessantly about it.

"Geez, Art, look at Kimi smiling at you," or "Hey Art, did you see how Mary was winking your way?"

Time crept by in the camps. Art's dad started giving Buddhist lessons on the weekends. He wasn't an expert but had a good grasp of the teachings of Buddha. Many Issei enjoyed spending time together discussing the practices which helped with the pain of incarceration. Camp administrators favored the younger English-speaking Nisei and placed them in positions of authority. This undermined the Issei, who were forbidden from voting or holding office in what passed for self-government in the camps. Overnight, generational roles changed. The Issei became depressed as the discipline they had worked so hard to create slipped away. The family unit was crumbling before their eyes. Their children were eating away from them and spending long periods wandering around the camp, sometimes ending in trouble. The strict upbringing was disappearing, and the Issei were searching for ways to cope and accept. Then there was the emotional toll of the loss of freedom. No one could walk outside without being followed by guards and at night searchlights followed them as if they were being stalked by a hunter. Art's sister Lillian was the most affected. She was very self-conscious about the lack of privacy. The pressures were coming from every direction, and Art wondered if and when something would give.

Art considered himself Christian, yet enjoyed sitting in on his dad's Buddhist teachings to see how the elders were staying calm during these upheavals. The teachings were of Honen and Shinran, the founders of The Pure Land or Jodo Shinshu Buddhism.

There was the underlying confusion between Buddhism and the Shinto religion. Art's father said he left Shintoism in Japan, that it didn't have a place in America.

But the Buddhist scriptures helped bring solace to the Issei, searching for a way of life in the harsh camp environment.

"Impermanence is the cornerstone of Buddhist teachings—nothing lasts, neither good nor evil. Thus, nothing should be grasped or held onto, no matter how painful it is to let go," he discussed with his group of elders.

"That's right. We must release clinging to our homes and livelihoods to prevent more suffering, dukkha, right?"

"Exactly. We must follow this path, not grasping at material objects or feelings. If we can rise above these attachments, we can achieve freedom from suffering. We must appreciate what we have—our families, newfound friendships, challenges from which we can grow and learn. It's been difficult losing our previous lives, but if we accept these changes, we'll achieve peace."

Art was attentive as his father spoke, soaking in the teachings. Since Buddhism taught that everything shall pass, both good and bad, he hoped this, too, would pass and perhaps they would come out better and stronger for it.

His father added that life requires effort. If not, entire lifetimes may be lived in vain.

"We will reach true happiness through generosity and virtue. Understand this and it will lead to the cultivation of compassion, to "feel" what others feel. We're all interconnected and we suffer in similar ways. Attaining greater self-awareness through mindfulness, we can see a glimpse of our true selves—the enlightened nature in all of us."

At the end they chanted *Namu Amida Butsu*, meaning, I take refuge in the Buddha. The discussions helped them accept their situation, including Art.

Through hard work, everyone tried to make the best of things in camp. The desolate landscape transformed into fertile fields under the backbreaking labor of the incarcerees. By digging ditches, they diverted water from the canal and victory gardens sprung up behind the barbed wire fences. Soon lettuce, strawberries, beans, and corn supplemented the meager rations the government provided.

The winters were especially formidable, as the coal supply was intermittent. If anyone asked, they were told everything was being rationed to support the war. So complaints were rare since everyone wanted to help the war effort. That didn't help Art's neighbor, Mr. Fujita, when his wife fell ill with a common cold. She had been painting the scenes along the canal where she must have caught a chill. Their neighbor on the other side brought her blanket, leaving only the thin sheet for her and her husband.

"Please take our blanket. You must keep her warm," the neighbor had said.

Her coughing worsened until one night the coughing

stopped and only gentle sobs of Mr. Fujita were heard. The next morning, they removed Mrs. Fujita's limp body, leaving her husband alone, with only paintings left behind to remember her.

11

ÉCUEILLÉ, FRANCE
1943

The men were becoming a common sight around Yvette's home. They came clad in woolen pants and khaki button-down shirts, sporting either a wool or leather jacket, topped off with a beret. Never did they arrive clean-shaven, but always became so in the early morning hours by the creek. Her mother continued acting as if all was fine, slipping out to give the men extra food when she thought no one was looking. Yvette wondered who these men were and where they came from. Distributing leaflets didn't seem to be of much importance, though Didier insisted getting the word out was essential.

"People must know what's being done or they will give up hope," he said.

Resistance activities were increasing, more explosions rocked railways and bridges and the stream of materials being transported into the cellar was steady, peaking Yvette's curiosity. One evening after her father left, she snuck over to investigate. There was a bright moon, lighting her way as she slipped through the shadows to the cellar. Once inside, she lit her lantern to head down the stairs. Taking care not to topple any of the wine or preserves, she moved the shelves just far enough for her slender body to pass. There were many more boxes than previously. After opening a few of them, she was satisfied her father was storing the explosives and guns used by the Resistance. Where were the supplies coming from? She would ask Didier on their next visit. He was reluctant at first, but she kept pressing until he caved.

"There's an organization, the Special Operations Executive—SOE, a British secret service. The Nazis infuriated us when they invaded our free zone. More joined the Resistance but we couldn't support them all. Churchill helped by creating the SOE-F, the French division. They're sending in arms, French francs and are parachuting in radio operators so we can communicate with London to coordinate our efforts. Now the Resistance and Maquis who weren't getting along have a central unifier and are fighting like an actual unit."

"But England abandoned us in Dunkirk. My father said Britain destroyed our ships near Algeria, killing many of our sailors."

"The Brits got trapped in Dunkirk and had no choice but to retreat. And they destroyed the ships in the Mediterranean to keep them out of the hands of the Nazis. We need the Brits—you should see the planes they use for the deliveries, these Lysanders or Lizzies, as they call them. They're repurposed bomber planes that can take off and land in tiny fields. It's tough flying. Lights are out of the question so they can only come during full moons and clear nights. Think how good those pilots are."

As he spoke, Yvette saw his infatuation with planes, these so-called bombers. His excitement was contagious and she too, became convinced France would win this war.

"Plus we've got 1000 planes from the U.S. including the B-26. They hold 2-ton bombs in their belly and are fast. There's a gunner in the tail and if the front is clear, it's like you're floating on air when you're tucked in the nose of the plane. Can you imagine what that must be like?"

She smiled at the passion in his voice and with his knowledge. Coming from a small village didn't keep him sheltered.

Didier continued, "The Resistance and Maquis come from two factions—those that were to be deported to work camps in Germany or Communists. At first, they had trouble working together, but their common goal to fight Nazis has forged an alliance."

Yvette thought about the broadcasts transmitted each night at 8:30 pm. Many French risked the consequences of being caught listening to the BBC. The "message personnel" would be included even though few understood the meaning except for members of the Resistance who eagerly awaited the hidden messages, ready to decode for the real meaning.

"Marcel est très malade," and "Antoine aime Brigitte toujours" and "Grandmère mange nos bonbons." Marcel is very sick, Antoine loves Brigitte forever, Grandma eats our candies.

These coded messages might indicate a parachute drop was arriving or a radio transmitter was coming in on the next Lysander drop. Then General de Gaulle's speeches encouraged the French not to give in to the Vichy government. These always heartened Yvette's father. He would bounce Robert on his knee or grab her mother and do a few twirls around the kitchen. It made everyone happy to see him lift out of his usual seriousness.

The weeks passed. Yvette met Didier many times, sometimes to collect leaflets, more often just to sit on the bench. They would hold hands, and discuss their dreams for the future. A future where the Germans were out of their country and everything was back to normal. Didier planned on taking over his family's small garage; repairing cars and equipment. It would be the perfect trade, and he wanted her by his side. Yvette loved thinking of that future but an unrest existed in her like there was more to do. As if the bread wasn't completely kneaded before someone wanted to put it in the oven. Was there something else waiting for her to discover outside of Écueillé?

January 1, 1944, tragedy hit their quiet town. The Gestapo arrested René Couet, captured along with the town butcher, and his wife. They took them to Chateauroux where it was well known that the Gestapo tortured the prisoners. No one knew how the Gestapo discovered these members of the Resistance, but now the need to keep their guard up was essential. No one could be trusted, townsfolk were denouncing their neighbors, friends, or even family members by sending letters called crow letters, which Yvette thought was a sad choice of words. Crows were faithful members of their group and would never denounce one of their own.

Had someone figured out meetings were going on in the café? Perhaps a snoopy neighbor had succumbed to the bribes of the Nazis. Yvette snuck to meet with a few of the Resistance members in the café, not sure it was safe to be there any longer. As an extra precaution, they met in the far back room behind the kitchen. Beside the table, hidden under a rug, was a trapdoor, which led to a cave to hide if need be. Plus, it was a convenient spot, since that was where they stored the surplus alcohol. Only the most trusted members were invited—Didier, Jean, Pierre, and Yvette.

"I was heading over to the post to deliver a truck part when I saw the Gestapo arrive in their black sedan. Four men jumped out, all dressed in those telltale black trench coats," Didier said. "Two came to the café and the two others to the butcher's shop. I recognized our fellow Frenchman, Roger

Picault, and Pierre Paoli as two of the four. They must have joined forces with the Gestapo as part of the Milice."

The Milice was an aggressive division of the Nazi-backed Vichy government made up of French, whose main purpose was to take down the Resistance. Known for using more severe torture tactics than the Nazis, they were an important aide in extracting information from their victims.

"What makes them more dangerous is that these Milice are French. They know our country and our people and are undermining our activities faster than the Germans. They've turned out to be more deadly killers than the SS!" Jean said.

"We'll have to stop all activity until things quiet down. We have two days to clear any incriminating evidence. That's how long a captured Resistant tries to stay silent under the torture."

"Meanwhile, we're following Couet's path. They've taken him to Gestapo headquarters in Chateauroux."

Yvette cataloged in her head, *That's where Fernande, my cousin lives. It's about thirty miles from here.*

"From there, he's going to be transferred to a larger prison in Limoges. That's our chance to liberate him," Didier continued. "We need cars to intercept the van transporting them. It's happening this weekend. We must have a foolproof plan."

"I'll come as a distraction. Drop me off near the edge of town and I'll pretend to have bicycle problems and flag them down for help.."

She waited as Didier and Jean considered her offer.

"It might work. We need some way to get them to stop so we can attack." Jean said.

"No, it's too dangerous. She'll be in the middle of the whole strike," Didier said.

"It's perfect; we have no other choice and time is of the essence," Jean stressed. "Yvette's in."

Saturday morning arrived. Yvette wouldn't admit it, but she was terrified. What was she thinking, to make such a risky offer?

They dropped her off at the outskirts of Chateauroux near the road heading to Limoges. Didier gave her a fervent kiss and made her promise to be extra careful. Yvette glanced over her shoulder as they drove away, now alone on the desolate road. Time crept by and Yvette wondered if something was wrong. Then she saw a van approach, but there should be another car coming from the opposite direction to help with the attack. She froze, should she carry on with the plan? Didier warned her not to draw attention to herself if she had any doubts, so Yvette continued riding down the road, praying she had made the right choice.

The van slowed alongside her. She wasn't sure why, didn't it appear as if she was minding her own business? A panic gripped her when one of the men in the van rolled down his window. But suddenly the van accelerated and sped off in a swirl of dust. Once again she was alone on the road, with only the company of particles of dirt descending around her. Within a few minutes, Didier and Jean drove up.

"Are you okay? If they'd stopped, who knows what would have happened? Good thinking, Yvette, since we had no way of contacting you," Jean said. "We were watching them transfer Couet and the others. Things were going as planned until two more guards jumped in the back with machine guns. We could have taken the driver and one guard, but not four men. It would have been suicide."

"We had to drive like crazy on the back roads to intercept the other car to tell them to abort the plan. We didn't know how to contact you and didn't want to risk their discovering your involvement. Thank God they didn't suspect anything." The panic in Didier's voice was palpable. She crumpled over her bicycle when the realization of what she'd avoided sank in.

So their mission had failed. From Limoges, they transferred the prisoners to Buchenwald. Once in Germany, little could be done for them. The resisters had worked hard on the rescue and felt dispirited, unsure how to re-establish themselves in Écueillé.

12

MINIDOKA, ID
1943

The classification of Japanese Americans as 4-C enemy non-aliens prevented the U.S. Army from accepting them into service. As the war progressed, the government began noting all those able-bodied men in Hawaii and the camps on the mainland. Early in 1943, the Selective Services made the move to lift the 4-C status and issued a call for volunteers. The plan was to form a special segregated unit—an all-Nisei regiment. Immediately, there were objections. Why separate them and not allow them to fight alongside Caucasian soldiers?

The project director at Minidoka camp offered the men two options.

"I understand this may seem like an insult. You can turn away and say if that's the way my country feels, I won't do anything for it. The other is to consider it an opportunity to prove yourselves."

Many of them agreed with the second option. Serving in a unit that was all Nisei, they would make a record as Nisei, instead of being dispersed among other units. Over 300 men volunteered immediately from inside the Minidoka camp. They would prove their loyalty to the nation.

Encouragement came from president, Franklin D.

Roosevelt:

"The proposal of the War Department to organize a combat team consisting of loyal American citizens of Japanese descent has my full approval. No loyal citizen of the U.S. should be denied the democratic right to exercise the responsibilities of his citizenship, regardless of his ancestry. The principle on which this country was founded and by which it has always been governed is that Americanism is a matter of the mind and heart; Americanism is not and never was, a matter of race or ancestry. A good American is one who is loyal to this country and to our creed of liberty and democracy. Every loyal American citizen should be given an opportunity to serve this country wherever his skills will make the greatest contribution—whether it be in the ranks of our armed forces, war production, agriculture, government service, or other work essential to the war effort."

Funny, Art thought—If Americanism isn't a matter of race or ancestry, why did they take everything away and place us in these concentration camps?

The War Department and War Relocation Authority (WRA) together developed a questionnaire to be filled out by all adults living in the camps. These became known as "loyalty" questionnaires, as a few of the questions appeared to put their loyalty to the U.S. under scrutiny.

Art sat down to answer the questions. It seemed pretty straightforward covering family members, level of education, religion, and languages spoken. But two questions caused quite a stir among many of the inmates.

"What about question number 27? Am I willing to serve in the U.S. Army and be sent anywhere for combat? After the way they've been treating me and my family? They have some nerve to ask that!"

"And what about the next one? Will I give up any allegiance to the emperor of Japan? Why I've never had any allegiance to Japan. It sounds like a trick question."

"Why are we the only ones required to complete these forms? What about the Germans or Italians?"

So the camp became divided. Art agreed with most of the guys that they should answer yes to both questions 27 and 28 and be willing to join the army. However, some others didn't agree, including his friend Henry. Henry had been studying law at the University of Washington before being sent to Minidoka.

"I'll fight for this country once they return our constitutional rights. They've got to let my parents and family return home. I answered Yes to both, adding the qualification—if they reinstate our civil rights."

Art understood what concerned these men, but didn't agree it was some type of trickery. After long and hard contemplation, listening to those around him, and considering all sides, he sat down to discuss the decision with his parents. His father was pensive without an immediate comment, but his mother was against it.

"Please don't risk your life for this country. They've no respect for us. Why would you want to display loyalty to them when they're treating us like criminals?" she asked. "And I'm afraid to lose you. You're my only son!" She was near tears, her hands trembling.

His father drew her to him. "He's a grown man now. We need to let him decide for himself."

For the next few days, the comments swirled around him. It would be easier to sit out the war in this camp, but what then? At least joining the army and fighting for their country would build some of the respect his mother said they didn't have. He met with some of the other fellows to discuss it.

"If we stay in camp, what will we have to show for it?"

Art asked. "The army will give us a record we can point to, to prove our loyalty, right? We can do our part plus get some training. I'll fight as best I can, so I won't have to answer to anyone for having been a coward."

"Are you calling me a coward? Because I want our constitutional rights restored first?" Henry stormed up, inches from Art's face.

"I can't help the way I feel."

"I'm not a coward!" Henry yelled, shoving Art with both hands.

Art lunged back, clipping him across the face. Henry returned the favor with a left toward Art's jaw, who ducked to miss the swing and it landed on Frank.

"Hey, who do you think you are, punching at us like that? We're willing to fight instead of sitting out the war in this stinking camp!" Frank yelled.

Henry spat red-tinged saliva and stormed off, clutching his jaw.

"I don't think either of us is winning this argument, just the U.S. government turning us against each other. Maybe he's on to something," Art said.

"Rotting in this camp isn't doing any of us any good. I'm joining if they'll take me," Frank said.

All his buddies nodded in agreement.

The words of President Roosevelt, who spoke of fighting for the freedom of speech, worship, want, and fear, inspired Art. And there was the closer purpose of proving his loyalty to his country. To show that facial characteristics and skin pigmentation had nothing to do with how loyal an American could be. So yes, joining was the only choice to make, and he was certain it was the right one.

The confined life in the camp was degenerating. Most of the guys gambled, smoked, drank, and swore—all a definite waste of time to him. The thought of being in uniform was attractive—egotism, perhaps. It gave one an air of authority and distinction, which would be a refreshing change. He worried about leaving his family. He would have to keep faith that the U.S. government would continue to provide, even though it was far from ideal. There wasn't a lot more he could do.

After days of hard contemplation, he dipped his pen in the ink and answered yes to both questions, and he was relieved he had. The War Relocation Authority decided those who answered no to questions 27 and 28 were disloyal. Even those that answered yes but added qualifiers "if they release my family" or "if they restore our rights" were considered disloyal. So Henry and all the others who gave 'incorrect' answers were segregated and moved to yet another camp, Tule Lake in California. They were to become known as the No-No boys. A deep rift between those that enlisted and the No-No Boys developed. Even the JACL(Japanese American Citizens League) denounced them. They had little to no support or understanding, including from Art, who had a hard time accepting their point of view, even as he listened to Henry.

"What about the civil liberties we studied in school? Don't any of you remember those? Sure, there's freedom of expression and religion, but how about the right to privacy, to equal treatment, and a fair trial? We've been thrown in here for committing what crime? When did we have a trial? Come on, this is a blatant disregard for the U.S. Constitution."

The guys listened half-heartedly, knowing Henry was making sense but also knowing that his attitude would only hurt them in the long run.

"The only way to prove we're good Americans is to buck up and fight for our country."

Most everyone nodded in agreement. Henry shook his head in despair.

"You guys don't get it. We can't get respect if we don't stand up to them. They can't strip us of our rights and then expect us to risk our lives for them. I want our rights returned first. I'm not a coward. I'd join in a heartbeat if they treated me as the American I am."

"Nope, I think we'll get more respect if we stand up and fight for and with our country. That'll prove to them they were wrong about judging us based on our race alone."

"But they're denying us the protection of the Bill of Rights. We don't have the freedom to live where we want in the forty-eight states and then they forced us into concentration camps without any hearing or charge of misconduct. They're tearing down the whole American system. They could deny these same rights to someone else six months from now for another poor reason as the one offered against the Japanese."

So Henry was sent off to Tule Lake, now designated as a segregation center. It was overcrowded, housing 18,700 people in a camp designed to hold 15,000. It became the largest and most conflict-filled of the ten WRA camps. Due to the presence of 'disloyals,' it became a prison camp, ruled by martial law. They reinforced security against the 'dangerous' inmates by increasing the guard towers from six to twenty-eight and protected the area by 1,000 military police with armored cars and tanks. Unannounced searches of barracks took place, and they curtailed daily activities. As one can imagine, tension built under the severe repression, and some inmates became bitter towards the U.S. completely losing faith in the nation of their birth.

The most divisive issue came in 1944. President Roosevelt signed a new law, directed at the Japanese

Americans in Tule Lake. It permitted an American citizen to renounce their citizenship in wartime. So under the duress in these repressive camps, some U.S. citizens turned their backs on their country, to go to an unknown land in Japan, hoping to find somewhere welcoming to their race. Little did they know what awaited them.

In contrast, the mood around Minidoka became close to festive with parties to celebrate the enlisting men. Women were in a flurry, making *senninbari*. Art's sister, Lillian, got a senninbari belt and ensured that 1000 women each placed a stitch of red yarn.

"A silent prayer accompanies each stitch to protect the wearer as he goes to battle," Lillian said as she offered it to him. "It will serve as a type of amulet or good-luck charm."

His heart melted when she offered it. He looked down at the white sash covered with red stitches, each placed perfectly aside from the next. He would wear it under his clothes with pride.

The excitement was exhilarating at the dances. The women swarmed the enlisted men. Art wondered if they feared they may never see them again and wanted one more dance. Then again, there wouldn't be many fellows around once they left.

Butch was spending more time with both him and Tom. During one dance, Art thrilled as she whispered into his ear.

"Promise you'll write and watch out for yourself. No heroics, but I know all of you will do anything to protect each other."

"We've become like brothers living in this camp. We know each other's families like our own. I'll be careful and promise you'll write back?"

"Of course," she murmured.

Art was sure she said the same to Tom, but still felt a special hope deep down.

While things were going swimmingly for all the enlisted men, things were much more trying for the families of the No-No boys. Other parents shunned them, whispering to one another, yet loud enough to be heard.

"Isn't it shameful about Hisa's son?"

"He'll make it harder for the rest of us left here in camp," another parent of a volunteer agreed.

The younger brothers were often targets of fistfights.

"Your brother is too chicken to go fight like my brother. Is he too good for us or what?"

"He's smarter. He knows we're captive under guards! Why's your brother so stupid he doesn't see that?"

Fists began flying, and fathers ran to separate the boys. No one knew exactly what to do to calm the volatile atmosphere.

It went on like this, but things became worse. Mrs. Shinoda's only son was sent to Tule camp after responding No-No to questions 27 and 28. They didn't spare the Shinoda family any of the degrading comments. Mrs. Shinoda, a quiet, delicate woman, had left behind her family in Japan to marry a man, sight unseen.

The following week, they found her body by the canal, her wrists slit—the comments from the others being too much for her to bear.

"Mrs. Shinoda was a kind woman but sad, telling me how she liked to walk along the canal, dreaming about being home in Japan," Art's mother said. "How she would laugh with her mother while they washed clothes together or prepared the evening supper. I hate to think of her poor mother in Japan getting this news."

Art was furious. If only their country had had some

faith in them instead of throwing them into these camps and forcing them to answer unfair questionnaires. He went down to the canal that evening—the setting sun glimmering red in the slow-moving water. He imagined the current carrying Mrs. Shinoda's blood and sorrow out of the camp, wondering how many more dead would join before all this madness ended. And would it all be worth it?

The men kept waiting for their call, but the Army had further suspicions. Each volunteer's record was checked and then rechecked in Washington, D.C., adding three more months to the selection process. Once cleared, a team of Army doctors came to Boise, Idaho for a screening exam to reject the unfit. Two hundred of the initial three hundred passed, including Art. It was a proud moment for him.

During the months while he awaited the call to duty, Art read everything about the war in Europe, putting aside his usual reads of novels like Death of a Salesman or Robert Frost's Poems. He delved into Ernie Pyles' war reports in the newspapers and listened religiously to Pyle's daily radio broadcasts. The war started in 1939, with Nazis and Russians invading Poland from either side. Germany continued its invasions, taking over Norway, Denmark then France. He read with fervor, wondering where the Nazis would stop. Then Hitler turned against his ally, Stalin, by sending the largest offensive force in history to invade the Soviet Union. The Soviets switched sides to join the U.S., Britain, and China in the war against Nazis and fascism.

Germany, Italy, and Japan formed a tripartite pact to become known as the Axis powers. Then Germany made its most fateful decision and declared war on the U.S. They destroyed merchant ships off the east coast of North America with their U-boats, sinking over 600 ships, and killing thousands of mariners. The war had entrapped the United

States from both sides between the Pacific and Atlantic oceans.

On April 30, Art received his orders. He and the first contingent of thirty volunteers were sent from the Hunt camp to the induction station in Salt Lake City, Utah. Upon arrival, they were issued uniforms and given furloughs to any point in the continental U.S. for one week.

"This is great. We can go to Seattle one last time," Art said.

"Yeah, let's go see all our buddies. One week in the city will be great." There was a tinge of doubt in Tom's voice.

Art shared the same concerns. Would they continue to face blatant prejudice despite wearing the U.S. Army uniform? They would soon find out.

The pullman took two-days, traveling through countryside neither recognized until they reached the West Coast.

"Look Tom, evergreen trees and blue skies like nowhere else."

They gazed out the windows in silence, as if speaking might break the magic. The train pulled into the Union Station in Seattle where they parted ways for the day. Art caught the bus at 4th and Jackson to head up Delridge Way to West Seattle. He stopped to pick up George's car, a '41 Chevy. George was still at Minidoka, but had given Art the key. George's car was going to be a great way to get around the city compared to the bus.

Art drove to the shed where they had stored their belongings. The lock was broken, the place ransacked, and most of their things were gone. He stepped over broken boards from the destroyed furniture. Everything was in ruin, the cash register's glass smashed and the keys jammed. He lifted a few remnants of clothes and uncovered his mom's sewing machine, which looked intact. He placed the machine into the trunk of the car. At least it had survived. His mother would love having it in camp and he wouldn't speak of the state of the rest of the shed.

That evening he went to pick up Tom, putting the shed out of his mind, dead set to enjoy their last few days of freedom. First stop, the Admiral Theatre to watch 'The Random Harvest', then visits with friends to favorite hang-out spots. It allayed their worst fears as everyone seemed thrilled to see them. Monday came too soon, and it was time to head back to Hunt. Art drove the Chevy across the Lake Washington bridge heading east, saying a silent prayer he would return someday.

It was exciting for Art to visit the camp, donned in his Army uniform. His mother's face lit up on seeing the sewing machine and his dad gave him a big grin and a deep bow. After seeing his folks and sisters, he swung by the hospital to find Butch. He had to turn the car into the Internal Security Division, but thought he would sneak a last trip in first.

"Let's go for a ride." He opened the car door for her and beamed as he saw the surprise on her face when they passed the gates to exit camp.

"How can we leave? Aren't we going to get in trouble?"

"Don't worry. I finagled a couple of passes. We're going to Twin Falls for dinner and a show. 'Hello, Frisco, Hello' is playing."

The evening was a perfect finale to a great week. Butch promised to write and fiddled with the buttons on his shirt while they said goodbyes. Art wondered if he dared kiss her, but didn't want to ruin their friendship. Maybe when he got back, he might gather up the courage to try. After all, he wasn't the only one she was promising to write. Sometimes he felt so unsure of himself.

The next day he and Tom boarded a train for Camp Shelby, Mississippi. They passed through Kansas City, St. Louis, then Memphis where they had a four-hour layover. It was here for the first time he met severe discrimination against Negros. All the train depots, USOs, theaters, cafes, and such provided "special accommodations" for "colored" folks. Even the buses and streetcars had "reserved" seats for Negroes.

"Where do you suppose we're to sit? We don't fit in either category," Tom asked.

"I asked the man in the USO. He thought about it for a minute then said we should go in the whites' sections. I hope we don't run into any problems. Pretty weird seeing such blatant separations because of color."

"Yeah, makes you think."

The rest of the trip was uneventful. The last leg from Memphis to Hattiesburg was hot and humid. From there, they hopped a bus to Camp Shelby where all the men were processed. Art learned every time they had a move in the army, they would get a short-arm test and some kind of shot. He passed, and it was onward to the 442nd Regiment.

In Shelby, they met the Nisei from Hawaii. Many of these men had belonged to the Hawaiian National Guard before being discharged after December 7th. Then the government reversed the decision after they saw how many men that removed from the military. It took a cautionary move, forming a special unit for these Japanese American soldiers, the 100th Infantry Battalion or the "One Puka Puka" ("One Zero Zero" in Hawaiian). The newly formed battalion was then sent to the mainland for combat training. Their performance became known amongst everyone as stellar. This excellent training record of the 100th Infantry

Battalion likely opened the draft to all Japanese Americans. The War Department took note, changing the designation of Japanese Americans from 4C, enemy non-aliens, back to 1A, available for service.

The 100th had started their training earlier in June 1942 at Camp McCoy, Wisconsin. Then in January 1943, they were sent to Camp Shelby for further training. The Hawaiians were ahead in their training, but that wasn't the only difference. The Japanese population in Hawaii, unlike the mainlanders, had not suffered the widespread forced removal and incarceration of their families. Though they were both Nisei, there was a significant difference in attitude between the two groups. The Hawaiians were more casual in appearance, playing ukuleles and singing. Their language was spattered with words the mainlanders didn't understand: "Pidgin English" it was called. They were louder and unruly in comparison to their mainland counterparts. The Hawaiians found the mainlanders too reserved and quiet, "stuck up" and acting superior with their proper English and fancy manners. Fights broke out. The Hawaiians took to calling the mainlanders "kotonks."

"That da sound you hollow head make when hit da ground! Just like sound when coconut bounce."

"Oh yeah, who you calling kotonk, you buddahead. Come over here and say it to my face."

"Like this?" asked one Hawaiian, as he planted a right hook across the man's jaw.

"Break this up. You soldiers are to fight together, not against each other," a captain yelled as he ran interference.

The mainlanders called the Hawaiians "buddhaheads." This was not just a religious reference, but a play on words as *buta* meant "pig" in Japanese. It looked like this regimental team wouldn't get past training.

Out of desperation, the commanding officer, General Pence, organized a dance for both groups. The Hawaiians were looking forward to meeting some 'kotonk' girls. They took buses to the closest incarceration camp in Rohwer, Arkansas. The atmosphere was raucous—ukuleles and singing until they arrived.

As they entered the gates, one Hawaiian asked "What's with the barbed wire enclosure?"

"Because this is where our families are living. Didn't you guys know we came from concentration camps?" one Minidoka volunteer exclaimed in sheer disbelief.

"We were forced out of our homes. Why we lost everything and our families are stuck in these camps for who knows how long!" said another.

"This is outrageous. You have whole families squeezed in tiny shacks. Why'd you guys volunteer to fight? I woulda made them release my family first," a Hawaiian yelled out.

"Some guys tried and now they're rotting in a prison camp. Besides, how else can we prove our loyalty?" asked Bill, whose family was incarcerated at Manzanar, in the California desert.

Many of the incarcerated families had set aside their rations to give the soldiers "dinner" before the dance and had cleared spots for the soldiers to sleep. But the Hawaiian's attitudes changed on a dime. They turned down all the offers, choosing to sleep in the buses or even outdoors instead of displacing the families already in such cramped quarters. The bus ride home was somber as the Hawaiians reflected on what they had seen.

"I wonder what I would have done. Would I have volunteered?" Daniel said to another Hawaiian next to him. "We weren't dragged from our homes and put into concentration camps. These guys still volunteered despite it all."

"They're proving themselves for all of us, for our people," another Hawaiian said.

Much to the officer's relief, a new found alliance developed, and the two groups became harmonious. General Pence organized more of the dances, and the bonds between the men continued to deepen. The Hawaiians saw their mainland counterparts in a new light. Respect and admiration developed, forming unbreakable friendships. What had started as animosity between these men had morphed from a military unit to one of a family.

The training continued harmoniously until August 1943, when a contingent of the 100th Battalion was sent on its way to Oran, North Africa to join General Mark Clark's 5th Army, 34th Division, "Red Bulls." The battles led them across the Mediterranean to Italy from Cassino towards the Arno River.

The men left at Camp Shelby continued training and tracked their 100th Battalion buddies with zeal through the campaign in Africa and then into Italy. They monitored news reports and movie reels daily. It became clear the men of the 100th were meeting terrific resistance from the Germans and suffering heavy casualties. The losses were so enormous they became known as The Purple Hearts Battalion. Hearing of injuries and deaths hit hard on those left in Shelby. With each death, it was as if they had lost a brother.

13

ÉCUEILLÉ, FRANCE
1944

The cold of winter kept the memories of losing key players in their Resistance suspended in the recesses of their minds. Didier was spending more time cooped up in his father's garage. The impending weather had slowed Lysander travels, putting a halt on supplies from Britain. Resistance members weren't being brought in or taken out without the planes. Yvette worried their cause was melting away with the retreating ice. Had all their efforts been in vain?

But as the emerging shoots of crocuses began to peek out from the bare soil, a noticeable uptick in Lysander pickups and drops started. Yvette's father went from despondent to almost joyful, even joking around with her mother and the rest of the family. The small enclave of Didier, Jean and Yvette began to meet at the bar again along with a few new members.

BBC reports hinted the Allies would invade at Calais, the shortest crossing from England. There were tanks seen building up in the region near Dover. The tension was palpable. Plus, good news came with the report—the Russians had liberated Leningrad after it was held hostage for over 900 days. Then in May 1944, the Allies gained ground in

Italy, taking Rome and Bologna. These reports helped bolster the French Resistance, giving new hope to their efforts.

One evening, as they were clearing the table after dinner, a knock on the door startled everyone, followed by a much more forceful pounding.

"Open the door now!" a voice said in French with a distinct German accent.

Yvette, alarmed, searched the room. Where were the Wolffs? Had someone reported them to the police? That they were hiding a Jewish couple?

"Where are they?" she asked, everyone knowing she meant the Wolffs.

"They went out for an evening walk behind the house," Yvette's mother said. "Quick, Madeleine, run up to ensure their room looks like yours. Hide any extra shoes or clothing that couldn't be yours."

Her mother brushed her apron and opened the door. A gruff man pushed past her, followed by the head of the *Gendarmerie,* the local police force, Mr. Gustav.

"What's the meaning of this?" Yvette's father had entered from cleaning the mill.

"We have reports you are hiding Jews in this house!"

A crow letter, the anonymous letter denouncing innocent people to the police, signed only by *The Crow, one who knows.*

"Absurd. Why would I endanger my entire family? Your tips are fallacious."

"Search the house and no one leave this room."

Yvette and her sisters sat obediently. Robert stared with enormous eyes, tears flowing down his blanched cheeks. Yvette's mother paced in the kitchen while her father, in defiance, tailed the men. Yvette heard them going into each room, throwing open the doors of the armoires, knocking on walls, checking for hidden alcoves.

"Did you get their room in order?" her mother asked Madeleine.

"I think so. I put his shoes around the outside of the window."

"Let's hope they don't open the shutters to look out."

There was more slamming of doors and shuffling of the cabinets. Was that the window shutter being opened? Would they find the shoes?

Yvette's mother's pacing became frantic. Yvette got up and wrapped her arms around her.

"Please, Mama. Sit here and try to relax. We may look like we're hiding something if we appear too distressed."

After a long wait, the men left as abruptly as they had come. Yvette's father sat at the table and buried his head in his trembling hands.

"They didn't find anything *this time*. But who tipped them off? Has someone said something? What about the children? Have any of you given even a little hint to one of your friends who would tell their parents?" her father asked, his face an ashen gray.

They shook their heads.

"Someone might notice you aren't around the house much. Maybe they suspect you're involved in Resistance activities," her mother said.

"How and why did they think we had someone hidden here?" her father asked.

"We'll have to be more careful." Everyone nodded in agreement.

Over an hour passed before the Wolffs came back.

"We saw the black car come down the driveway. It looked suspicious, like an SS vehicle. We hid in the bushes on the hill until we were sure they were gone."

"You did right. I can't imagine what would have happened if you'd been here," her father said.

"Keeping us here is too dangerous. We must leave."

"Nonsense. They won't be back now. They've searched the house as well as all the outbuildings. I hope they'll think twice before heeding another of those letters. Besides, where would you go?"

Yvette was relieved they didn't find her father's stash of weapons in the cellar. The shelves were a clever disguise but weren't perfect. The Nazis were getting more clever at finding such hiding places. What if Resistance fighters had been found hiding there? Yvette shuddered to think. Sometimes she felt someone was watching out for them, so far.

Spring arrived, along with a marked increase in activity around Yvette's home. Many more men were flowing in and out of the cellar and there was a palpable energy, almost radiating off her father. He listened with fervor to the BBC radio, mumbling about stopping Germans from moving north. Yvette read in her flyers that the Resistance was blocking roads with felled trees and she heard explosions as bridges and railways were destroyed. Non-violent acts of resistance were occurring as well by factory and industrial workers. Forced to produce war materials for the Nazis, they slowed their production to a snail's pace and railroad workers went on strike. Why was so much destruction and dissidence happening?

June 6, 1944. D-Day. Now it all made sense. The instructions to do anything to impede the German's movement north towards Normandy, put Yvette's hometown in the center of the activity.

"The Americans and Allies have landed on French soil," her father said. "The FFI has laid the groundwork. Now together we can push the Germans out of our country. Towns are being liberated. Onward to Paris!"

What events would take place next? The expectation and apprehension were thick in the air. Encouraging updates filled the newsletters:

English and Canadian troops advance toward the Seine River. The Allies have made significant progress in pushing the Nazis out of Calvados. The repulsed Germans flow back in disorder, some even crossing the river by swimming. Retreating enemy motorized columns stretch for miles.

Another report stated several Allied troops were north of Marseille. Was there another operation in the wings to free up the southern wall the Nazis had secured in that region? The region was seeing an increase in Allied and FFI maneuvers. The entire country was bracing for the next move.

A few days later, Didier mentioned he would be gone for a couple of days. His aunt, who lived in Oradour-sur-Glane, needed some help with her tractor. It wouldn't take more than a day or two. Yvette packed up some fresh milled wheat and eggs for him to give his aunt. They exchanged a long intense kiss, awakening areas of her body with unfamiliar aches and throbbing sensations. She could hardly wait for his return—it was the 9th of June.

Yvette waited with anticipation for Didier's return. Monday, Tuesday, then Wednesday passed with no sight of Didier at either the café or the fairgrounds. She became very concerned about the Nazi roadblocks, spending hours at the café, running every scenario through her mind.

"What about the roadblocks?" she asked. "They'll wonder why he's not at a work camp."

"His papers are in perfect order," Jean said.

"News travels so slowly, I'm going crazy waiting."

Wednesday afternoon, Yvette's father came home, his

face pale as if he had seen a ghost. He fell into his chair and told what he had heard at the café.

"The Nazis entered Oradour and massacred the entire village. Men, women, and children—all of them rounded up, shot, then set on fire!"

"When did this happen?" Yvette's mind raced, wondering if Didier had been there. No, he must have left before this atrocity occurred.

"They entered the town on Saturday, going door to door, forcing everyone to the fairgrounds. The pretext was they needed to check everyone's identification and search the homes for weapons. Of course, the townspeople cooperated, but they razed the entire town to the ground. The people were burned alive- locked in barns or the church. Think about that. We don't know why this happened. What made the Nazis enter a sleepy village like Oradour and kill over 600 people? My God, it could have been Écueillé." Her father sank further into the chair, as if trying to curl his body into a small ball of grief.

Saturday morning, Didier would have arrived at his aunt's on Friday to spend the weekend. Her stomach began turning over and the room faded. She stumbled, grabbing the edge of the table to stabilize herself. She stood frozen, not knowing what to do.

"What is it, Yvette? Did you know someone in that village?" her mother asked.

"Yes, I know someone who went that weekend, he must have been there." Yvette couldn't believe her own words. Had he really been there? She left the house, seeking solace in the fields with the animals, wrapping her arms around Belle's neck. She sobbed into the soft fur, soothed by the horse's aroma, leaning her entire being against the solid warmth of the horse.

"How did this happen? Why did he have to go that weekend? What about our dreams?" she murmured to Belle, whose velvet nose searched across Yvette's face as if trying to snuff out the source of her friend's sorrow.

Yvette stayed outside until well past dark, drained and weak. After settling Belle into the barn, she went back to the kitchen. The room was quiet and empty, save for a bowl of soup her mother had left on the table for her. Yvette was relieved for some time to herself and tried to eat the warm soup. Maybe that would help settle the ache in her stomach.

Her father entered the kitchen, so softly that she hadn't noticed him sit across the table from her. He took her hand in his, asking if there was something else. Yvette spilled everything—how she had joined René Couet to help distribute Resistance news. How she had fallen in love with Didier and their plans together for the future, once things returned to normal. To run the small garage and start a family right here in Écueillé and how he had left Friday to visit his aunt in Oradour.

"Oh Papa, how can this be? What shall become of us now?"

Her father looked deeply into her eyes. He appeared shocked at first as she mentioned helping Mr. Couet, but his stern face softened.

"You could have been picked up when they took Mr. Couet away. Yvette—how could you take such chances? Didn't I warn you not to get involved in these affairs?"

Just as he said this, he saw her despair.

"I'm sorry, *ma mignette*. Didier was a fine young man. I'm just worried about you, your mother and I would be devastated if anything happened to you. The Nazis can be cruel to their captives. We couldn't have lived with ourselves...." her father said, his voice trailing off.

His grip on her hands was beginning to hurt.

"I'm sorry, I don't know my own strength at times. Your news shocked me."

Her mother had entered the room and overheard most of the conversation. She went to the cupboard and took out their small stash of *eau de vie*, a potent liqueur made from the grapes left over after winemaking. Not saying a word, she filled small glasses with the honey-colored liqueur. *Eau de vie* had a way of making everything better from a cough, sore throat, upset stomach, or a broken heart.

14

Being part of the 442nd made Art swell with pride. This was their chance to prove they were red-blooded Americans of Japanese ancestry. Strong bonds and an unbreakable trust had built among them. There had been controversy in camp about whether to join. Would an all Japanese American regiment mean discriminatory treatment? If they proved their loyalty, then America might change its opinion of them. Or not.

Art recalled the African Americans who fought valiantly in WWI and for longer than any other combat unit. *Weren't they called the Harlem Hellfighters?* But upon their return, racism was worse than ever. Lynchings occurred, some of the men were even lynched in their military uniforms. *What motivates someone to hate or fear enough, to kill an innocent person based on skin color alone? Can't we appreciate the differences and realize we can be stronger if we embrace the diversity instead of trying to destroy them?* Art had to put those thoughts out of his mind. He had volunteered and here he was, in the 442nd. It was a full-fledged, all Japanese American regiment with three infantry battalions, the 522nd Field Artillery Battalion, the 232nd Combat Engineer Company, an

141

Anti-tank company, a Cannon Company, a Medical Detachment, and even its own Army band.

Initially, the shoulder patch for their uniforms was designed by the War Department, a yellow arm holding a red sword, a detested insignia. Another patch designed by Sgt. Miyamoto, had a white hand holding a torch of liberty against a blue sky, framed in white and red, which was more acceptable. Their motto was "Go for Broke" a Hawaiian pidgin phrase, meaning "shoot the works" or "go all out."

I'll go for broke and hope this time, things will work out for us, Art thought solemnly.

They assigned him to the 1st Platoon, Cannon Company, which would provide close artillery support to all three infantry battalions. That sounded good—it would enable him to keep tabs on everyone. Unfortunately, his other buddy, Tom, was in the 522nd Artillery, which would be four to five miles behind the battalions. He would be lucky to see Tom at all once they started the battles.

Captain Robert Shorey was their commander.

"Men, the Cannon Company consists of drivers, gun and auto mechanics, ammunition and supply personnel, communication and radio specialists, and above all, cannoneers: men with strong backs to load six howitzers with up to 1000, 35-pound shells a day," Shorey said.

Captain Shorey was only eight years Art's senior. He had been a civil engineer with Shell Oil before entering the Army. With his boyish face and gentle smile, he looked more like a pal you would join for a game of billiards than to follow into battle. Fingers crossed, he would be a good leader.

"Art, you'll be a radio operator."

That sounded better to Art than hoisting shells.

"You'll be on the front lines with the platoon leader. It's your responsibility to radio back coordinates to the gunners. Here's the radio pack. It weighs in at thirty-five pounds."

Art groaned silently to himself. Maybe being a cannoneer wouldn't have been so bad.

During training, he learned the inside and out of a cannon, an M-1, 105mm howitzer, to be exact. There was so much information—setting up the cannon in firing positions, reading maps, using a compass, and pinpointing gun positions on maps. They also gave him an M1 carbine rifle. He'd never shot a weapon before and wondered if he could shoot another human.

The training was tougher than anything he had ever been through. His slight body developed strong firm muscles as a result of the hikes, up to twenty-five miles in eight hours carrying 60-pound packs on their backs. Each man transformed into a soldier as the training physically and mentally challenged the men of the 442nd. They practiced night maneuvers to avoid using any light which would expose the convoy to the enemy. Art became accustomed to driving the dark roads, feeling his way over the bumps and curves, like reading braille. Lead vehicles had a small light that illuminated only a few feet in front and successive vehicles followed the white, painted on the rear bumpers of the lead. Thus, no light would be seen by any reconnaissance planes or potential attackers.

A few church families came from nearby Hattiesburg. One man in particular, Earl Finch, befriended them, becoming like a "one-man" USO. He had tried to volunteer in the Army but was rejected due to a heart ailment. He helped out by offering hospitality to the soldiers so far from home. Art was invited one Saturday afternoon and Earl's mother prepared some fine southern fare—fried chicken, buttermilk biscuits, and sweet potato pie.

"That's the best meal I've had in a long while," one soldier said.

Art nodded, loosening his belt to make room for one more piece of pie.

The following day, Art and the other men returned to the home, bearing roses in appreciation. This small token of gratitude made these soldiers stand apart from the others. A newfound respect and friendship developed between them. Earl brought food and supplies when he heard of things lacking to the men in Camp Shelby as well as for those in the incarceration camps in Rohwer and Jerome, Arkansas. He was certain their forced removal to camps was unconstitutional.

"Earl took candy and toys to my little sister and the other children in our camp," a soldier said. "He arranged for rice and tofu to be delivered when he heard about some of the older Japanese not being able to adapt to the Western diet."

"Right, but he's taking risks for us. I've heard Earl's being ostracized by many of his neighbors. The Deep Southern whites don't like it when their kind mixes with us. Don't forget this is Jim Crow country and they don't like anyone who's not like them," another soldier added.

Art's face flushed as his blood pressure rose. How dare someone judge the kind actions of Mr. Finch and his mother.

"Will they ever see us as Americans? How can anyone be so cruel and ignorant?" Art said.

"Watch it, Art. That's how people get hung from trees out here."

"Well, it's got to change, and I plan to prove them wrong."

The chaplain, Rev. Higuchi, decided to help add some goodwill to the community by forming a musical group, predominately of Hawaiians, to perform at the local churches.

Few people in Mississippi had seen anyone of Japanese ancestry and even fewer Hawaiians. He grouped together a steel guitar, a ukulele plus several regular guitars and a few vocalists performing songs like Across the Sea, Ku'u Ipo, Blue Hawaii, Don't Fence Me In, and Ka Lei e. They were a hit leading to a feeling of community and an understanding spread among the locals. Perhaps exposing the naive population would help quell the prejudice against the Japanese, rampant in the U.S. After all, knowledge is the best weapon.

Then there were the parties, among which the Cannon Companies became legendary. During the beer busts, the Cannon Company song would get belted out:

"Imua lanakila e (before winning e)
Hear our battle cry
Onward we go to meet the foe
Go for broke we roll
In God we place our holy trust
With a prayer for all
Fire all the cannon
Forward to victory
Fight on, fight on, Cannoneers!"

Within a few more months, they were boarding trains to Camp Patrick Henry in Virginia. From there, ships were to embark from the Chesapeake Bay, destination: Naples, Italy. It was May 1, 1944. The men of the Cannon Company were in line alphabetically, duffle bags and rifles by their sides. Art was excited to see the Red Cross offering donuts and coffee, for it might be a long time before he'd get to indulge again. He stocked up before boarding the S.S. Samuel Johnston, a converted Liberty ship. Propelled under a steam turbine engine and over 400 feet long, it was the biggest thing he had ever been on.

They left by nightfall the following day, joining a convoy of other ships escorted by destroyers. Ships covered the sea as far as the eye could see. The accompanying destroyers were to protect against attacks from German submarines prowling the U.S. coast. Art was relieved the voyage got off to a smooth start until they encountered the wide Atlantic.

The seas were rough, almost every man was sick until he found his sea legs, and a few unfortunate never found those legs. Exercises such as abandon-ship and anti-aircraft drills helped keep their minds off the voyage. Art whittled away many hours playing chess with Frank, who carried a small chessboard with him wherever he went. And there were the weekly amateur shows. A fellow cannoneer from Hawaii performed the funniest one.

"Oh my God, look at *Sergeant Kaneshiro*. He has the biggest falsies I've ever seen!"

There he was, on top of the hatch cover, doing a hula dance about Princess Pupule. Pupule meant crazy in Hawaiian, and the song described this "crazy princess" that loved to give away her... papayas! He cradled those falsies in his hands as he danced, accompanied by a ukulele and ocarina, the howls of laughter helping to ease the tension in the men.

Hours were spent gazing at the open sea. Though no one spoke of it, Art was sure everyone was thinking the same thing. What were they headed into? Which of them wouldn't make it back? Art fingered his senninbari, hoping somehow, the prayers of a thousand women would grant the intended luck.

As they approached the Mediterranean, passing the Straits of Gibraltar, things became tense. They announced warnings of hostile aircraft and submarine attacks, as a few other ships in the region had seen threats.

Art spotted Oran and Algiers as they passed the North African coast.

"Operation Torch was the name of the landings in Africa," he recounted to Frank. "That's where General Eisenhower and the Brits drove out the French Vichy forces."

"Is it still under Nazi control?"

"No. It took over a week of fighting but the French Resistance helped secure Tunis, which opened the route to the Middle East," Art proudly stated, glad he had read Ernie Pyle's reports. "It was a tremendous victory for us. It freed up the passage into Italy and the Vichy joined the Allies. Right after that, Hitler ordered his troops to occupy the rest of France. I guess he didn't trust the Vichy to keep the south of France secure. Last September the 100th battalion went to Oran to join the 34th Red Bulls and they've been fighting in Italy since, building up quite a reputation. The battles have been tough—Sicily didn't come easy. The 100th fought through July and August of '43, finally pushing the Germans out to open the way up Italy."

Frank smiled at his friend. "I'm glad you kept up with the news so well. It helps explain what we are getting into and why."

After twenty-eight days at sea, the ship arrived in Naples, Italy. Art looked out at the Italian coast. He was astonished, having always imagined the Italian beaches to be beautiful, but in front of him was a coast in complete ruin. Destroyed ships littered the beaches and only shells of once beautiful buildings were left standing, crumbling rock seemed to tumble into the sea, creating zigzag obstacles for anyone attempting to cross.

Their ship was too large to dock in the port, so barges ferried them ashore. The men scrambled down cargo nets into smaller transports. Art hesitated a moment as he looked down at the seemingly endless mesh of ropes. From the ship, the barge looked more like a dinghy, much too tiny to hold all these men. With a big inhale, he glanced around the safety of the ship he had called home over the past month. He went over the side, nestling first one foot, then the next, into the ropes down the rocking boat. Art held tight while his body swung out, then crashed back against the side of the ship as it lurched in the waves. It seemed forever before he felt his buddies grab his pants and drop him into the barge.

15

ÉCUEILLÉ, FRANCE

The next morning Yvette couldn't face going into town. She was at a loss, wondering what to do or where to go. She tried to stay busy, to keep her mind off Didier. But the visions of him, trapped in a barn and not able to escape, rattled her to the core. With no relief in sight, she returned to the cafe where they had first met. Upon arriving, Didier's friends embraced her and continued to discuss the tragedy at l'Oradour.

"A young boy survived the attack to tell the story. On Saturday afternoon, the Nazis arrived and gathered everyone in town, separating the men and the boys from the women. He tried to stay with his mother but they hit him with the butt of a rifle and dragged him to a barn. The Germans started shooting, aiming for their legs. He hid behind a couple of the men. Then the Germans locked the doors and set the barn on fire. Everyone panicked, their legs paralyzed, not able to get up. He managed to kick loose a few boards in the back and squeeze out," Jean said.

"Imagine if they had caught him," Yvette said.

"Yeah, he was lucky. For two days he hid behind bushes, terrified the Germans would find him. When he was certain they had left, he crept out. Only six people survived out of 642 residents, over 400 being women and children."

"Didier was there but could have been out on an errand. Maybe he didn't get caught in the siege," she said. The others shrugged their shoulders, shaking their heads.

"He would have come back by now," Jean whispered softly.

Yvette clung to a slim glimmer of hope he had escaped the atrocity. She rode to the fairgrounds every day in hopes he would magically appear on the bench, grinning at her like before. Eventually, she gave up, knowing he would never appear. No one had heard from him. The answer was clear. Her last trip to the fairground sent her home with a heavy heart. It was hard not to just give up on everything.

She fought to pull herself out of her despair, others had suffered worse losses. She sought solitude during a long walk around the farm. It was quiet in the hills behind her home, among the soft grasses and wild daisies. The sun warmed her back as if Didier were wrapping his arms around her, filling her with his fortitude and courage. There was a gentle breeze caressing her face, taking her thoughts back to the park bench sitting with him. She heard his voice carried in the soft current: "This is so much bigger than us. We must stop the Nazis before it's too late."

Yvette looked around the countryside, which seemed so peaceful at the moment. These hills had become a favorite place for the Wolffs to sneak off for a bit of relaxation. What would become of them if the Nazis won? And of all the other refugees and young French men and women fighting for the cause? At that moment, Arthur flew to the trees above, cawing loudly. He kept flying from one tree to the next, staying just in front, as if to encourage her to continue on a path. Yes, she had to keep fighting and abandon any thought of failure. Dwelling on Didier and sulking around the house wouldn't accomplish any of their dreams, but did she have the courage to risk her life? There was only one way to find out— it was time to join back.

The determination must have shown on her face when she entered the Café des Sports. Jean gave her a big grin, grabbing her in his burly arms.

"I was hoping you'd come back. We're devastated by the loss of Didier too, but he would've wanted to see the fight continue. We've a new job for you if you're up to it."

"I'm ready. It's taken some time, but I know it's right."

"We're glad, just promise to be careful and don't let your anger get a hold of you. Think through your actions or the consequences could be deadly. There's a Maquis encampment a few kilometers north of Écueillé. I can't tell you anymore for your protection. There are about a dozen men from the region, avoiding deportation to Nazi work camps. They've joined our resistance efforts. We need you to bring them supplies, mostly food, since weapons are too dangerous for you to carry on a bicycle."

"I can do that. Just point me in the right direction."

16

ITALY
JUNE 1944

Trucks left Naples bound for Bagnoli, about ten miles west. After bivouacking, which Art learned meant to make camp, they opened crates upon crates to unload their gear. The men had the tedious task of removing the grease that had protected the equipment against the seawater during the voyage. Then they tested and retested the gear to ensure its proper operation once in battle.

On June 6, they left Naples for Anzio, aboard small landing craft boats. The air was abuzz with news of the Allied landings at Normandy lifting everyone's spirits.

"Not so fast men, the war is far from over," the colonel said. "We still have to push the Germans out of Italy. Along with the Brits, we have the help of the French Expeditionary Corps, led by Marshall Juin Alphonse. These men are Goumier, Moroccan Berber tribesmen to be exact who are excellent mountain men. They've helped guide us over the steep terrain here in Italy."

Landing in Anzio rubble was all that remained from the battles. So much destruction rattled Art once again. Within minutes, orders were to move out before he had time to sort out his emotions.

From there, the 442nd headed to Rome in convoys of trucks and jeeps, but mostly on foot. Art marched behind a jeep towing a howitzer. It had been raining for weeks, washing out most roads, slowing their progress. He trudged solemnly behind, his calves aching with each step as his boots sucked down into the mud. Things were miserable, but at least they weren't being shot at... yet.

They were following the path of the 100th who had spent the last nine months working up the boot of Italy. The Eternal City—Rome, freed of the enemy, had come at a substantial cost to the men of the 100th.

The Germans had declared Rome an "open city" thus sparing it from destruction. It took Art's breath away when he entered the historic city, just before dawn. The moonlight twinkled against the ancient buildings and ruins, bringing them back to life — the musty odors adding to the effect. He saw the Coliseum and two thousand years of history opened before him. Stories of gladiator fights and Christians being thrown to the lions, first thrilled, then repulsed him. He imagined the sandals worn by these bygone Romans sinking into the nooks and crannies in the timeworn cobblestone roads he was marching on today. Someday he hoped to visit the town under better conditions.

After 75 miles, they arrived in Civitavecchia, north of Rome, for a final bivouac. Here they met up with the 100th Battalion, who would serve as the 1st Battalion alongside the 2nd and 3rd of the 442nd. They would retain the 100th designation to conserve their reputation. After all, the 100th had just received the highest honor the U.S. Army had to pay, the Presidential Unit Citation, for their fighting in Italy, presented by General Mark Clark.

"All of you Americans of Japanese descent have demonstrated true Americanism and true American citizenship on the field of battle. The 34th Division, the 5th Army, and America are proud of you. You have reached the highest standards of American fighting men," said General Clark.

The 100th was now known as the "Purple Hearts" Battalion, based on their ferocious fighting and high casualty numbers. As the 442nd joined, it replenished many of those lost in the earlier battles of the 100th. Now the 442nd Regimental Combat Team was in full force as a complete regiment of all Japanese American soldiers. The only exception was the officers, who were predominantly Caucasian. Art heard fellow soldiers concerned about being in an all-Japanese unit. Would they treat us differently? Art wasn't sure what to expect, but he felt safer being surrounded by his own kind, people he had grown to trust amid all the prejudice found in Seattle. He surprised himself as he had never felt animosity towards the whites he had lived with most of his life. Many things had changed since that fateful day on December 7, 1941. He wondered if he would ever feel comfortable and trusting of others besides his own again.

That evening, the 100th tried to prepare the new soldiers for the battle ahead. They had the men's undivided attention.

"The Nazis are methodical and dangerous. Just when you think they're retreating, they'll attack. They booby-trap trees, doors, even dead bodies. You can't be too careful—don't ever let your guard down."

The newcomers were keen to listen to what the war-experienced 100th had to say.

"Don't fasten the chin strap on your helmet. An explosion could blow your helmet off, taking your head with it."

"Don't light a cigarette at night, unless you are under cover. Remember, it's not just you, but your buddies' lives at risk as well."

"Learn the sounds of the enemy—their rifles, grenades, artillery, and tanks sound different from ours," warned yet another soldier. "Dig a foxhole if you are on the line—deep enough so you can sit on your helmet to look around, but duck your head if trouble starts."

Art cataloged it all, knowing it was good advice to save himself as well as anyone around him.

Over the next two weeks, the men tried to regain the stamina lost on the sea voyage. The terrain here was different from their training grounds in Mississippi. Plus, now the instructions were to not carry full packs.

"I don't want to see anyone carrying more than a day's ration, a poncho, underwear, and socks. Keep the socks in your armpits, it's the only place they can stay dry. You'll carry your ammunition and weapons. That will be all you can manage and even that may be too much. You need to be able to run and fight and crawl in combat."

Art contemplated his thirty-five pound radio backpack. He hoped he wouldn't need to run too much with that weighing him down. Looking around, he saw steep hills covered by short, scrubby bushes, leaving little area for cover or protection. Everyone felt vulnerable as they walked along the narrow trails, each bush an ideal hiding spot for a sniper waiting to use them as target practice. Worse yet, the enemy had observation posts on the hilltops and could see them for miles. It was an exercise in physical as well as mental endurance.

He was busy working with his leader to become familiar enough with each other so words wouldn't be necessary. If his leader needed something, he had to know exactly what it was and deliver it as quickly as possible. The entire team had to learn to work together as a fine-tuned instrument—when one lever moved, the other ones had to move in perfect succession.

June 26, 1944. Art woke up to his first day of battle. It was sunny and calm, the air smelled fresh as he mulled over what the day had in store for them. He had a mixed set of emotions—a downright fear of the violence of battle, of possible mutilation, and yes, even death. But the fear combined with the excitement to use all they had learned in training. They were a well-oiled machine, ready for top performance. No regiment would operate better—he was sure of it.

The plan was set. They were to take Belvedere and Sassetta, to gain control of Hill 140. The hill had a German outpost that needed to be taken out. The 100th Battalion was to sneak behind the German line while the 2nd and 3rd Battalions would approach from either side. As the team assembled, the tension was palpable. Faces were harrowed, though there was the rare one grinning, or was it a grimace? Art had never felt such tension. His head was bursting with thoughts of what they were going to be facing. Was their training good enough to beat the Germans, would he ever see his beloved Seattle, make his home with a wife and family? He kept seeing flashes of his father, reminding him to not bring shame to the family, and his mother trying to smile through her tears. Then Chibi, clutching Prince's stuffed toy—she had brought it back out since the news of his enlisting. He shook his head, trying to clear it. *I need to concentrate on what's happening here!*

First, the jeeps headed out with Captain Shorey and his driver, followed by the tanks and artillery. Next the soldiers marched in line, every man silent, only the crunching of the coordinated footsteps audible. A "clear ahead" signal was sent down from the front.

The Cannon Company's job was to destroy any enemy tanks. The jeeps towed the howitzers as Art followed behind on foot. They were heading down a straight road, keeping a close eye out to either side. His skin was afire as every nerve was on edge, ready to react if needed, each step more grueling than the last.

One foot in front of the other. Use your peripheral vision to watch for any unusual movements. As the bushes rustled in the wind, he was sure he saw the enemy crouched behind each one. *Just my imagination,* he thought, as his lips moved in silent prayer. It took all his willpower to continue up the road.

Then an explosion hit the forward jeep, knocking out the driver and Captain Shorey. Everyone jumped off to the side of the road, digging with their hands, helmets, bayonets, and anything that would help make a hole for protection. Shells kept exploding and the smell of sulfur enveloped them, making it hard to breathe.

"I thought we had a clear ahead!" Art heard someone yell.

"No one can be sure of anything out here!" another man yelled back.

Art saw Captain Shorey help his injured driver to cover in a shed. Shrapnel had pierced both of the driver's legs. As another shell exploded over them, Captain Shorey threw his body over the man to protect him. Once the shelling stopped, he helped carry the driver to another jeep, which would take him to the aide station. The actions of the captain moved Art. He was an impressive commander. Respect welled up inside of him, a white officer, risking his life for a Japanese American. Race clearly wasn't an issue for him. He hoped everyone saw soldiers only, losing pettiness over minor differences in appearances.

The Germans were using 88mm artillery weapons, known as the anti-everything gun, as it was effective against tanks, infantry, and aircraft. The gun was accurate, lethal, and versatile with a high-pitched whine before the shell landed and exploded. Entering each village, the soldiers were on high alert, listening for any suspicious noise. It was impossible to know if the Germans were still there or not. As they entered Sassetta, Art thought, *It's too quiet—there should be a few sounds of activity.* He wanted to hear the clatter of dishes or smell the aroma of food, but nothing, just eerie silence... then he heard it. The shrill of artillery—*The Germans **are** here.*

He couldn't pinpoint the exact direction it was coming from, but the explosion went off about twenty yards from him, missing any targets. Everyone dove for cover until the German tanks were sighted and their location pinpointed. Art's team was called in for firepower. He radioed back the coordinates, and the field artillery and Cannon Company rained fire down on the German troops, forcing them to retreat. One more village had been liberated.

"Geez, it's awesome when the artillery clears out those Germans. Then we're able to do our work," said a rifleman in the 2nd Battalion.

It looked like the infantry-artillery team, newly formed for WWII, was an effective force.

On the 3rd of July, they crossed the Cecina River on the approach to Hill 140. Enemy fire was unrelenting, Germans entrenched on the top of Hill 140, rained artillery on them from above. Little protection was available to the 442nd to approach the Hill, which was surrounded by low growing wheat fields.

The going was slow, taking days to gain only a few

yards, and German resistance was relentless. Machine gun and mortar fire were taking down soldiers and even tanks while overwhelmed medics tried to no avail, to pick up men who were falling on all sides. Art never imagined fighting could be so violent and brutal, with almost 100 men killed and 300 more wounded.

Art closed his eyes in sorrow as he thought of the flood of telegrams from the War Department going to loved ones back home. He pictured those blue stars changing to gold in the windows of their loved ones, imprisoned behind barbed wire. How would those families feel, losing their sons to a country that had stolen their homes, belongings, and even their citizenship? Was all this worth it? He could only hope so.

The noise was constant, and the sky lit up in never ending explosions, allowing only a few winks of sleep at night, dozing off from sheer exhaustion. The Cannon Company was called on to pour fire attacks on the German troops who were defending the area. Art felt the weight of being on the front lines as he radioed location coordinates back to the cannon operators. Their howitzers fired hundreds of rounds at enemy artillery positions, knocking out gun after gun. It was exhausting, never seeming to let up.

It happened on July 4th. Art was on the front line, radioing locations to attack. The antennae on his radio made him a sitting duck. The bullets seemed to be passing closer and closer. As he lay flat in the foxhole, that darn antennae would spring straight up, marking his location. The machine gun fire was coming from an area about a hundred yards away. Private First Class Nakamura crawled within fifteen yards and lobbed hand grenades in, neutralizing the enemy. More machine gun fire started from another location. Once again, the private crawled to a point and began firing clip after clip of ammunition with his rifle. He kept the enemy pinned until his platoon retreated to safety. But while exposed to the enemy, they shot him in the head, killing him instantly.

Art felt a stabbing pain in his gut, followed by the taste of bile. He looked down to see if he had been hit, the feeling was so intense. There were no wounds, no sign of blood. Could seeing the soldier get hit have caused such a visceral reaction? He fought back the urge to vomit. He and the platoon were safe, but they had lost a fine soldier that Fourth of July, 1944. Art searched the faces of the others who had seen Pvt Nakamura get killed. Everyone's eyes turned down, not able to look at one another. There never seemed to be time to work through these feelings as he heard Lt. Shorey yell to get moving.

The troops finally secured Hill 140 and they continued the battle toward Pisa. Orders were to provide cover for the 34th Division near Luciana. The Cannon Company was called to take down targets in town. Art went with the forward observer, radioing back coordinates in rapid succession. They fired over 500 rounds, opening a free zone to allow the men to clear landmines the Germans had planted all around the town. Because of the cannons and the engineers, the battalions could enter the town along with the men providing the supply details, whose job it was to restock essential ammunition to the battalions. Art held his breath as these men laid their lives on the line, running the gauntlet of artillery shells along the open roads into Luciana. It looked like they were racing through an invisible maze, turning and darting every which way, while explosions and bullets ricocheted around them.

The morning of July 7th, Art heard the news about fellow cannoneer, Cpl. Aoyama. He was a forward observer working in tandem with Art.

"One of our forward observers got hit. He was crawling through to reach Hank, who had been hit. Mortar shells and gunfire were exploding all around him. He started giving first aid when he got hit and went down, both his legs blown off. No one realized the severity of his wounds as they took him into the aid station. He kept saying he was fine. Go tend to those other guys, I can wait, he told the medics. By the time they got to him, he had bled to death. They said he must have been in excruciating pain, but he wanted everyone else to get help first," a private said.

It hit Art hard to hear this quiet young man whose family was interned at Heart Mountain had died. He was one of their most gung-ho members, thrilled he had been accepted even though he was quite near-sighted. He was a remarkable soldier, someone you wanted by your side during these battles. Yet another heartbreaking loss. It was getting more difficult by the day to justify these deaths. And the orders to move out kept coming.

The 442nd fought its way up the Italian coast to the Arno River. They encountered heavy resistance from each town until reaching the river. The number of casualties was huge at 1,272, with 239 men killed in only forty miles. Finally, they had a short rest for a couple of weeks. It was great to get a shower, a change of clothes, and solid sleep. Catching up on letter writing and receiving mail and packages were the biggest treats.

Art settled down after breakfast to read his letter from Butch.

Dearest Art,

I follow every battle with such intensity, people are teasing me, however they pack into my room every lunch hour for the latest broadcasts. A battle takes on significance because you may be a participant. An hour doesn't go by Art, that I don't think of you, hoping and praying you are safe. I know you have courage so even though you feel fear you will meet whatever comes staunchly and thoughts of personal safety are far from your mind, so I am dismissing all except hopes for your safety, which will remain my foremost concern.

Thanks so much for the anklets (socks to you). Imagine me, running around in silk—at least up to the ankles.

Kato sent me a clipping from one of Chicago's papers, which has a glowing account of the 442nd combat team. The headline was as follows—"The Japanese yanks are fighting brilliantly in Italy" Really makes us proud to know what and how you boys are doing over there.

I am all packed and ready to leave in ten days. I can hardly wait to be free of this degenerating existence.

I went down to visit your family. Your parents are so proud of you, Art. I share their pride and have every faith that we will not be disappointed.

Ho! Ho! So you think you can grow a beard! I know you've been fighting like a man, but you shouldn't let that go to your head or face.

Fondly, Butch

Art loved the subtle, flirtatious manner of Butch's letters, wondering if something could have happened between the two of them. Now she was moving away, heading out to New York on a WRA release program. Being a nurse, she had doors open to about anywhere. And he suspected she wrote this way to some of the other guys.

They sent the instructions to reassemble the units. The time for rest was over. Now it was time to confuse the Germans as to where the next attack would come. The 442nd was to display an impressive force of strength south of the

Arno River, while the 5th Army and the British Eighth Army would establish their positions without detection. The Germans had a heavy defense north of the river with even an enemy observation post in the Leaning Tower of Pisa, which overlooked the river. Orders were to preserve the Tower if possible. Patrols on both sides were intense. Dismantling the heavily mined and booby-trapped south bank was very dangerous for the engineers.

"Until we clear the mines, if you are the lead, crawl on your belly. This will spread your weight to lessen the pressure—mines are pressure sensitive. At the same time, tap the ground in front with your bayonet. If you tap a mine, mark it—toilet paper around a rock works good, then the next man can see it."

Reconnaissance patrols found an enemy nest that the Cannon Company helped clear out. The patrol continued until it got caught between two enemy machine guns and mortars. Men were killed or wounded on both sides. The medics, under the flag of truce, retrieved their men as the German medics also came out under the flag. They exchanged a few words between the two forces and they each retreated with their wounded. What a shame this couldn't serve as an example, settling war with simple words.

Finally, the plan succeeded. Air observation confirmed the Germans were withdrawing north to the Gothic Line. Along the way, they destroyed most of the bridges crossing the Arno river to slow the Allies advance. However, the engineers worked diligently to build new crossings over the Arno, as well as to remove the hundreds of mines scattered along the river banks. The Allies began crossing the river within a few days following the German withdrawal. The 442nd took a deep breath of relief. They had succeeded in flushing the Germans to the Gothic Line.

The next orders came from Generals Eisenhower and Mark Clark. Two battles were being fought in Italy and France. They pulled the 442nd out of Italy to join the forces in the south of France after a brief rest in Naples. It only lasted a few days, but gave everyone a welcome break after the past weeks of intense fighting.

Art headed out to visit Pompeii with his buddy, Frank, for a history lesson. He had read about Pompeii, the ancient Roman city destroyed in 79 AD when Mt.Vesuvius exploded. But to actually see the ruins and the bodies frozen in time was incredible. They walked around the half standing buildings, admiring small glimpses into Roman life. There were beautiful mosaics still visible on the worn walls, an oven used by bakers, and even a dog buried alive left to guard the master's home.

Art wondered what France had in store and there was a galvanizing sensation that the war was nearing its end.

"I think we'll be heading home soon. Paris is liberated and the Germans are being pushed back to their country," Frank said.

"There's talk the Nazis are getting more desperate and aggressive. They want to preserve as much of the land they've conquered as possible. I'm worried we're heading right into that mess," Art said with a furrowed brow.

17

ÉCUEILLÉ, FRANCE
POST D-DAY

Yvette was eager to get involved with the Resistance again and, in a way, keep a connection to Didier. With the plan set, she would return in the morning to pick up the food and deliver it to the Maquis encampment. The camp was only eight kilometers away, a quick trip on a bicycle.

Yvette woke to menacing dark clouds rolling across the horizon. *Everything in my life has felt threatening these past few years, as if a dark cloud has followed me.* Since the Nazis had invaded *their* country, everything around her had been turned on end. It was selfish to wallow in self-pity, but damn it, her whole life had lost direction. Instead of focusing on herself and what *she* wanted, she realized helping others filled this emptiness. She left the desolation and anguish behind in the trail of dust as she pedaled off on her bicycle.

She looked forward to the ride. Even if it rained, it wouldn't slow her down, quite the opposite, as the crisp, cool air helped her cycle even faster. Yvette went around to the back door of the Café des Sports to collect the supplies. She tucked the food in the two saddlebags on her bicycle, then headed towards the town of Heugnes with a renewed sense of purpose.

She smiled, remembering going to dances there with her friend, Odette. The tents assembled by the townsfolk were never quite large enough for the crowds that came. Young men and women from the surrounding villages gathered for these weekly events. Each town would hold a dance, rotating throughout the summer, so rarely a weekend went by without one occurring somewhere.

She entered a tent. There wasn't much elbow room, so she squeezed into a spot along the side of the canvas. A musette echoed out from the one-man band playing an accordion, tapping his foot on a small drum of sorts.

Someone grabbed her arm, "Yvette, come, dance!"

She laughed as she looked to see who her suitor was. Oh good, Jean-Michel, one of my favorites! *she thought.*

They moved to the center of the tent, leaving the others backed up along the sides, still looking for suitable partners. Yvette loved to dance and rarely missed one of these. Her skirt swirled around her legs as her partner guided her around in circles, intertwining between other dancers, on occasion knocking into them.

"Excuse us," one of them would say, not noticing or caring whom they had bumped.

These weekly dances gave Yvette a chance to make new acquaintances, even though Écueillé had a fair amount of men near her age. As she saw it, there was no such thing as too many dance partners.

Her smile disappeared as fast as it had appeared. Up ahead, a German car pulled out from a farm, likely searching for Jews, or raiding a garden and stealing a chicken or two. Her mind returned to the present. Those dances were a thing of the past now that the Nazis were here. Fortunately, they hadn't looked back to see her cycling towards them. How would she explain all the food she was carrying? She thought she looked pretty innocent, but she couldn't be sure. She pedaled on with determination, this unspeakable violence against innocent people had to be stopped.

Oak trees lining either side of the road cast shadows, making it hard to avoid the ruts and bumps with her old bicycle tires. Her supplies were packed tight as sardines, so she doubted there was any problem with them. She couldn't say the same for her derriere, which was getting pretty sore bouncing on the hard leather seat.

The wheat was turning from green to gold, and the sunflowers were in full bloom. It was turning out to be a beautiful day, not too hot since the sun remained hidden behind the clouds. There were no other cars about, so she relaxed and began making large loops along the road. Whiffs of honey-like scents flowed across her face from the surrounding fields. She put the sight of the invaders' car out of her mind. Why spoil such a perfect day?

Once she arrived at Heugnes, she followed Jean's directions, scanning the side of the road for the '4 km' post marker. There, just past the church on the right, was the white post with a faint engraving. It wasn't clear, but it looked like it had been a four some time ago.

"Go about five hundred meters beyond the post. There will be three towering oaks grouped together," Jean had instructed her.

Other than that, there was no indication of a trail. Yvette got off her bicycle and pushed it alongside her, heading behind the trees. The woods became thicker as she worked her way down into the valley. Not sure if she was on the correct path, she heard the snap of a branch. She spun her head to the right and her eyes locked with the determined eyes of a man about ten meters beyond. He was unshaven, with an angry look on his face, as he brandished a large stick of some sort. She should turn back, maybe this wasn't the right place. The fellow looked menacing, as if he was thinking of hitting her, or worse.

The man approached closer, tapping the stick against his hand. An icy shiver went down her spine and her legs were poised to sprint. *Oh, wait, the code Jean told me to use. How could I have forgotten?*

"Thomas, mon frere?" *Thomas, my brother?* Her voice was quivering and its high pitch surprised her. It reminded her of a cat whose tail has just been stepped on. The man dropped the stick to his side as a slight smile crept over his lips.

Was he laughing at my voice? Is it time to make a run for it?

"Marguerite, enfin ma soeur." *Finally, my sister,* was the correct reply, as Jean had told her. Yvette, who had been holding her breath, released it with a heavy sigh. The first contact had been successful.

She followed the curious man deeper into the woods, still unnerved by their initial encounter. He led her to a clearing where light filtered through, revealing clothes hanging from trees and lean-tos assembled for shelter. A dozen or so young men were attending various activities. Some were cleaning rifles and guns, others were whittling sticks, and a few seemed to be doing very little, resting against rocks, looking at her with interest. She never imagined these many men were hiding away. Most of the village had feared the Nazis had taken them away, but now she understood. She recognized a few of the young men—Jean-Michel and Patrick both from Écueillé. If only she could tell their families, it would give them some relief, but everything had to be kept quiet for fear that a collaborator might be in the midst. It would be difficult, as she often crossed their mothers in town who were having a hard time keeping hope.

Yvette unpacked the supplies with the help of her contact, Thomas. They spoke few words, which was for her own good. The less she knew, the better to ensure her safety and theirs. She wanted to talk to Jean-Michel, oddly she had just been thinking of him. It had only been a few years since they last danced, yet it seemed a lifetime ago. She smiled at him, but he turned away. Was he ashamed to be hiding here? He looked like he had aged ten years in this short time.

Yvette left the same way she had come, hoping that she would return soon with more food. It didn't seem as if she had brought enough for those many, and they looked thin and hungry. Some clothes might be nice as well to replace the torn pants and tattered sweaters they were wearing.

A palpable euphoria was sweeping over the country since the invasion at Normandy. The dread once enveloping the country was melting away, a dread similar to that of the 1793-1794, Law of Suspects. During that year, French revolutionary committees could arrest and turn you in as a traitor, simply from a mention by a neighbor. You would either rot in jail or be killed, usually beheaded. God forbid a word was muttered against the Revolutionary tyrants such as Maximilien Robespierre during his reign of terror.

Life under Nazi occupation felt the same, making the French wonder how this was happening again. No one felt safe, local police or your neighbor could report you as a traitor. The Vichy government had persecuted Protestants, Jews, Freemasons, Communists, homosexuals, anti-fascists, and foreigners, sending innocent civilians to prisons, concentration camps, or executing them on the spot.

Now it looked to be coming to an end. The Vichy officials had moved to Germany attempting to establish a government in exile. Police in the Vichy government were changing camps to join French civilians. The Maquis and Resistance groups had gone from scattered guerrilla fighters to form the French Forces of the Interior (FFI). These groups combined to sabotage railways, create roadblocks, and pass key information to Britain.

Yvette had heard about a woman in Valencay, a town close to Écueillé.

"Papa, do you know anything about a woman, Pauline? I understand she's involved with our Resistance fighters?"

"I know of her. Why do you ask?"

"I'm impressed that a woman is doing such things. Is it true she has over a thousand fighters in her organization?" Yvette's eyes were ablaze with curiosity and her father caved, filling in the details.

"Well, I'll tell you what I know. This woman's working for our cause and risking her life. She's actually British but French-educated, making her an ideal agent. She parachuted to an area near Valencay and is working with the French SOE," her father recounted.

Didier had explained the SOE to her.

"SOE, or Special Operations Executive, is a secret British organization created by Winston Churchill to support the French Resistance. They drop agents into France along with weapons, transmitter radios, and money," he had said.

"It's true, she has over a thousand maquis under her," her father said. "It's no party trying to keep them all in order, but the groups are finally working together to harass the Nazis and impede their movements to help the Allies. She works with another network, the Stationer, which covers an enormous territory from the Loire River, south past Limoges and over to Vichy even."

The thought of a woman doing this made Yvette swell with pride. She only knew her by Pauline, a code name. At her next visit to the Maquis camp, she would ask her contact, Thomas, about her.

18

ONWARD TO FRANCE
1944

The reprieve in Naples was ending. Daily briefings keeping the men of the 442nd current on the movements of the Germans were foreboding. The Allies had liberated the Normandy and Mediterranean fronts yet the Nazis weren't relenting, holding on like a pit bull guarding what was left of his bone.

"The SS 2nd Panzer division is moving from the east to central France," the commander said, pointing to the map. "They've been ordered to hold the region and to quell any uprisings by the French Resistance and the Maquis. They're killing on sight, no questions asked, and innocent civilians are getting caught in the middle. We've heard of mass hangings in the town of Tulle and complete annihilation of another town, Oradour sur Glane."

Art exchanged glances with Frank. Leaning towards him, he whispered, "What makes someone lose all humanity and do such heinous acts?" Frank just shook his head in dismay.

The commander continued, "As you know, the Allies are in Normandy and the French have freed the ports along the Mediterranean which has opened up an alternate route for fuel and supplies. Meanwhile, the Germans have retreated into the Vosges mountains. They've set up a strong defensive line and don't want to lose this foothold. That's where we're heading to join the Seventh Army. The 36th Division needs reinforcements."

On September 11th, the 442nd headed out in ships. Destination: Marseille, France.

When they docked into the Marseille harbor, Art was overtaken by emotion. People covered the streets, celebrating their freedom. Even the severe winds known as the "Mistral" kicking up swirls of dust couldn't quell the elation of the French people.

"Let's go check out the crowd at the corner. I can hear music." Frank grabbed Art by the arm, his eyes sparkling with a renewed sense of joy. Art ran alongside his buddy, maybe joining the celebration would pull him out of his gloom. After all the misery of the past few months, it would be uplifting to share the excitement with the liberated civilians.

They found a carnival in full swing. Old men, women, and children were rejoicing, their faces covered with smiles oblivious to their war-weary bodies and tattered clothes. The lack of military-age men was obvious, still either in Germany at labor camps or continuing the fight in the Resistance. Old age didn't stop a few from climbing up to pull down the swastika banners.

Some townsfolk had dug out their traditional costumes of Provence, somehow still intact after all the bombings and fires. Determination was written across their faces. Nothing could dampen their pride of being French. The women wore lace caps resembling stiff doilies atop their heads and brightly colored skirts. The men donned more classic attire—black pants with wide red waistbands. Holding hands in a circle, they moved to the music of a violin and a sort of flute. Many years had passed since they had celebrated like this, and Art became lost in the reverie with them. Music was releasing the emotions these people had kept bottled up, in a way that words could not. Expressions ranged from poignant to passionate, some sobbing from the release of the pent-up anguish suppressed during the Nazi occupation. The music pumped out in beat to the rhythmic swirls of the women's skirts. The sight was both beautiful and heartrending.

But no respite for the weary serving in the Army. No sooner had they begun to relax than they were being corralled back to the meeting areas.

"Everybody load up, we're heading north to the beautiful Vosges mountains."

The 442nd boarded open trucks for the nearly 500-mile trip, forming convoys that hauled them up to the *Epinal* region close to the border with Germany. The sunny coast faded as the trucks headed north along narrow roads, climbing into valleys toward dark, menacing clouds. Before long, those clouds opened up, releasing a downpour. The trip was exhausting, and the trucks were so crowded that no one had room to sit down, all lined up like sardines in a can. Art tried to sleep. Propped up against the shoulders of whoever was next to him, his legs throbbed and he was drenched to the core. The first night, the convoy stopped near an open field for the men to bivouac. Art looked around to find Frank.

"Let's go for a quick walk to stretch out our legs," he suggested.

"Sure, but only if you play a game of chess with me later."

"It's a deal."

"I sure miss the beaches of Marseille. After everything we've gone through, I was hoping for a longer break. A couple of days would have been a real morale booster."

Art commiserated, yet wondered if moving wasn't better than dwelling on the experiences of the previous months. Seeing death for the first time had been tough, it was better not to think about it and keep moving forward with their goal—annihilate the Nazis.

They found a few areas of high ground to pitch the tents, but even the highest ground was deep in mud. C-rations of canned beef stew were served. As Art sank his teeth into the brown mush that tasted more of tin than beef, he yearned for rice. And he wasn't alone. Most of the men dreamed of steaming bowls of the sticky white mounds to scoop up in chopsticks or shovel into the mouth with a splash of tea. He finished the can without a complaint.

Frank pulled out his chess set as Art got the tents assembled. No sooner was the pup tent up than a torrential rain soaked the ground under them. So much for chess, another game washed out. The canvas tents gave little protection, and Art shivered through most of the night. He wondered what was in store for them as they continued the long and miserable three-day trip to the Vosges. It was getting colder and wetter the further they climbed.

On the third day, they arrived outside of a small town, Bruyeres, with a population of less than 3,000. Art went on a reconnaissance mission. Peering over the hill, he saw the village sitting in a valley. Four cone-shaped hills rose several hundred meters, covered with thick forests, encircling the town of red clay rooftops. From their vantage, they saw the Germans in fortified strongpoints on each hill, looking down into the valley, establishing a perimeter of defense that would be formidable to reduce.

The men were dumbstruck by the dismal state of the surrounded town. A couple of even more dismal appearing men — skinny and bedraggled, whose faces wore expressions of complete exhaustion met them.

"We're with the Resistance and are assigned to work with you. We know the lay of the land so will help guide you around the Nazis. Back in June, orders came down from London to block the German army's route to Normandy before the Allies made their landing. Our Maquis attacked and succeeded in halting 10,000 Nazis in their tracks. They were furious at not being able to join their forces against the Allies. The battle was terrible - so many killed on both sides. In revenge, the Nazis annihilated Bruyeres with flamethrowers. They got my best buddy Gaston, tortured, then dragged him back to town and beat him to death in the town square, right in front of us. We're regrouping now and are grateful to see you men here."

Art could only nod his head, understanding now why the village sat in ruin and contemplated the bravery of these French civilians.

"They've eaten our provisions, emptied our wine cellars, and taken anything that suits their taste, *les merdes Boches*," the Frenchman spit out the last words, his expression transforming to intense ferocity.

"The bombing has been non-stop. To leave the shelters, we must hug the walls of any standing building, just to find a bit of food."

"The local hospital's overrun with wounded, the town has little water or food and we've only a prayer of hope left ... until now," the other says, with expectation in his eyes.

Art studied these men, creases of determination ingrained in their faces. Then to the dark village, its electricity cut and surrounded by Nazis on all four corners. Together they faced what looked like an insurmountable battle.

They returned to the rest of the unit with their report. Camp had been set up in the forest, each soldier in a foxhole to provide some protection from the intermittent showering of shells.

Art tried to dig a foxhole deep enough, but the near frozen ground had no mercy. It took close to an hour, chipping out an inch of crunchy mud at a time.

"Damn it, I can't make a dent in this icy dirt."

"Try aiming the shovel sideways, it worked for me," Frank said.

Art saw he was set up close to Frank. That suited him just fine—maybe they could get in a game of chess before calling it a night, though he wondered how Frank managed to still have the set. As he went to procure a game, the sudden whine of an incoming shell, much louder than the others, broke the silence. He and Frank dove into their respective foxholes as the shell exploded. It was the closest one yet. Art felt the ground shake and the heat of the blast wrap over his face. A small shelf of ground had protected him from a concussion and any shell fragments. He crept out of his hole, calling out, "Hey Frank, you okay?"

"Yeah, that was way too close!"

The shelling continued for hours. The men stayed in their foxholes trying to get a few hours of shuteye between the explosions and the unrelenting rain.

The next morning, it was still raining. Art crawled out of his foxhole, which had accumulated an inch of water. He was soaked from head to toe, but everyone was in the same state.

The men circled around the commander for an update on the situation.

"The next battle will be tough. Bruyeres is only 50 miles from the German border and Hitler's orders are to hold it at all costs," he said. "It sits in this valley, surrounded by four hills which we will call hills A, B, C, and D. We have to take all four to free the town, which won't be easy with the Germans secured in those hills. They can see anyone attempting an approach."

He pointed to each hill on the chart. It looked like an impossible job. How many more men would die? Would his number be called up this time? Art checked for his senninbari, knowing that each soldier was doing the same with theirs.

That evening the Reverend Higuchi delivered a short sermon, crouched under a tree for some shelter from the merciless rain. He prayed for men to become brothers after this terrible war. Art wondered how things were going back home with their families locked away. It didn't seem like a good start to "brotherly love."

Art had a fitful night of sleep, worrying about his family and the upcoming battle. If he didn't return home, would his family be alright? Being the only son carried many responsibilities, he should handle the affairs with his father getting on in years. His family had lost everything they had built over the years, and it was taking a toll on his father. With his fingers intertwined around his *senninbari*, he finally got a few hours of shuteye.

The battle commenced at daybreak. They were attached to the 36th Division, whose leader was General Dahlquist. Art went out with a team to support the battalion whose objective was to capture Hill B. Between them and it stood an open valley with little cover for an approach. The Germans had blown down trees and other debris to block the roads to slow their advance. The Cannon Company was called in to clear these blockades.

Once the roads were clear enough to pass, the men moved to the base of the hill. The terrain was tough to cross—tall trees and undergrowth impeded the movement of the cannons. The enemy artillery burst above the trees, sending a shower of metal and wood splinters driving down on the men. Art felt them hitting his helmet, like being bombarded by huge hail or bricks.

Italy had been brush-covered hills, but here were steep mountains, covered in dense pine forest. The rain hadn't stopped for 20 days and fog had settled down to the ground, enveloping the region in a cold, blinding blanket. The Cannon Company's job was to support the battalions in the open areas, but once they entered the woods, it was too dangerous to fire the cannons. Art's frustration grew as he tried to protect his buddies once they dropped into the woods, out of his view, limiting him to watch from the base of the hills.

Art moved back and forth, giving support between the 2nd and 100th battalions. He walked between the white tapes the engineers had laid to mark off minefields. He kept a close eye on the ground, searching for the thin tripwires used to trigger explosives. Continuing on a gravel road flanked by black skeletons of trees, the smell of smoke and burning wood still lingered in the air. He moved off the road to allow a bulldozer to pass, watching as it shoved aside a roadblock of trees and rocks with amazing ease. He kept constant vigilance from the corner of his eye to avoid getting hit by a sniper.

"Okay, our rifle teams have flushed out some Germans," an infantryman said.

Art received coordinates and radioed back to the guns who quickly fired off for direct hits. They chased the Germans across the fields to the next hill.

The days following were the most intense fighting the 442nd had seen, much worse than in Italy. Trying to fight in the mountains controlled by the enemy often led to hand-to-hand combat. Moving between the trees was backbreaking, as the terrain was steep and slick with mud. Besides being shot at by machine guns, mortar shells exploded in the tree canopies, sending searing shrapnel and splinters from the trees. These lodged into the soldiers like hot knives, plus there were mines and booby traps in the underbrush. It was clear the Germans were trying to hold Bruyeres no matter what, and so far, they were succeeding.

The going was slow—men slipping and sliding up the steep hill while mines exploded under them. Art heard yells, screams, and cries out for mothers. He stopped, dumbfounded by all he was experiencing, searching the faces of the others. *Are they having as much trouble as me, enduring this?* Expressions were either blazing with fury and determination or dull and lifeless, as if drained of any emotion.

Then he saw Ben, another member of the Cannon Company. He had a vacant stare, cutting right through Art like a zombie.

"Hey, buddy. How are you? Let me help you get down to base."

Ben didn't speak, just gave a drop of the chin resembling a nod.

Art grabbed his elbow to help guide him. Ben's legs slumped, and his feet dragged along, leaving deep ruts in the mud. Art mustered all his strength to get him to the base camp, where a couple of other guys helped him to the medic tent.

"Looks like another one with battle fatigue. It must be murder up there, several men are coming back like this," the medic said. "He needs to get out of here, but good luck with that. Dahlquist says the best thing is to send them back to the front. That will knock it out of them, he says. I say take him to a tent and cover him as well as you can."

They each hooked an arm under Ben's shoulders. They pulled back the tent flap, but the canvas was saturated so no relief was found inside, just the same mud and puddles.

"Let's settle him in this foxhole. I'll keep an eye on him," Art said.

He covered the foxhole with tree branches and built up the surrounding ground. What amazed him was the endurance of the human body. Everyone was freezing and wet, teeth chattered when anyone spoke, and muscles trembled under their skin uncontrollably. Sleep was intermittent at best, no more than one to two hours in a twenty-four-hour period, along with the constant threat of being wounded or killed. The only thing that kept everyone going was sheer willpower. And keeping their boots on.

Art hoped the lull in fighting would hold, and he headed to the makeshift camp. His feet squished in his soggy socks, reminding him of better days playing in the mud as a young boy. He flashed back to his mother's anguished face, following the tracks he left in the house. It seemed like yesterday but was long ago and far away. He slipped down into a foxhole, landing in a couple of inches of cold water, and paid no mind, his body still trembling from the cold. Or maybe it was fear. He awoke to a familiar voice cursing outside.

"I shouldn't have taken off these boots. Dammit, now my feet are too swollen to get them back on. God damn it all," Captain Shorey yelled.

Shorey looked dismally down at his discolored toes. They had all the indications of trench foot from being perpetually water-logged. Every soldier knew the danger—the feet would become swollen, then infected, sometimes leading to gangrene and even amputation. Boots would have to be cut off if the foot had swelled too much. The next day, they took Captain Shorey to the General Hospital back in Marseille.

On October 18th, they briefed the men.

"We're going for an all-out assault on those hills.

Navigating through the thick forests is near impossible, but we have help from the French Forces of the Interior. They know these areas like the back of their hand and will guide us. We have two assigned to each of the battalions."

Art looked at these Frenchmen, who would lead them through the forest. They carried the same look of determination as the others he had met, willing to risk their lives for the mission.

First, the chemical weapons provided smoke cover, followed by artillery from the Cannon Company. This allowed the riflemen led by the Resistance, to charge the hills. These local Frenchmen guided the battalions through the woods, not following any apparent path, slithering between trees like a fox returning to her den. Galvanized by the fortitude and courage of these men, the troops surged forward. Their expert guidance shortened the battles and saved many more lives.

Hills C and D fell in succession over the next two days. Artillery attacked the tops of the hills, and machine guns and mortars cleared the lower slopes until the troops met in Bruyeres.

"Now we must neutralize hostile fire in town. It will be a house-to-house battle. Cannon Company will fire on the German weapons, fortified buildings, and armored vehicles," ordered the Colonel.

Art went with another observer to an upper story of a burnt-out building. From there, they had an eagle-eye view of the town. Other observers posted to surrounding buildings completed a circle of surveillance. The enemy hid with their artillery behind solitary walls left from destroyed homes. From Art's vantage point, they reminded him of the toy soldiers and tanks he played with when a boy. It was easier to send instructions to take out these targets if they didn't seem like humans, but inanimate objects. It was part of the separation helping him cope as they killed these young men. Not seeing them for who they were, made it easier to send instructions on where to aim the next cannon attack.

After nine days of constant battle, Bruyeres was liberated. As the 442nd entered the town, Art heard a few of the townspeople sound an alarm.

"Wait, these are Japanese! Aren't they with the Germans?"

"No, they're wearing U.S. uniforms, they're Americans. We're saved, our village is free!"

Art was glad he had studied some French so he could enjoy this moment. These villagers recognized them as Americans, not Japanese, but good ol' American boys. Just what all of them were fighting so hard to prove.

Bruyeres was liberated but news came that the Germans had retaken Hill D. Three companies went back to attack again. In the meantime, the rest of the units took a break. Frank rushed over to Art, chessboard tucked under his arm.

"How about a game? It'll help get our minds off everything."

"No, not right now. I'm beat, I need to send off a letter—it's been too long since I've written." Art felt a twinge of guilt when he saw the disappointment on his buddy's face. "We can play tomorrow," he said to reassure Frank.

Art settled against a tree, sitting on his helmet, and began writing to Butch. He had received a letter from her and wanted to reply as soon as he could. He read it again before deciding what to say.

Dear Art,

I arrived here in Rochester on the 7th. The Mayo clinic is located in the center of town. Before I left, I went to see your mother. *She, like the other mothers with sons overseas, was worried, but I had just received a letter from you, so I told her all about what you said you were doing. Lillian and Chibi saw me off at the bus.*

Received a letter from Mable today. They visited Seattle recently but received a cold shoulder from most in their old neighborhood. One garage door even had "Go Home Japs" painted across. They still think they will return but I prefer to stay out this way.

I'm sorry to hear you're in the machine gun squad. Be sure and have the darn thing turned away from you before firing. And when you are shooting, don't forget to tie the cork to the gun with a piece of string. That way you needn't keep hunting for it and save lots of valuable time. Just a sisterly advice, you don't mind, do you?

I thought you were in the Field artillery? How come you walk? Shall I talk to the General or something?

Love, Butch

Art closed his eyes, thinking about her. At one time, he had fantasized she might wait for him, but now she had left Minidoka for the East Coast. Her letters seemed to be affectionate, like she cared about him. Would he ever see her again?

October 22, 1944. All four hills had been taken, but the fight wasn't over. The battle continued east to the towns of Belmont and Biffontaine. Art was with the forward observer, sending back coordinates and relaying fire orders on his radio. A counter barrage by the enemy came in from over the ridge, bracketing him between two curtains of fire. Shells exploded in the trees and objects crashed down around him, bouncing off his helmet and ricocheting in every direction. Then it hit— a searing pain in his back knocked the wind out of him and his legs collapsed. He dragged himself to cover as trees burst into flames, sending burning branches down on prostrate soldiers. After what seemed like an eternity, movement returned to his feet and legs.

Hearing moaning to his left, he stayed low, crawling on his hands and knees to the soldier, rolling him over.

"No, my God, no," Art said.

It was Frank. His helmet was gone and pieces of tissue were hanging off his cheekbone. Art moved him to a protected area in the rear.

"Don't worry, buddy, I'll get you some help."

He watched as the medics loaded his best friend onto a stretcher and carried him down to the aid station. His back still throbbing, he turned to find his team.

"Hey Art, over here. Get out of the line of fine."

He joined a couple of soldiers under a jeep to wait out the attack. When the barrage slowed, they emerged, and one soldier lifted the tarp over the vehicle.

"Sweet Jesus! Look, this vehicle is loaded with 105mm shells."

All three of them turned pale, thinking about the consequences if it had been hit. The entire truck would have exploded, blasting them across the hill.

Art's back was still burning, so he headed down to be checked by the medics. They had set up a lean-to, built into a hill. Tarps were strung over branches to form a roof of sorts, under which they arranged cots for the wounded. Art winced as he bent to enter the improvised treatment area.

"The shrapnel entered right next to your spine. You're one lucky soldier! But it's too dangerous to remove. I'll sprinkle in some sulfa powder and throw a couple of stitches to close the skin. If you can tolerate the pain, I recommend leaving it," said the medic.

"Sure, I hardly notice, how about some aspirin or

something?" *I can't complain about a little shrapnel, but I'd love to stop this throbbing.*

"Here's some pills for the pain. Come back if it worsens."

Art swallowed a couple of the pills and then went to check on Frank, who was sedated and connected to an IV line for fluids. His head was covered in bandages, only his nose and eyes peered out. There were chest wounds as well. It didn't look good to Art. He sat by him for a few moments, resting his hand gently on Frank's arm.

"Frank, it's me Art. I'm sorry I didn't shield you from those damn shells! You pull through this and you'll get to head stateside, out of this hellhole."

Frank seemed to groan under all his wrappings, or at least Art thought he had heard something.

"Hang in there, I still gotta beat you at chess. You've been my rock, I need you," Art whispered, trying to encourage him. He wasn't good at expressing his emotions but scared he was losing him, he kept blubbering on.

"He needs his rest. You better get some yourself," a medic said.

Art tried to straighten his slumped back, then headed out. He found a boulder to lean against for a few moments of shut-eye. It wasn't safe near the foxholes, besides they were filled with mud, so with his back aching, he propped himself up on his helmet.

It was impossible to sleep. Every time he dozed off, visions of Frank's face appeared, either smiling over a game of chess or with chunks of bloody tissue hanging off his cheeks. No rest for the weary as he jerked back to reality by the sound of mortar. The attacks had started up again. He shook his head to clear the echoing sounds of Frank's moans and grabbed his gear. As he reached down to get his helmet, the shrapnel lodged in his back twinged. He headed out with his platoon, following the orders to fire on some Nazis identified on a hilltop. At the end of the day, Art ran back to check on Frank.

"Oh no, sorry. He didn't make it through the night, but he put up a good fight."

Art dropped his head, not able to believe it. Why hadn't he protected him and why hadn't he played that last game of chess? He stumbled out of the medic tent, his legs weak and his head reeling until he fell against the nearest tree, slumping to the ground. The stress of the war was taking its toll on everyone, but he was worn out. Frank had helped him manage so much of it, by being the friend always there with a smile. His desire to learn was contagious, and he sure played a mean game of chess. How was everyone expected to keep moving under these conditions? Wasn't there any time to process the toll of losing a friend like Frank? He wasn't aware how long he had laid against that tree, but commotion nearby jarred him back to reality.

He headed to Frank's foxhole to get the chess set, fingering through all the pieces. If only he had played that one last time, remembering the disappointment on Frank's face. If only he could go back in time. Squatting down, he reached for the king and placed it high on a rock, surrounded it with knights, and imagined Frank regal, looking down on the troops.

"You're on your own now, men. I can't be with you any longer, but I'll be watching over you from up here, so make me proud."

Art winced from the wounds in his back and stood to give a firm salute to his imaginary buddy high on the rock, then gathered the rest of Frank's belongings. He'd send those to his parents, envisioning another gold star being raised.

19

FRANCE
1944

Yvette braced herself as she aimed her bicycle towards the Maquis encampment. The questions she had for Thomas circled in her head, bouncing with each rut her tires dropped into. Who is this Pauline, and do you know her? Are the stories about her escapades true? And could she meet her? Upon arrival, she began asking.

He hesitated, cleared his throat, and lowered his voice to a whisper.

"I do know her. She's head of our supply source, working under the guise of a cosmetics saleswoman. She manages Maquis with Resistance groups—a total of 1500 persons. The Nazis have a one million francs reward on her head."

"That's incredible. With people like her, we'll win this war yet. How I'd love to meet her."

"She contacts me when a shipment arrives to restock our ammunition."

"Can I go with you on your next run? I'm sure I could be of help," Yvette asked.

Thomas walked a few steps away, his head shaking from right to left as if saying no to himself. Yvette crossed her fingers he'd see it her way. After some contemplation, he returned.

"I guess I'd be less suspicious if we looked like a couple. I'm going in two days to pick up a delivery."

"Perfect. Where do we meet?"

Yvette memorized the instructions and then waited, butterflies fluttering in her belly for the entire wait. She was both excited to meet this remarkable woman and terrified of the possibility of getting caught with the cache of weapons they were to collect.

It was another gray day. She climbed into the old Peugeot 201. The car had a powerful stench of damp leather mixed with body odor. How hard it must be to keep clean living out in those woods. Still, Thomas had a confident, determined look, and Yvette tried to keep her mind off the aromas. She blinked, fighting back the burning sensations in her eyes, concentrating on calming her nerves. Deep breaths usually helped, but it was becoming more difficult to focus lately.

The drive to Valençay took just over an hour. They passed through Luçay-le-Mal, the hometown of Yvette's mother, then continued towards a smaller village, Dun-le-Poilier.

"Her headquarters were in a house on the other side of town," Thomas said, pointing across the valley. "Last month, the Germans tracked her there, attacked, destroyed all the supplies, and killed over twenty maquis. Pauline escaped, hiding in the field behind the house. Now she's set up a few miles out, taking refuge with an older couple."

They drove up to a small farmhouse, and an attractive woman came out to meet them. She was exceptionally cautious, directing them to park their car behind some trees, out of view from the road.

"It's taken this long to get restocked from England, but we're back in action," Pauline said. "I've arms and ammunition for you."

Yvette watched the petite woman run to a shed, sliding the doors open to reveal stacks of cartons. What a feat for her to manage such an extensive organization. Yvette thought of the courage it took to risk everything and keep returning after the close call last month. And with a bounty on her head to add to the peril. But here she was with a grace and elegance that could convince anyone she *was* a cosmetic saleswoman, the perfect cover. No wonder the Nazis hadn't caught her yet.

Thomas mentioned Pauline was also an integral part of running escape lines for downed British and American pilots. First, they transferred them to a safe house near Paris, then they would either be guided over the Pyrenees into Spain or up to Brittany, where French fishermen would sail them back to England. It was an elaborate puzzle of people, each risking their lives at many levels. Not only were there the safe houses hiding them along their paths but also the guides who led them on the long, arduous routes.

She helped Thomas load over fifty arms, ranging from revolvers to submachine guns, grenades, plastic explosives, and ammunition into the trunk of the Peugeot. The old car groaned under the weight of its load. Then, to add misery to the poor car, they covered the entire cache with wood and topped it with bricks. If stopped, they hoped it would look like they were transporting building supplies.

Rain began pelting down on the trip home and Yvette nodded off to the rhythmic sound of the wiper blades. She jolted awake when Thomas cursed and slammed on the brakes. Horrified, she opened her eyes to three men in German uniforms standing in front of the car, ordering them to get out. One of them thrust her door open with such force that the door jolted to the side with a thump. He looked at it with disgust, jiggling the door to settle it back in place.

It took all her strength to step out of the car, her legs felt like overcooked noodles. The Nazis looked menacing, hovering over her. She tried to keep herself from trembling, but her lips were quivering. Did it look like she was mumbling to herself? They would think she was either disrespectful or mental. The tall one stood guard over them as the other two started searching the car. He spoke broken French, enough to ask what they were doing. Thomas tried to explain they were bringing back supplies to work on the house. The tall German seemed to understand, but looked skeptical. He grabbed Thomas by the arm, pointing to the trunk. *"Offten!"* he yelled. It was clear what he wanted.

Thomas reached in to get the keys out of the ignition, not taking his eyes off the Nazi. He walked to the back of the car and opened the trunk. The bricks had jostled around, exposing the wood planks. Yvette gasped at the sight, and Thomas glared in her direction.

She couldn't help it, what if they found the guns? What would they do? Could she run fast enough, trying to dodge their bullets? Bribery might work, but what did they have?

Her eyes glued to Thomas as she said a silent prayer. Or maybe it was out loud. She was so upset it was hard to tell.

Yvette stood to the side of the car, the rain streaming down her hair, soaking her back and chest. Frantically, she thought to herself, is there anything to divert their attention? As she looked down, she noticed her blouse becoming quite transparent, clinging to her curves. Wondering if this might serve as a distraction, she gave the Germans as close a coquettish regard as she could muster. This quickly drew their attention away from the task at hand. She rubbed her arms as if trying to keep warm, which compressed her breasts further forward. They became captivated, glancing only quickly at the bricks in the trunk. The tall German, less affected, tried in vain to maintain discipline between the other two soldiers. It was clear their attention was now transfixed on the young woman, whose breasts were their greatest concern. He yelled for them to get back to their vehicle and off they went, the two Germans looking wistfully through the rear window of their black sedan.

Once they had lost sight, Thomas grabbed his coat to throw over Yvette.

"That was clever, but it wouldn't have gone so well if they'd been SS or worse yet — Gestapo. Who knows what they would have done to you. You shouldn't have taken that risk."

"But they weren't and we deflected them from finding our stash," she argued.

"True. If they'd traced the guns to Pauline they'd have figured she was back in action. Thank God, you were able to distract them." He was absolutely giddy.

Yvette smiled to herself. Thank goodness those soldiers were gullible and easily distracted.

20

VOSGES MOUNTAINS, FRANCE
OCTOBER 26, 1944—0300 HOURS

They woke the men of the 442nd after only a few hours of rest. The promise of a respite from the battles cut short.

"Every man report to duty now. We have a crisis at hand. The 1st Battalion of the 141st Regiment is encircled by the enemy 3 km from here. Earlier attempts to rescue them have been unsuccessful. We're counting on you 442nd men to bring them down," General Dahlquist said.

"Remember, this isn't any regiment. Their roots come from the Texas Revolutionary War of 1835, when Texas won independence from Mexico. *Remember the Alamo* was its battle cry. Orders are from President Roosevelt himself. I don't care what it takes, we must get these men out."

"Psst, Art. You know, General Dahlquist sent them up there and now they're trapped. He expects us to clean up his mistakes," a soldier whispered.

"How come they don't use their own guys to help the battalion? Why use our outfit?" another soldier asked.

"Is it because we're Japanese and expendable?"

The Texas 141st became known as the 'Lost Battalion' and hope for their survival was becoming dim. They had no food, water and ammunition was dangerously low. There was some grumbling among the 442nd, but they knew what they had to do.

It was pitch black when they set out from Belmont, each man groping the backpack of the forward soldier, eyes straining to see the attached white cloth. The pace was slow, as each tree and bush was checked for booby traps and trip wires. The men slipped and slogged on the steep, muddy path with the added threat of Germans hiding in trenches with their machine-gun nests camouflaged under brush. These formed hidden trap-doors so as the 442nd passed by, the Germans would jump up, attacking from behind. It was hard to know where they might spring up next.

The engineers kept ahead of everyone, ensuring the roads were covered with logs and rocks to provide traction for the tanks. Which wasn't an easy feat. Each tank passing would sink down into the sodden ground, requiring constant reinforcements. Bulldozers were on hand to pull the tanks out as they inevitably got stuck in the mud.

The 442nd marched on, through violent attacks from machine guns and mortar fire. The enemy shot into the tree canopies sending explosions down on the soldiers. After two days, they gained a mere 1500 yards, losing countless men and materials along the way.

Art didn't think he could be more exhausted, cold, and wet. He cursed the army, General Dahlquist, and the 141st for getting trapped, but all in silence. Not a sound was made as the men continued into the early hours.

The rain was relentless, with the only change at night, when it was mixed with snow. It had been days since anyone had any actual sleep. A few innovative men propped saplings and brush around boulders, using mud to keep the water out, to allow a bit of shut-eye. Art leaned against another boulder to doze off, his vivid dreams providing an escape. He's back in

Minidoka, waltzing with someone. He's not sure who, but her hair smells of cooked rice. An explosion bolts him awake. A short catnap was all anyone could get.

At daybreak, Art's team was called in for firepower. The regiment continued moving towards the 'Lost Battalion.' The trapped men sent an update on their situation.

"They're starving us out and aren't wasting any men or weaponry against us. They know we're trapped. But we refuse to surrender."

An attack plan was set—but would it succeed or fail?

"The 442d's 2d Battalion will approach from the left flank, the 3rd—a frontal attack, and the 100th will come from the right," the commander announced.

The advance to the hilltop was near impossible. The Germans defended it with all their might, but the Americans of the 442nd had their orders and the assault continued.

Art watched a private fix his Browning automatic rifle around his shoulder and climb toward the enemy, taking out one machine gun and then another. Meanwhile, the rest of the company followed suit. They dug the enemy out of foxholes with bayonets and lobbed in grenades. Up ahead, the Cannon Company pointed all six guns at fifty Nazis tucked behind a roadblock. An explosion of black smoke shot into the sky, then tree trunks and miscellaneous body parts rained down in front of them. Cheers roared out about the direct hit, but the sense of death dampened it. How could one not be shaken by the youth and innocence of each dead man. Moments later, another disaster hit.

He was in the wrong place at the wrong moment. A shell screamed into the trees over his head, hitting so hard his helmet blew off. Art recognized him—it was Uetaro who had demanded to be buried where he fell instead of being sent home with the other killed soldiers.

"The people of this country have shown me more respect than those in the U.S. who only have hatred and discrimination for us," he had said.

Art thought of the family receiving the news of their son's death. Not being able to have his body returned would magnify their sorrow a thousand-fold. Was it the right choice? There were many unknown equations in this war.

On October 30, the 'Lost Battalion' was rescued. Their ordeal of seven days was over. Out of the 275 Texans, only 211 are left. The 442nd was down by almost half, having lost 814 men during the rescue, with 121 dead. It was the worst fighting they had encountered since landing in Europe. The men were drained and demoralized. The only uplifting moment was the actual rescue, seeing the grateful faces of the 141st men.

"We fought with all we had, but no way were we going to get out of this on our own. Thanks to you men of the 442nd, we'll never forget this."

"Want a cigarette?" asked a 442nd soldier, reaching into his jacket.

"Oh, man, do I ever. You know, you guys are honorary Texans now."

Art felt a surge of pride at the thought of being a Texan. Had they finally made a dent in the psyche of a die-hard American?

"That's great, how about a dry change of clothes and a solid night's rest?"

The troops headed down the mountain to base camp, looking forward to a small reprieve.

General Dahlquist had other ideas, ordering them to continue chasing the Germans through the forest to secure additional territory. The battles continued as the 442nd drove the Germans off the hills to finish the job of the 141st. It took another nine days before they had a break. After three weeks of nonstop combat in the Vosges, the 442nd had lost 140 men with over 1,800 wounded.

The confirmation the Germans were withdrawing came as fires exploded in St. Die and Corcieux. The Germans torched everything to leave nothing behind. It was a dismal sight to see St. Die, one of France's oldest cities, left a pile of smoking rubble.

The Combat Team finally had a respite. They assigned houses for the soldiers to billet, providing hot showers, dry clothes, and boots. Art collapsed in a bed, finally not lying in semi-frozen puddles. He tugged with all his might — first the right, then the left boot. But his wool socks stuck glued to his feet - should he dare pull them off? What might lie beneath? Peeling the socks back like one might remove the skin from an orange, he breathed a sigh of relief. His toes had color and had feeling as he gently touched them, one by one. He knew not to rub or try to warm them too quickly. Before he knew it, he fell into a deep slumber.

But all good things must come to an end—after only four days, they sent the 442nd back out. This time to provide a defensive line at the base of the forest that the Germans still occupied. The Cannon Company fired thousands of rounds into the hills to dissuade the Germans from attacking. It was a success.

After a month of fighting, the 442nd lost more than half of its men. Many were in hospitals, some never to be entirely well, while others joined back on the lines before being released, reverse AWOL. They would leave treatment before being deemed recovered—to join back with their troops.

Upon the release from the 36th Division, the commanding officer read a letter from General Dahlquist.

"The 36th Division regrets that the 442nd Combat

Team must be detached and sent on other duties. The period during which you served, October 14 to November 18, 1944, was one of hard, intense fighting through terrain as challenging as any army has ever encountered. The courage, steadfastness, and willingness of your officers and men were equal to any ever displayed by United States troops. Every officer and man of the Division joins me in our best personal regard and good wishes to every member of your command, and we hope that we may be honored again by having you a member of our Division."

Art was humbled and felt a deep pride in what they had accomplished. The tragic loss of life made the moment impossible to enjoy, but the recognition helped the men know the lives lost weren't without purpose. All the soldiers agreed it was from the help of Colonel Pence who led them, always by their sides and supporting their actions. Yes, he had been a top leader during the battles in the Vosges. Even back at training in Shelby, he had said, "If other troops pick on you, just get back at 'em, and don't take anything lying down." That made them feel like any other soldier, not second best, as some other officers treated them. Now what lies ahead?

21

ÉCUEILLÉ, FRANCE
AUGUST 1944

As the Allies pushed eastward towards Germany, the enemy's mood became more volatile with each kilometer of land lost. They destroyed anything that got in their way. Their goal to keep as much of occupied France as theirs was paramount. The Resistance continued to curtail the German movements by sabotaging bridges, communication lines, and attacking isolated German forces. These actions eased passage for the Allies and the joined effects were taking a toll on the enemy.

The repercussions of the Nazi's desperation echoed in the Milice and Gestapo, with more violent reactions against Resistance activity. The Normandy invasion had liberated the north of France, including Paris, but the fighting south of the Loire River was mounting to a ferocious level. With General Patton on one flank and the French First Army on the other, the Germans were trapped. And like wild animals, they were protecting their domain.

Yvette's father, now aware of her activities, gave his advice.

"Don't do more than deliver food to the Maquis. They take greater risks than the Resistance and can get unruly.

"But since the two have banded together, they've grown from 100,000 to over 400,000. And we need to finish pushing the Nazis completely out of our country," Yvette said.

"True. The south of France around Marseille is liberated but the Germans are established in the Vosges mountains. They would love to steal the Alsace Lorraine back again"

After dinner, Yvette's father pushed his chair away from the table. "I'm going out for an hour, no longer."

Hours passed before Yvette heard him come in.

"Papa, where have you been?"

He looked bedraggled, dried dirt caked into the creases along his forehead and streaks of sweat ran down his cheeks.

"Here, sit down at the table and let me clean you up."

She dampened a cloth to wipe his face then poured two glasses of red wine and sat across from him.

"I was at Mr. Denis' house when Nazis came pounding on the door. We had no choice but to do as they demanded. Some Maquis had planted explosives and destroyed a bridge. Trees fell and blocked the road out of town. You know, the one to Valençay. A German convoy of twenty cars near Écueillé got stopped in its tracks. The soldiers were in a frightful mood, storming into town, beating on doors, and demanding men open the roads. Meanwhile, they marched another group of men and women to the town hall and locked them in. They say they'll kill them at dawn."

"They dragged young and old out of their homes to open up the road. This is why villagers despise the Maquis. Innocent townspeople have to bear the consequences. So at dawn, the prisoners, including the priest and mayor, will be shot as a reprisal for the road blockage," he continued.

Yvette's father had been one of the men who helped

clear the road and had worked through the night.

"The worst part is the prisoners. We'll use force if we can't reason with them for their release."

What kind of force would her father use against Nazis? He would need more help, otherwise it would be suicide for sure. They had to break them free before dawn.

The priest was a close family friend, not only to them, but to most of the families in town. He knew about the Wolffs and came to give private communions to the couple when possible. And the mayor, why he was also the town veterinarian. How would they function without him? Last month, when Belle was limping, he found an abscess in her hoof. He cleaned it out with his pick and packed it with care. He was a wonderful doctor—they couldn't lose him.

Full of worry, Yvette heard every movement as her father left and stopped by the cellar on his way out. Was he taking some guns? A tightness grew in her chest. Should she try to go along? She focused on the ticking of the kitchen clock. Time crawled by until it was impossible to wait any longer. She started to slip into her shirt and pants when she heard the door open.

"Oh, Papa, you're back already. What happened?"

"We were lucky. The German lieutenant in charge was a Protestant pastor. He was a calm, good man who decided not to follow through with the killings. They've released the prisoners, the road's clear, and the German convoy's on its way!" her father said, sinking in a chair, a look of relief washing over his face.

The morning sun emerged, glinting its light through the kitchen. Everyone was coming down for the start of the day. Yvette's mother was heating water on the stove, and even the Wolffs had come down to join for breakfast. Yvette smiled at her father, who winked back. It was going to be a beautiful day.

She celebrated the release of the hostages in her head. Humming a tune during her daily chores, the day flew by. It was late afternoon before she headed to town, hoping a few items remained at the store. On her last trip, she had waited over 30 minutes, only to see the store clerk place the sold-out sign on the counter. Cycling to town, she hoped for better luck today.

The ride into town was quiet. Nazis were passing through on their return to Germany, traveling by foot, in a car, on a few horses, or even an occasional tank. If she was lucky, her path would stay clear until she made it back home. She rode around the square, noticing a gathering at the hotel Lion d'Or. Seated outside was a squadron of French soldiers, sporting tall leather boots signifying they belonged to the cavalry. Wondering where their horses were, Yvette got in line at the store across the way, which was abuzz with news.

"Have you heard? The Nazis are out of Paris at last. Our beautiful city is again French," said a woman, her face beaming with pride.

"Our cavalry is following on the heels of the Germans eastward. With Chateauroux liberated, the Nazi flag is down and ours is flying again in the town hall. We have squadrons in place throughout the region. This group is staying here tonight and then continuing in the morning. It looks like we're finally rid of those Nazis, once and for all."

That seems unlikely. Father has concerns and Thomas said smaller groups of Germans are still on the attack, Yvette thought.

She purchased a few grams of salt and sugar. Before heading out the door, she smiled and said her pleasantries to the other customers. It was getting late, close to 8:00 pm. While heading to her bicycle, she saw the mayor running towards the hotel, waving his arms frantically.

"Germans are approaching Écueillé. Alert the soldiers now!"

Two German tanks approached the town square, followed by a file of German soldiers on either side, rifles at the ready. Yvette scanned the area, frantic, realizing she was trapped. Soldiers from both sides, French and German, stood blocking the roads. Her eyes darted around the square, looking for an escape path. It looked like they might start shooting at any moment. She slipped off her bicycle and crept around a building, pressing her body against the stone bricks, attempting to blend in with the wall. Her fingers dug into each nook, the lime and sand mortar cutting into her hands. Closing her eyes, she darted to the next building adjacent to the town hall, where a few people had taken refuge under the stairs.

"Yvette, come next to me. You'll have some cover," said her cousin, Jeanne.

"I need to get home to warn my family," Yvette said.

"They'll be fine as long as the fighting stays in town."

The French cavalry tanks had lined up—one on each road facing towards the town square. The Germans had fanned their tanks inwards from another road. As soon as Yvette dove for cover, the shooting began. Shells illuminated the sky, first green, then turning a bright red, exploding into the surrounding homes and businesses. Yvette saw one pierce the pharmacist's windows above the shop where he and his family lived. She prayed they had taken cover in the cellar, thinking of their young son, Luke, who would bring her orders out. Jeanne's hand pressed firmly on her shoulder.

"Don't do anything silly."

"I need to see if they're alright. What about little Luke?"

"Getting yourself killed won't help anything. We need

to wait here."

Soldiers fell on both sides from rifle and shell fire. The sounds were deafening. Screams and shouts filled any silence between the blasts. Yvette's ears throbbed in her head and the smell of sulfur engulfed her. She squeezed her eyes to control the stinging. A loud thud and the sight of a shell tumbling toward the stairwell alarmed everyone.

"Oh my God, we must get out of here."

"Where can we run? We risk being seen and they'll shoot us."

Yvette felt a heavy arm tugging her further under the stairs. *Well, this must be it. I wonder if these stairs will provide any protection.*

Everyone held their breath. Minutes crept by.

"Wait, it hasn't exploded, it's a dud! Someone up there must be looking out for us."

Yvette's stomach was tied in knots, like a rope was pulling from both ends. She heard Jeanne gasp and followed her gaze to see Jeanne's house engulfed in flames. There wasn't any way to save it.

Fires were breaking out around the square, windows shattering and walls collapsing. The entire area was aglow in red. The beautiful statue of the girl in the fountain tumbled down as if she had fallen to her knees in despair. Smoke and ash rose, making it hard to see what was happening and screams continued with an intense fervor.

Eventually, the explosions and shooting slowed. Only a few bursts were heard from stored ammunition triggered by the fires. Creeping out from the staircase, Yvette peered around the half-destroyed building that had served as their fortress. French soldiers were running from building to building, checking for the injured.

"The Boches have surrendered! Everyone come out

now—we need the areas cleared so we can fight these fires," a soldier yelled.

"Run to the post office and alert the postmaster to telephone surrounding towns. We need more fire trucks to come help. We can't handle this alone," another soldier added.

People were running right and left. Some running in circles, confused about what to do next. Yvette beelined to the pharmacy where she found Luke kneeling next to his mother, sobbing.

"Let me see if I can help," Yvette said as she placed her hand on him.

She rolled his mother over. This kind woman, always quick with a smile, was gone. Yvette held him in her arms, rocking him back and forth. How do you console a young boy who has lost his mother? She turned to see his father limping towards them.

"No, no, she can't be dead!" he exclaimed, the stern pharmacist clinging to his wife's lifeless body. Yvette left them to mourn. René curled up by his mother's side. Tragedy had hit their quiet town on a level never seen before.

She followed a line of people taking the injured down the hill to the church. A make-shift hospital had been set up inside. Moans of agony instead of hymns seeped out of the nave. Bodies of the dead leaned along the outside wall as if waiting for their turn to enter for mass. She didn't want to see who might be there, looking away from the bodies laying in a row, covered with makeshift shrouds. Peering in the entrance, there were plenty of volunteers tending to the victims, the doctor in the center aided by the town nurse. She headed back into the center of town to retrieve her bicycle and get home. Her family must have heard the battle and would be worried.

Additional fire trucks had arrived, dousing the remaining flames to embers. Her hometown was smoldering under toppled walls and caved-in roofs. To her amazement, her bicycle was still standing—it was close to 1 a.m. and with ash falling, she weaved her way home through the debris.

22

BACK TO ITALY
MARCH 1945

The next destination sounded great to Art—the French Riviera. Well actually, he would be stationed in Sospel, in the Alps about an hour from the famous city of Nice. But close enough for him. Their orders were to guard the 18-mile front from the Riviera to the mountains along the French-Italian border. It was between the coastal town of Menton near Monaco to the ski mecca of Piera Cava. It wasn't a well-known front, but was important nonetheless. The Germans could burst through the line and recapture Marseille at any time. They were sitting across the border in Italy, waiting for their opportunity.

The 442nd was assigned to three main areas along the old Maginot Line—the 100th battalion near Nice, the 3rd near Sospel, and the 2nd in Piera Cava. The Germans shelled almost daily and snipers shot at their patrols from locations across the valleys in Italy. In return, the Allies sent over intermittent fire from the Cannon Company and the 522nd artillery.

Art was attached to the 3rd battalion about ten miles from Sospel, in the Maritimes Alps, on a particular Mount Grosso. They set up their operations post in an old turret. Dry, proper tents replaced muddy, frozen foxholes, but German shelling soon punched holes in the canvases. The men, being creative, figured out a simple solution. They made dugouts in caves which kept them dry and protected.

Being stationed in the mountains made getting supplies formidable. The trails were too narrow and steep for vehicles, so mules brought up everything, including meals. After a few weeks, Art became familiar with each mule and developed a friendly relationship with them, especially one he called Bessie. She was brown like the other mules, but had tips of red in her coat, setting her apart from the rest. It became quite the joke as she would bray when she approached the camp, the *hee-haw-hee-haw* sounds making everyone smile, especially Art. She wouldn't stop until he came out to greet her. He traded cigarettes for cubes of sugar, and she grew accustomed to her reward for climbing the steep mountainside.

"It's the least I can do after she sweated up with our food," Art said defensively. He was a bit embarrassed as the guys teased him about his new French 'girl.' He did love the way she nuzzled her soft lips against him and how she smelled like fresh grass (but wouldn't admit that to anyone).

It was Thanksgiving Day, and the troops got a surprise turkey dinner, served in a Mermite can. He carefully opened the insulated tin to remove the smaller containers filled with the feast. It was warm and tasted choice to Art. Memories of gathering around the table in Seattle with his family brought a lump to his throat. He pictured his father carving the turkey and his sisters, encouraging him to hurry. For now, Art had to be satisfied with this turkey in a can. He leaned back against a rock, admiring the view of the Maritime Alps, happy to be alive and to have a warm meal. After being under constant attack, it was surreal to relax and let his guard down. Sure, there were still explosions around, so caution was vital. But the Germans were easy to spot, hiding in houses below them in the valleys.

Relief came with passes for breaks to Nice and Cannes. Art was excited at the thought of practicing his French. He showered and shaved, found a freshly pressed uniform, and headed down with a couple of other soldiers. They were to stay in the Hotel Helvetique, which was open to them. Settling in the bar, they focused on finding the best spots for dancing.

An elegant older woman with a young girl approached them. The older woman introduced herself as the owner of the hotel and her daughter, Jeannette. She hoped their stay would be pleasant and if they needed anything to just ask. Her graciousness to the uninvited guests impressed Art.

"When the Nazis took over our hotel, they ate and drank our best, leaving nothing behind," Madame Durville explained. "It's a relief to have the Americans here now!"

We appreciate your hospitality and will try to not cause too much trouble," Art said. "Can you suggest any places to dance?"

"There are a few places down the street where you'll find a warm greeting." Or at least that was what Art thought she said, his French being only fair to middling.

The weekend flew by, and soon it was time to return to Sospel. Madame Durville packed sandwiches for their trip back and Art was already planning his next visit. Madame Durville had taken him under her wing, almost as a surrogate mother.

As the holidays approached, every soldier waited with anticipation for mail call. The letters gave them such morale boosts, especially Christmas Day. Art received a box of candy from home, and Butch sent a couple of books. Sitting down with some buddies from Minidoka, he shared the letter with the news about the camp and its goings-on.

> Dear Art,
>
> Remember Henry? He's been at Tule Lake since responding No-No on the questionnaire. It has been tough down there for everyone. They are being treated like criminals, much worse than us. President Roosevelt signed a new law that allows them to renounce their citizenship. After the way our government treated him, he decided it would be better to live in Japan. His parents are encouraging him as they are Japanese citizens and want to move back. He's making a mistake, but over half the people at Tule (over 5,000) have renounced already. There isn't any legal help for us to make the best decision. Plus, there's talk the camps will be closing and many of us are afraid of what we'll face back on the West Coast. I understand to a point, but have faith in our country and its people. Many good people don't share the bigoted, prejudiced opinions of some.
>
> People are afraid of heading back with no money, no income, and no place to live. It will be tough, but nothing compared to the men fighting this war. After all, you boys are putting on a very impressive display of courageous fighting for life, liberty, and freedom for everyone. The news reports say the 442nd has received more decorations than any of the other units. We are so proud of you. I couldn't imagine leaving after everything you have done.
>
> Love, Butch

"I think the No-No Boys are getting what they deserve, chickening out instead of joining like we did. It's an insult to all our buddies who've died or been injured," one man said.

"I think I understand how they felt about fighting for a nation that judged us on our looks only and didn't trust us.

They're American too," Art defended, thinking of Henry's dilemma.

"Hmm, sorry Art, but I don't see it. Signing no to the questions made them suspicious at least, and if they want to go to Japan, so be it."

"But they were born in the U.S. Their parents are from Japan and may be influencing them. You've heard how rough the treatment is at Tule. They're locked up there without any information from the outside. They remember their neighbors taking advantage of them—buying their goods for pennies, spitting on them and telling them to go back to Japan. Why, we went through it too," Art continued, defending their position. "We must support our country and save face for everyone left behind. We have nothing to be ashamed of— sorry, I don't get it."

They could have debated all night but agreed on one thing: that *they* had made the right choice. Art went back into his tent, taking care not to wake his tent mate, who had hit the sack earlier. He slipped into his bag, pulling it over his head to keep out the cool night air. It wasn't long before he heard the clanging of dishes.

Funny, who'd be cooking now? The earthy scent of a dashi broth made Art's mouth water. *Is someone making ozoni soup, my favorite New Year's treat?* He stumbled out of bed, following the enticing aroma. A woman had her back to him, stirring over a stove. He pulled a chair up to the table in anticipation of a delicious hot bowl of traditional Japanese soup. The woman turned to him, smiling. But the next moment her face melted away, exposing raw muscle and bones, her eyes protruding out and her teeth gaping out of her lipless mouth. Her dress and apron transformed into an army uniform, shredded into strips of burnt green cloth. The odor of burning skin and fabric replaced the pleasant memories of the soup. Art jumped up from his cot, yelling in confused terror. *Another bad dream, but this one seemed so real. I could almost taste the soup.*

The next day was New Year's Day. This was going to be tough for all the guys. It's a family day for the Japanese—a time to come together and celebrate the opening of a new year and to eat delicious treats like the ozoni soup from his dream. His father explained the significance of the mochi cakes, an important component of the soup.

"The round cakes signify harmony in our family and the stretch of the sticky rice is for long life."

We all need some luck for harmony and long life right now, Art thought.

Art visited Nice whenever he got a chance, staying at Madame Durvilles' hotel. He developed a strong tie with her and her family. They invited him to share many meals and forged a friendship that he hoped would last well past the war. The daughter became like a younger sister to him, helping fill the void from being so far from his sisters. They would walk along the Promenade des Anglais, where he would buy them ice cream. Sitting on benches facing the Mediterranean, she tutored him in French, and he helped her in English. They spent many afternoons laughing like he had done with his sisters.

"Your French is improving," Jeannette said, trying to encourage him.

"Aren't you being a bit generous in your compliments?" Art chuckled.

"Well, we do need to work on that accent!"

The next instructions were tough for him to take, but all good things must come to an end. The 442nd left the Port of Marseille, heading back to Italy once again.

General Mark Clark had requested the return of his

favorite infantry for a critical mission—to create a diversion on the western end of the Gothic Line.

"We're back to the same place," groaned a soldier.

Art understood the frustration and noticed most of the men shaking their heads. It was only eight months ago they'd crossed the Arno River and liberated Pisa. Since then, the Germans had held back all Allied attempts to break through the Gothic Line. The line started north of Pisa at the Ligurian Sea and ran some fifty miles diagonally through the Apennine Mountains to the other side of Italy to meet the Adriatic Sea.

The soldiers lined up to get updates on their assignment from the lead colonel.

"The Germans are feeling the pressure—the Russians are pounding them in the east and we're approaching with the Brits from the west," he said. "We won't get complete defeat until we drive them out of these Italian mountains. Field Marshal Kesselring used Italian slaves to build trenches and gun pits into the solid rock lining the mountains. There are over 2,300 machine-gun nests facing down on us."

Art exchanged anxious glances with a few of the other soldiers. The thought of the enemy well entrenched in the sides of the mountains reverberated memories of previous battles. A soldier pulled Art aside, concern washed over his face.

"They're safe and snug in concrete reinforced emplacements and our planes and artillery haven't made a dent yet. What do they think we'll do?"

Art was about to say it would be something risky when the colonel wrapped up his speech.

"They've been impregnable thus far, but now we've arrived, right men?"

The 442nd gave out a hesitant cheer. They had fought

the enemy in the Vosges forests of France, helping to open the gateway for the 7th Army's invasion of the German Rhineland. It was time to finish the job.

Art looked up at the saw-toothed Apennines, rising some 3,000ft from the Ligurian Sea. The task looked impossible. These mountains differed from the Vosges mountains, which had been covered with trees and thick greenery. These were bare of any vegetation, save for some scrubby growth here and there. There wouldn't be any place to hide.

"After much deliberation, Colonel Miller and I have developed a new plan. Since the previous frontal assaults have failed, we'll approach from behind for a surprise attack at dawn," Colonel Pursall said. "It will entail scaling those cliffs and will be dangerous. Some men may fall but not a sound can be uttered for us to succeed."

The soldiers looked at one another, dumbfounded at this decision, and murmurs swept across the group.

"That's what they're asking us to do? It's impossible," a soldier said.

They sent the 3rd and 100th battalions to commence the night offense. It was April 4th. Art's fellow soldiers smudged their faces and hands with soot and taped their dog tags together to prevent any jangling noise. They loaded up with full battle equipment, facing an eight-hour climb, up an almost vertical, shale-covered mountainside. The men climbed on their hands and knees, a few falling, remaining silent in the night. They succeeded in sneaking up behind the sleeping enemy at 0530, taking them by surprise.

While they began the rear approach, the other groups took their positions. Art saw many fresh faces, replacement men who filled the void made by the fifty percent casualties suffered in the Vosges. These fresh soldiers were being thrown into the fire, without even a few days of warming up allowed.

The Cannon Company was ordered to provide artillery fire to flush the enemy out of the gun emplacements. Art worked his way to the front alongside his platoon leader. Glancing at the clouds enveloping the mountaintops filled him with anxiety, knowing the enemy was camouflaged within the mist.

Art radioed back coordinates, watching his directed shells explode near the top of the mountain while return fire from grenades and machine guns was unrelenting. The men had to navigate the mines scattered throughout the area—the Germans had spent the last five months fortifying their installations. No wonder the Gothic Line still stood.

Men charged forward and others fell back amidst the smoke and flashes of explosions. It looked surreal to Art like they were in a complicated dance. Bravery was everywhere across the hills.

One of the most horrifying sights was seeing Private First Class Munemori make a frontal attack through direct fire. It was April 5th. He took out two machine guns with grenades, but as he headed to join two other soldiers, a grenade bounced off his helmet and landed right where he was headed. Throwing himself over the grenade, it exploded, killing him, but his sacrifice saved his two fellow soldiers. That was the spirit of the 442nd.

There was a forceful counterattack by the enemy, but they achieved the first day's objectives with the early hour's climb up the cliffs and the coordinated frontal attacks. In just thirty-two minutes, the 100th/442nd reduced the mountain fortress which had withstood Allied assaults for five months. But it was a short-lived triumph since there were still many strongholds to clear.

The next day, the Cannon Co. fired smoke and explosive rounds at the next hilltops to be captured, followed by more of the same for the next few days. The battles continued up the boot of Italy towards the Po River.

As the troops headed towards the towns of Carrara to Aulla, an Italian partisan joined their march, sharing a story. "It happened in the town of San Terenzo, south of La Spezia, near a naval base. Last August, some German soldiers took a truckload of farm animals—a few cattle, some goats, chickens, and a pig. Well, we didn't think of the consequences, we just wanted to get the animals back. In the chaos, we killed most of the Germans. A few days later, in retaliation, the 16th SS Panzer Division entered the village, killing 159 innocent citizens, including the priest, women, and children. Only one seven-year-old girl survived, hiding under the dead bodies of her parents," he said, his knuckles blanched from clenched fists.

The men had heard many stories like these on their marches through France and Italy. The suffering of innocent people living in these countries was beyond comprehension. Marching through the countryside, it was hard to fathom the devastation. Entire towns destroyed, burnt-out fields speckled with dead farm animals left to rot, and people who had lost more than anyone could imagine. All this in the name of racial cleansing. And to what end?

The 442nd shared the same background—the strong codes instilled by their immigrant parents. Do what is right, have respect, loyalty, self-control, and courage. He heard his father's voice reminding him before he left, *"Gaman my son, and don't forget where you come from."* Art felt continual support from the other soldiers as they too, carried similar teachings with them. Endure the unbearable with patience and dignity. And it was so much to bear.

The men marched on, driven by the desire to end all this suffering and destruction. Battles raged on until Carrara was liberated. It was April 17th, and they had chased the enemy as far north as Aulla, blocking the Germans from escaping via the naval base. There was no way for them to retreat. The Germans, who had fought so fervently from Salerno to the Po Valley, had reached their end. On April 25th, Aulla fell, and the Germans began surrendering by the thousands.

The Po Valley campaign claimed the lives of 101 Nisei soldiers, wounded 922 and left three missing in action. They awarded the 442nd Regimental Combat Team the Distinguished Unit Citation signed by Chief of Staff Dwight Eisenhower. Ironically, he was the same man who had refused the 100th Battalion when they were deployed to Europe, saying he doubted their ability and loyalty.

Art looked around at the men of the 442nd, thinking back over the years of giving their all. He peered through blood and tear-stained eyeglasses and proudly thought, *There is no longer any question of loyalty or fighting skill of our men. No one can judge us by our race now.*

23

ÉCUEILLÉ, FRANCE
AUGUST 30, 1944

Thinking back to that decisive day—June 22, 1940, Yvette recalls when France agreed to the armistice, forcing it to succumb to occupation forces. The French Vichy government aided the German military authorities in rounding up Jews, anti-fascists, homosexuals, Jehovah's Witnesses, and others. They "vanished" into *Nacht und Nebel, "night and fog."* The Nazis picked up these so-called "undesirables" and shipped them off to Drancy and other detention centers. Then it was on to concentration camps such as Dachau and Buchenwald.

Now with the Allies' invasion and the strong resistance from the French, the local Vichy and police force were switching camps. No longer were they harassing French civilians into confessing or snitching on a Resistance sympathizer. The Germans were losing the war, and no one wanted to be affiliated with them. People knew who had been friendly with the enemy and their actions would not be overlooked. Women who made the mistake of being "cozy" with German soldiers, had their heads shaved bare and paraded around town, labeled as "horizontal collaborators."

Relief was sweeping across the country as Jewish victims began to emerge from their underground hidings. The

Wolffs weren't brave enough to leave the house yet, but didn't run as fast up the stairs when visitors came knocking.

"We hope to return to Holland to find our daughter— she was only eight years old when we were separated," Mrs. Wolff said. "The International Red Cross has lists of missing persons and we hope to find her name. We never would have had this chance if not for your kindness. You risked your own family to hide us. We'll never be able to repay you."

"Just let us know that you find Anna," Yvette's mother said, taking Mrs. Wolff's hands in hers.

Yvette's father was heading out that evening to a Resistance meeting.

"Do you still need to go?" Yvette asked.

"This war isn't over yet. The Nazis want to keep as much of our country in the east as they can. Don't worry, it won't take long. Just need to get a few plans in place to slow them and their supplies from getting to Alsace."

The Germans wanted to regain the strip of France known as Alsace, between the Vosges mountains and the Rhine River. Originally French, Germany took control in the late 1800s, until it was returned to France at the Treaty of Versailles. The Germans were yet again trying to establish it as theirs, entrenching themselves in the Vosges mountains. The Allies were attempting to liberate the mountains once more.

This time, her father didn't return as usual, and it was well past midnight. Yvette's mother was pacing the kitchen. "What about the curfew? How will he get home?" her mother asked.

Yvette was sitting in the kitchen counting the minutes, imagining the worst. German troops retreating through the region were in a vile mood. The Maquisards were setting explosives, blocking roads, and shooting at them from the forests. Since they were familiar with every nook and cranny in the area, they could attack then disappear into the woods. This enraged the Nazis who sought revenge in the cruelest manner. Many innocent people ended up on the receiving end. The ticking of the kitchen clock seemed slow compared to her heartbeat.

A knock at the door broke the silence, sending a wave of panic through the room—no one came at this hour of the night. Her mother opened the door a crack and then allowed a young man to enter.

"We've found your husband—shot dead behind the bushes at the corner. He must have tried to hide, but the Nazis have their dogs tonight. We told him to stay with us until morning, but you know Maurice. He wanted to get home to you. 'What if the Nazis went there and found the Wolffs,' he had said. 'They would kill everyone.'"

"We must bring his body back without being seen. I'll get a few others to help, but you need to find a place to hide him," he said as he headed out the door.

Yvette's mother stood motionless, staring at the door. Yvette was in disbelief.

"Why would they kill Papa if he was only walking home?"

"It was after curfew and he had his FFI armband and pistol," her mother said. "Go clear an area in the garage where they won't find him. I must go help to bring him home. Time is of the essence. Our miseries and worries will have to wait."

Yvette walked the path to the garage she had taken thousands of times. But this trip was different. She saw her papa working next to the shed, loading grain and taking Belle to the field, doing all his regular chores. Visions of him smiling, his eyes twinkling as he winked her way, kept flooding her mind. Yvette was overtaken with the knowledge she'd never see him again.

With thoughts swirling in her mind, she entered the garage. Her mother said to find a good hiding place for him, for his *body*, to put him out of sight, like he was an old piece of furniture.

She moved some barrels that lined the back of the room. Once they were rolled back in place, no one would be the wiser. It was an inconceivable thought to put him there, in that cold, dingy corner. He deserved so much more after everything he had done for his country, his family, and his community. She turned to see a few of her father's trusted friends pushing a wheelbarrow with a lump under a blanket. That's when everything went black.

She woke up in the kitchen, her mother placing a cool towel over her forehead.

"What happened? I was clearing a spot in the garage. Is Papa there now?" Yvette wasn't able to say the words that he was dead.

"Yes, behind the barrels was the perfect spot. The Germans should be leaving town soon. Then we'll have a proper burial."

Yvette looked around the kitchen at the familiar faces of her father's friends. Why did he go out last night and how would they get by without him?

There didn't seem to be any time to mourn his passing. Life without him added a tremendous burden. He had been the one to run the mill, and now most of the work landed on Yvette's mother. Even with neighbors helping, it was insurmountable along with the other home and farm duties. They made the tough decision to close the mill. How would they make enough money to support them? With so many mouths to feed, it wasn't certain. At least they had the land and a few animals.

Yvette found herself lingering in the cellar, missing the conversations with her father. Since he had found out about her activities with the Resistance, he had given up trying to discourage her. He seemed to enjoy having someone to share the news as it unfolded. Now she found herself there alone, wondering how or if to go on in Resistance efforts.

The censoring and fake news from the Nazis were being lifted. Newspapers were printing accurate reports about the situation in their country instead of the previous propaganda and lies from the Vichy. With the Nazis out of the area, the Vichy had little power over anything. In fact, the controlling parties of the Vichy had fled to Germany, and the remainder were trying to switch camps.

It was a warm evening. There wasn't much left to do until supper, which gave her a few hours of free time. The Wolffs were out walking in the back fields to stretch their legs and get a bit of fresh air. There was little reason to hide any longer. They waved at her as she rode off on her bicycle. She was going to see if there was anything new at the café. She joined a few friends in the back room, who had gathered around the most recent press release.

"Things are progressing well on the war front. The Allies, along with the FFI, have pushed the Nazis out of Paris. We're so close to liberation that I can almost taste it, yet there are still occupied areas under severe tyranny. Those Nazis are more brutal against our citizens, blaming us for aiding the Allies and the Resistance."

Stories about the horrors committed by the Nazis on the French population were non-stop. Jean opened the paper across the table.

"Look, here's a story regarding the liberation of Issoudun, that's less than fifty kilometers from here. A few months ago, some Maquis tried to hoist the French flag in town. Nazis came storming in, shooting at the crowd. Innocent citizens, trying to hide in the public restrooms were shot on the spot. None of this could be published at the time, no notification of names, funeral arrangements, nothing. Now with the names finally published, the families and friends can grieve in public."

Everyone nodded in agreement. At least the truth was coming out.

Yvette read reports from an American journalist, Ernie Pyle. He documented the liberation of Paris on August 25, 1944—the wild celebrations and expressions of gratitude and the profound relief everyone felt. Yet somehow the singing and dancing seemed sacrilegious, when many would never sing and dance again. He credited two leaders in particular for the success of the war—Generals Eisenhower and Bradley, both direct and kind men. Yvette found his writings sincere and accurate.

"How cruel my father can't be here, he gave his all to the fight."

"It's tough not having him here to celebrate with us. I hear they'll be naming a street after him near where he was shot down."

Yvette nodded, deep in thought. So many people were killed or their lives ruined. Like the Wolffs, separated from their daughter and forced to flee their homeland, just for being Jewish. The Nazis had been proven wrong but it had taken too long and so many lives lost. When would humankind realize hate and fear undermine society and that good will prevail in the end?

Good news continued until close to Christmas. Then reports came out that Hitler wasn't giving up yet. As the Allies continued from Normandy, towards Belgium and the Netherlands, the Germans took everyone by surprise, attacking via the Ardennes forest. War-fatigued American soldiers had a weak defense in the area, overconfident from their previous successes. Would they be able to stop the Nazis from gaining access to Belgium's harbors? They reinstated curfews and France braced for yet another round of battle, as a dread blanketed their country yet again.

The battle in the Ardennes, known as the Battle of the Bulge, raged for over a month until the Allies triumphed against Hitler. Yvette read in the paper a quote by Winston Churchill, *"This is undoubtedly the greatest American battle of the war and will, I believe, be regarded as an ever-famous American victory."*

Yvette pondered these unknown soldiers who had come so far to fight their battles. She had never met an American, but imagined what they must be like. She had overheard people describe them, how tall Americans stood, how they swaggered about, always with a cigarette in hand. And how they were quick to smile but couldn't utter a word of French. It intrigued her, and she hoped her path might cross with one someday.

After January 1945, the Allies were taking more and more victories. German soldiers were surrendering by the thousands, Italy was liberated and Mussolini hung dead in the town square of Milan.

Then the day everyone had waited for—May 7, 1945. Blaring across the radio came the news of Germany's complete surrender and Europe erupted in celebration.

Yvette joined her family, hearing yells and whoops from surrounding homes. Mr. and Mrs. Wolff were dancing around the kitchen. Mr. Wolff even picked up Yvette's mother to give her a twirl, her face beaming as the years of terror lifted from their country once and for all.

The German occupation and the intense fighting

during the war left France, its economy, and its infrastructure devastated. Food continued to be scarce and most of the people were still starving. It would be tough going as their country from cities to small villages had been torn apart by the Nazis as well as the Allies. In some towns, almost every farmhouse had been destroyed. The Allies had little choice but to blast out each one as a precaution, knowing the Nazis used the homes as artillery or observation stations. They hoped the farmers had vacated beforehand. Their return was heart-wrenching to see, as livestock wasn't only their financial support, but many had been with them for years and were a part of the family. Yvette had seen one neighbor return to his farm, laying himself over the head of one of his dead cows. His hand caressed the dismembered neck and his body trembled in grief. Behind him, only half the farmhouse was left standing and the fields were covered in black soot.

Then there was a shortage of able-bodied French men who were still in German work camps or had taken up arms against the Nazis. Many hadn't returned or were languishing in hospitals, missing body parts or their sanity and oftentimes both. Without enough capable men, the country had an enormous obstacle in trying to rebuild. It was going to take years and much patience to regain what they had lost during the years of occupation.

There was little left of the town of Écueillé—the square had been bombed and burned. Many buildings were left in ruin, businesses were closed, and employment prospects were dismal. Cycling her bicycle around town, Yvette saw phantoms of days past—René tending bar at the Café des Sport, women milling around the bakery with warm baguettes in hand, and the pharmacist's wife running a medication out to a needy patient. Lost in thought, she almost ran into a tree. Quickly regaining her balance, she brought herself back to the present.

It wasn't easy. The painful memories continued to haunt her. Visions of her father and her beloved Didier seemed real. She still felt the security of Didier's arms around her, his lips murmuring their plans, promising he would always be there for her. Life without Didier seemed unbearable. Thoughts of him being shot and likely burned alive in that garage with the other men of Oradour haunted her. His trip was to be a brief stay over the weekend.

"I'll be home by Sunday or Monday at the latest," he had promised.

But the SS had changed everything. She had kept hope, even imagining she saw him coming around the bend towards her home more than once.

To try to shake these images, Yvette stayed busy around the farm. Her mother had started working in the shirt factory, the only business in town that was hiring. There were only a few open positions and widows of war heroes had priority.

After almost two years of staying invisible to the outside world, the Wolffs were able to return to Holland. They departed on foot, the same way they had arrived, eager to reach a larger town, where there would be help for Jewish refugees. The hope of reuniting with their daughter was all everyone could think of.

"You must write as soon as you can and let us know of any information about your daughter," Yvette's mother said.

"We're forever indebted to you. If only Maurice could be here today, he deserves to see how his hard work paid off," Mrs. Wolff said.

Many tears were shed before they headed down the street. Yvette and her family watched as the two figures disappeared over the horizon, carrying one suitcase and the small satchel of food Yvette's mother had packed for them. It was hard to see them go after everything they had been through together. In some ways, it seemed like yesterday when the two of them appeared alongside her father. Mrs. Wolff, her stout build alongside her spindly husband, terrified of being in a foreign country with Nazis threatening their very existence. How glad Yvette was that her father had brought them into the folds of their family.

24

THE CALM IN ITALY
1945

The army transferred them to Leghorn, or Livorno, to stand guard over German POWs. On May 9th, 1945, the Germans formally surrendered, ending the war in Europe.

The war was over. A mix of emotions overwhelmed Art. He was both elated and somber. There was a deep pride in the job the 442nd had done, having proven their loyalty to the United States. Newsreels shown before movies and newspaper articles displayed the heroism credited to the 442nd. Letters from home were full of clippings commending the "doughboys" of Japanese American blood. Yet interlaced between the accolades and cheers were the memories and images of the faces of his fallen buddies. The dichotomy was tearing him in two. Should he be content? Was it pride or ego taking control? He had seen terrible things and lost good friends.

A bunch of 442nd soldiers got together for a bull session. It didn't take long before their lost buddies came up in the discussion. Whiskey and beer were flowing like water.

Art thought back to the gravesite he had visited in Castelfiorentino, Italy. There were many other final resting places for the men of the 442nd—Epinal, Sospel, Marzanello, Nuovo, to name a few. All those headstones formed a dizzying array of white symbols, each representing a young soldier who would never see home again. He had stayed only long enough to leave flowers at the grave of Tom's brother, who died fighting in the last days of the Italian campaign.

The whiskey burned his throat. It felt like the punishment he deserved for surviving. Pretty soon, it felt warm, and he forgot his worries, beginning to feel light as a feather as if he were floating among white clouds. Or were they headstones?

"Hey, Art. Over here—get away from there. Good God—you're drunk," Tosh said, rushing to catch Art, who was nearing a precipice.

"You almost fell over the ledge, buddy. What's got into you?"

Art tried to mumble he was fine, but all he saw were white headstones hovering around him, some flying right at him. He ducked for cover, stumbling over rocks and then falling right onto Tosh.

"Let's get you some coffee and you tell me about this."

"That ssounds good—I could ssit a sspell," Art said, his words slurred.

"I don't know what you're saying, but come sit down here."

Tosh poured some hot water into a tin cup, stirring in instant coffee with a bit of sugar and powdered milk, just like Art liked it.

"Thankss, Tosh, you're the besht." His lips felt swollen and dry. Coffee had never tasted so good.

The next day, Art's head was throbbing. He sat on his cot, cradling his head in agony. Why did he drink so much and how did he end up in his cot? He had flashes of Tosh, smiling over a cup of coffee. Then he saw them again. Those white headstones, hundreds of them, lined up for miles. He shook his head, groaning again since that made his head pound even more. Maybe more coffee, yeah, that would help. Art struggled into his boots and headed to the mess tent.

He wondered if the other guys felt the same guilt for having survived. He looked at their faces, solemn or devoid of expression. Only a few slapped each other on the back and grinned. Should he go talk to them or join with the few celebrating the defeat of the Nazis—pushing his feelings deep down where he wouldn't be able to find them? Would he forget that way?

By late afternoon, he started to feel like himself, the headache had subsided, and he could eat. Tosh was being kind, not razing him about last night. He was from Seattle too and they shared the difficulty of coping with all the loss.

"Hey Art, Tosh! Join us, there are some celebrations in town," one fellow yelled.

"Another time, I have a couple of things to do," Art replied.

"Like what's more important than getting out of here and cutting loose a bit?"

"I need to write a few letters while I have a free moment," Art tried to sound convincing.

"And I need to talk with the chaplain. I've got some questions about letters to families I want to write," Tosh added.

"Suit yourselves."

Art crawled back into his tent, found his notepad, and started on a letter. First, to his mother, she'd be relieved to know he was safe and coming home. Hmm, heading home. He wondered if that would be back to the dreadful camp in Idaho. The war wasn't over with Japan, so he might get herded back to camp, wearing his U.S. Army uniform with the blood stains of the sons of families locked behind those barbed wire fences.

There were rumors the U.S. government was going to close the incarceration camps. Where would his family go? There wasn't a home or any semblance of normal life left for his parents in Seattle. They were too old to start from scratch after losing everything in the incarceration.

The second letter would be to Butch. She had written, without fail, throughout the war. Hearing about the activities back in the States had helped keep him connected.

The third letter would be to his English teacher, Mrs. McKenzie. She was the rock that cheered him on. Her letters convinced him that there were many following the actions of the 442nd and that it duly impressed them.

So Art felt this was more important than carousing around with the guys. Maybe he was missing out on a historic event, but he couldn't knock out the pit deep in his gut, rocking him with guilt.

After a quick note to his mother, he settled in to write to Butch. He was disappointed she had moved to New York, but it didn't surprise him. With her nurse training, there were many jobs available in areas less hostile to Japanese Americans. He pulled out her last letter, unfolding the worn creases carefully.

Dearest Art,

Your letter arrived this morning. I am glad you can write to me about the pangs of homesickness, loneliness or whatever adverse feelings you may have. I know that telling someone lightens the load and since you have enough to carry without the above, I am happy when I can help carry some of them.

Really Art, I am proud of you. To me, you are at once a grown man with the ability to face responsibility and a very small boy—somehow, deep down, bewildered by it all. I like both qualities. I'm so full of admiration and pride.

I was ever so glad to hear of your objective attitude towards the job you are doing. Whatever you do, don't learn to hate. It's a pity one learns to take human life so impersonally, but that is part of this business of war and I think it is better than hating.

Keep your 'beard' brushed.

Love, Butch

Art grinned, thinking of this lovely nurse, Butch. Her teasing ways had supported him during the war. Sure, she wrote similar letters to other guys, but it made him feel good. He penned out a short letter, letting her know how important she had been to him.

He stepped out of the tent to stretch his legs a spell and looked at the village below. The Europeans were beginning to relax and celebrate the simple pleasures of life since the war had ended. No longer hiding behind closed doors, people were gathering in cafés, restaurants, and outside in the streets and parks. Alongside the locals, the 442nd was enjoying the switch to a non-battle service. The slower pace allowed time to enjoy a warm shower, the feel of a clean uniform, and a hot meal. The relief to not worry about getting orders to pack up and head out on a moment's notice, after you had just hit the sack. And not sleeping in a muddy foxhole was the best.

But the horrors of the Arno River, the Vosges mountains, the battle for the Lost Battalion, and the return to the Apennines of Italy where the deadly climax to the end of the war occurred lived fresh in the soldier's minds. Art wasn't able to shake the fitful nights, filled with images of playing chess with Frank, visions of battlefields covered with corpses, and men crying in agony. It was hard to understand and cope with the death and destruction. There must be better ways to solve the world's problems. Racism and fascism had reared their ugly heads and what had been accomplished? Once again, it proved that narrow-minded differences in race or religion will be overcome and that the good in humankind will prevail. He was sure if people experienced how terrible war was, they would do anything to avoid it.

The ongoing war in the Pacific against Japan lay heavy in the minds of the 442nd soldiers. How was that going to end?

Art finished with a letter to his English teacher. It relaxed him to put his thoughts on paper. After one last stretch, he went back into the tent.

Dear Mrs. McKenzie,

Now that the war is over, our outfit is in a garrison style of life. That means we have a permanent installation. We all want to get home, but there are prisoners by the thousands coming through here, so they have to be taken care of first.

The boys are gradually relaxing from the combat tension. At evening time, I hear the guitars strumming soft sweet melodies of Hawaii. We have some really talented boys here as in all outfits. Our first sergeant plays his accordion for us and each night before our movie, the band plays. I don't know whether our outfit is different but we prefer sweet swing to jive.

Would you find it surprising if I told you we didn't celebrate V-day? We were glad to hear the war was over, of course, but there was no cheering or loud celebrating at all. As I stood at attention hearing the news, all I thought of was how cruel war is—that I was standing there yet so many of our buddies weren't there to share in the historic moment.

We shed tears, remembering them. Victory felt anti-climactic.

That's '30' for today. I'm enclosing a page from Stars & Stripes that tells where we are and what we're doing.

Always,

Art

Leaning back and taking in a deep breath, a calm washed over him. It did help to write, maybe talking to someone would too. There was always the chaplain...

A head popped into his tent, causing Art to jump.

"Hey Art, want to join us to see the film in town? It's 'The Face in the Window.'"

"Sure, a change may do me some good," he replied, trying to calm his racing heart.

As they headed off to the theatre, the guys broke into song, 'The Erie Canal' which had become a popular ballad amongst them.

"I've got a mule, and her name is Sal,
Fifteen miles on the Erie Canal.
She's a good old worker and a good old pal
Fifteen miles on the Erie Canal."

The verses reminded Art of the mule, Bessie, who he had befriended in the Alps of France. He wondered what had become of her and hoped she had returned to her rightful owner once the Army was finished with her service. What a sweet animal she had been. It seemed cruel to take these animals to use as the military needed, without regard to their well-being or that of their owners. Art believed animals were sentient beings with needs and feelings. He felt the familiar tug in his chest like when he left Prince with the veterinarian in Seattle. The military ripped these animals from their families with no regard for what would become of them.

Days turned into months. Art filled his time reading books, writing letters, and going to shows when not on guard duty. He toured Italy where he found dance halls and met a few pretty—but too eager to marry a GI—Italian girls.

A letter arrived from Art's father.

Dear Son,

As you may have heard, Minidoka is closing. We didn't want to come here and now we have nowhere to return. This has become our home and we are very concerned what waits for us outside of these fences. It will be hard to abandon the community we have created here—the friends, the gardens we've built, the baseball fields. As I look around, I'm amazed at what we have done with this desolate land.

Some dining halls and bathroom facilities are closing, making us walk to the other side of camp for meals or to shower. We have no choice but to leave.

Some people are heading east to avoid the painful memories from the west coast. There have been some incarcerees shot at and fires set to their homes when they've returned. But your mother and I feel it's where we know best. There is government housing in Renton, just south of Seattle. We hope we can start up some sort of work and begin again. There is so much to do and I am but an old man now.

They are giving us $25.00 and train tickets, so at least that's set. Your sisters will help, of course, and we are waiting with impatience for your return.

Your father

Art felt helpless, stuck in Italy, awaiting his

release orders.

His buddy Tom returned from his service in the 522nd Artillery. Art hadn't seen much of him during the war and even less towards the end. They separated the 522nd from the 442nd after the battles in the Vosges to provide artillery fire for General Patton as he invaded Germany.

"We ended up in front of a prisoner of war compound called Dachau. I guess it was one of many compounds. Anyway, we shot the lock off to open the gate."

"We've heard about the prisoners you found. What a horror." Art recoiled in disgust.

"Yeah, plus we passed piles of dead bodies buried under snow along roads in Germany. Those poor people, forced to walk for miles in freezing rain and snow with little food or clothing. The death marches were the end of many innocent people."

Tom also had more information about the situation in Minidoka.

"After three years, close relationships formed, and now for a second time, bonds are being torn apart by forced removal, this time in reverse. My folks, as well as yours, have nowhere to go. There were a few lucky farmers who had a kind neighbor who cared for their land, but our families have lost everything."

Art nodded. "I heard some Filipino neighbors worked the Fuji's strawberry farm, paid the taxes, and have returned it to them."

"Right, some families were lucky, but not that many."

"My parents want to go back to Seattle to welfare housing. This is some treatment we're getting after fighting here in Europe." It shocked Art that his parents were expected to start with nothing. After all, it was the U.S. government that had taken everything away in the first place.

"My folks are heading east, away from those terrible memories. Me, I'm heading to Wisconsin. There's a school that accepted me. I want to be an artist. You know how I love taking photographs," Tom added.

Art was jealous. He had little to no motivation, and going back to Seattle was going to be challenging. There was a shortage of housing and racial covenants worsened the situation by restricting Japanese to living in only a few areas in Seattle. West Seattle was now off-limits, and he feared the housing in Renton would be shabby and crowded. Why couldn't his parents return to the home they had worked so hard to create in West Seattle? Maybe they should consider heading east as well.

November 4th, 1945. Art's release came, and he headed up to Naples to get new clothing and shots before boarding the Mariposa. It would be a comfortable passenger ship compared to his original passage. After the trip across the Atlantic, he landed in Newport News, Virginia on November 22nd and boarded a train to Fort Douglas with some fellow soldiers.

The train took a thirty-minute stop in Huntington, West Virginia, and they dashed out to buy some magazines, cokes, ice cream, and potato chips.

"Hey, I heard about you fellows fighting over there in Europe. The stories being told about your outfit are amazing—just wonderful, the 442nd right? My brother's in the Pacific fighting those Japs. You guys aren't like that, right? Sit down here a spell and talk about it," the storekeeper requested.

One of his buddies stiffened at the word *Jap*, his hands balling into fists. He looked ready to punch the man. Art put his hand on his friend's shoulder, trying to calm the outrage. The store keeper was oblivious to the harm words could provoke.

"We'd love to, but our train is heading out."

They grabbed their friend and hustled out of the shop.

"Don't pay any mind to him," the other fellow said as they jumped aboard the train.

"We should be proud he sees we aren't the same and knows what we've done in Europe. We're as American as he is," Art reminded him. "Or more."

Art arrived in Fort Douglas to await his release orders. After three days, his last orders came—he was heading home. He boarded another train, bound for Renton, WA, and a new chapter in his life.

Art had barely set down his Army duffle bag before he was whisked off to see his dad's friends at the barbershop. His father was so excited and proud, it made Art swell with happiness. All the Issei were circling him—oohing about his medals.

"There's the purple heart!"

"This is a bronze star! Tell us how you got that, my boy."

"What's this one?" asked Ito-san, one of his father's closest friends.

"Why, that's a good conduct medal," replied another man.

"I wouldn't have expected any less from one of our boys," another added.

Art just nodded, as being humble had deep-roots within the Japanese culture. Besides, it was hard not to feel guilty about surviving. Ito-san had lost his oldest son in Italy. Yet there he was, praising Art. Perhaps it helped soften the blow of losing one's child, knowing others made it home to tell the story. Art wondered if these heart-wrenching emotions would ever dissipate. But he didn't want to forget his fallen buddies or the devastation to those countries from the long years of battles.

The flashbacks continued. The smallest sudden sound or even the scent of a match would trigger one—visions of trees exploding above him or the determined faces of his buddies changing to shock upon realizing they had been hit. Some of them would drop upon impact, blood spewing from their body or seeping out from under their helmet. Others would try to push through until they fell in their tracks. The lucky ones kept going, but others would get hit again and again, their bodies ricocheted about. Art's knees would buckle, forcing him to stop in the middle of what he was doing to find a quiet place to regain his composure.

"What did you say? What was this badge for again?"

Art tried to utter a few words, pulling himself together to save face for his father.

"Yes, um—that's the bronze star." Art's thoughts were drawn back to the present. He glanced around, sensing relief from the warmth of his father's hand on his shoulder.

Art worried he might never shake the images and wondered if something was wrong with him. After all, the war was over and life must go on. He cringed at the sight of a chessboard. Was it battle fatigue? No one spoke about it. He felt like pouring out his actual feelings, all the memories—but would people call him weak? Look at his dad—so proud, what would he say?

No, no one even considered these things, so he would bury the visions forever, fearing they would keep resurfacing.

Art wondered why people were still judging him based on superficial characteristics, like his face and *slanty* eyes (which weren't slanted if one really looked). Now that irked him, inside he was more American than those who looked the part.

Why does human nature need to put people into categories and then decide their entire character based on it? Would he be safer to stay in his group of Japanese, with people who looked like him and didn't fear him? It was enough to confuse the best of persons.

Art had imagined a different homecoming, even visions of congratulations from his neighborhood in West Seattle. Was it crazy to think fighting in this war had earned the trust of other Americans? Hadn't they proved their loyalty? What about all his buddies who had lost their lives in Europe? Why didn't everyone see they sacrificed everything, even when their families were behind barbed wire?

It was a far-fetched dream, but there were multitudes of stories of soldiers returning home to parades and accolades. Those, of course, were whites returning home to families who never left their homes under the disgrace the Japanese Americans had been forced to endure.

Art became lost in hopelessness and despair. The Army had provided structure, and the war kept everyone focused. Sure, it was tough going and he wouldn't go back for all the money in the world, but now he didn't know what to do or where to turn.

Not having many skills made getting a job tough. Art tried to restart the flower business as they had before the war, but Bethlehem Steel wouldn't lease the land back to his family. The only thing available was a job in a frozen foods plant, packing vegetables. It was a slow-paced, boring job.

Art became apathetic. He went to and from work but lost the desire for his old loves—reading and dancing. He asked a few girls out on dates, but even that left him feeling empty. It was like he had left all his fortitude in Europe.

Things went from bad to worse. Since the pay was low at the cold plant, everyone took a few boxes of vegetables home from time to time. The boss called him into the office at the end of a shift.

"I found this box of peas in your locker. Is it yours?"

"No, I've never seen it before." Art felt his face turn red.

"Well, here's John. He overheard you say you were taking some of these boxes home. Do you deny saying that?"

"Gosh, boss. I'm sorry. It was only a few boxes to help out at home. We don't have much since the war."

"Everyone's in the same boat, you know."

Except *everyone* didn't lose their homes and get sent to camps, then forced back out with only $25.00. Art thought to himself, biting his tongue to not blurt the retort out.

They fired Art on the spot. He wasn't sure he could sink any lower—he had brought shame to his family. Disappointing his father crushed him more than losing his job.

It happened a few weeks after Art lost his job. Being sent to camp and losing everything he had worked for caused his father severe stress. Then, moving back to an unknown future had taken a toll on him. He suffered a fatal heart attack a few months after they arrived in Renton. Art's father was gone.

"It was too much for your father to bear. He had dreams of succeeding in this fine country, providing his children with the things he didn't have in Japan. He felt he failed us—I think it broke his heart," his mother said, her head bowed in shame.

"None of this was his fault. He gave us his love and support during these ordeals," Art said. "I hope he knew how much he meant to us, to me. Why didn't I ever tell him? It wasn't his fault. If he hadn't had a Japanese face, it would have been different. If this country hadn't mistrusted us. They destroyed my father and left us with nothing to show. After all these years he'd worked here."

Art had little time to mourn his father's passing. He was now head of the household and his first job was to find someone to perform his father's Buddhist funeral service, or at least be willing to try.

Beginning in the A's, Art worked his way down the list of funeral directors in the Yellow Pages, but no one was willing to even discuss the possibility with him. It was quite a slap in the face, being treated with such disgust at the mention of Buddhism. Nearing the end of his rope, he dialed Walkers Funeral Home, in Renton. The gentleman on the other end of the line paused for a long moment, then the kind voice replied. Art's muscles tensed. Was he going to make a snide or callous remark like some of the other places?

"If you can help me, I'm willing to give it a go."

Art felt the weight lift off his shoulders. His father would get the final farewell he deserved.

He went to the funeral home to meet with Mr. Maurice Walker. The man with the kind voice had a gentle demeanor to match, soft wrinkles around his eyes deepened with concern as he spoke.

"I'm very sorry about your father's passing. Your family has endured countless challenges over the last few years. I hope this modest gesture may help heal your wounds."

The man's candid words took Art aback, only nodding as he followed him into the office.

"I'll need you to guide me through the entire process. I'm not familiar with Buddhism and know even less about how they might conduct a funeral service."

"We'll learn together. I don't know the funeral customs, but I will talk to his friends."

Art pieced together information from his mother and

a few family friends. He visited the Seattle Buddhist Church to meet with the priest and organize the service to be held there.

"I'm impressed with how you've handled these affairs. I think this would be an ideal profession for you. There's a large niche to fill for your community."

Art had never considered working in the funeral business. It was an important stage in life that required respect and dignity. After seeing so much death during the war, this work wouldn't bother him. He noticed an internal calmness grow as he went through the process of arranging his father's funeral. As if a storm battering him had dissipated, leaving his soul tranquil and calm. Maybe this would be the break he needed.

Thus, Art made the second most important decision in his life. The first was to enlist in the Army and now he had chosen a career. Thanks to the G.I. bill, his college tuition was covered. He was heading off to mortuary school in Cincinnati in a few short weeks. Not having extra money, he planned on hitching across the country.

Art and his friends were having a picnic on the banks of Lake Washington, enjoying sushi and cucumber salad with a few beers, shooting the breeze about life since returning from the war and camp. Art hadn't felt this satisfied in years. He looked around at his good friends, who had put their lives in each other's hands, now rewarded with an unbreakable, lifelong bond. He wasn't looking forward to leaving them, but it was the right choice.

"You know losing my dad was tough but the stress of planning his aftercare... Geez, I want to help other families navigate that so I've decided to become a mortician. I'm heading off to school in Cincinnati. I'll have to thumb it to save dough."

"I watched you go through that, wondering what I

was going to do when my folks pass away. It's a great idea," Tosh said.

"Are you sure it's safe to hitchhike? Our faces are still scorned. You might meet up with some nasty people. I don't want you to get hung from a tree somewhere," Kimi said.

"That won't happen. I've seen a lot worse in the war. I'll be fine."

"But hitchhiking alone through those Midwestern states. Why can't you take a train?" Kimi added.

Art was thoughtful, not wanting to make light of his friend's worry. He took in a deep breath, locking the familiar aromas of the surrounding cedar trees, knowing how much he was going to miss all this.

"We don't have the money for a train ticket. My mom's having enough trouble making ends meet with Dad gone."

"We'll watch over her and your sisters, but be careful," Tosh added.

Kimi locked her arm in his, surprising Art with her sudden amorous move. He glanced at her, wondering if starting something now made sense.

The other guys had paired up with their respective dates. Art hadn't noticed, but he and Kimi were the odd ones out. He'd always been fond of her. Maybe a long-distance friendship wasn't such a bad idea.

The next few weeks were a whirlwind of events between packing and ensuring his mother and sisters would be okay on their own. Lillian was old enough and clever too, so he had complete faith she could run the household. His romance with Kimi was building but didn't have a solid foundation yet. The separation would give them both time to get to know each other, nice and slow through letters.

This time, Art left Seattle of his own accord, instead of

under the sharp eyes of armed guards. He headed down the familiar route of Rainier Ave. to Highway 10, confident this was the right choice to make for a successful career. He'd be back in Seattle in a short ten months, back to where he'd always belonged. With trepidation, he stuck out his thumb, eastbound to Cincinnati.

25

FRANCE
1946

The years since the end of the war crept by for Yvette and like most of the French, she was desperate to return to a semblance of normal. People avoided talking about it. The affirmative nod or exchange of glances spoke volumes to the shared memories of those who had survived the war. The papers covered the trials of collaborators and the Nazis and exposed the horrors of the death camps. They had known about camps, but no one had imagined the atrocities which occurred behind those gates. How could the world come to grips with knowing these events had occurred? And how would they ensure nothing like it would happen again? The country looked inward, trying to understand how this happened. The Nazis had ousted their government and ordered the destruction of a part of their population based on race, religion, or lifestyle. Shouldn't there be tolerance of others? After all, the situation could be reversed at another time. Your specific trait, such as your religion or lifestyle, could be the reason for persecution in the future. Everyone's rights needed to be protected.

The trials took place in Nuremberg to bring to justice the Nazis who had committed these crimes against humanity and countless other war crimes. The outcome was a disappointment with few of the accused facing just punishment. Most of the convicted received less than twenty years in prison. The familiar names of Hitler, Himmler, and Goebbels committed suicide instead of facing judgment. The trials attempted to convince the German people of the harm Nazism had done and to ensure it never reared its ugly head again. Yvette doubted the lessons would endure. History has shown that memories fade into the shadows until a new demon arrives to challenge humanity's conscience. The wrong leader had a way of creeping back into the folds of society and, before anyone was aware, would drag them down into an abyss of evil.

Due to the paucity of available jobs, Yvette and her older sister Madeleine searched for work outside Écueillé. A Count and Countess were hiring for help with the homes they had kept during the war. At the start of the invasion, they had escaped from Paris to their small chateau tucked away in the south of France. There, they had remained safe until the end of the war. Now was the task of getting both homes back into working order. The Nazis had commandeered the Paris home, leaving it in shambles with no wine or champagne left in the cellar. Like other French citizens, they had been through the worst and were happy for the freedom to rebuild their lives and Yvette was relieved to leave Écueillé and her shattered dreams.

The Count and Countess were a kind couple, bringing the two sisters on the trips back and forth between the homes, never demanding much work of them. Yvette enjoyed living in the beautiful quarters and their chores were simple. She served breakfast to the couple and then cleaned the home. The afternoons were often free to walk the gardens and listen to the birds sing among the many flowers. It had been years since she had heard birds sing. Had she been too distressed to pause and listen, or had the poor birds been as fearful as they? Now birds perched in linden and horse chestnut trees, chirping their songs of love. It was surreal compared to life during the war.

It was a lonely existence being away from home, but their mother appreciated any extra money to supplement the government's meager stipend. Their oldest sister, Renee, had married Pierre and they lived in Écueillé with a brood of their own. At last count, she had three children, or was it four?

The Count and Countess were lovely people to work for, but something was missing. She couldn't stay in this job forever and needed to find work with a solid future.

Good news came in a letter from her close friend Odette. There was a job opening at the tobacco factory in Chateauroux where she worked. It was a highly sought-after job in a government facility offering great benefits. Her application was accepted immediately, thanks to government grants for families of war heroes. The added perk was that her cousin Fernande lived in Chateauroux. Odette found her a small room to rent across from the factory. It was time to start a career and was in an ideal locale, not far from Écueillé, taking just under an hour by train.

Yvette said her goodbyes to the couple who had supported her for the past two years. They had provided her with the needed time to accept and put the losses from the war behind her. She moved into the room across from the tobacco factory to start her new life, post-war, post-Didier, post-Papa. She wasn't sure how it would turn out, but it was time to move on.

The job was tedious but provided her time for reflection. The schedule entailed long hours of rolling cigarettes from 9 am to 12 pm, a lunch break for two hours, then back for the afternoon shift, 2 to 7 pm. It became meditative for her. With each cigarette rolled, another worry was put to the side. Or sometimes she thought of each as a soldier, wrapping the remains with love before placing it in its final resting place. It gave the day some purpose, more than just the monotonous rolling of tobacco, even if only in her imagination. Back at her apartment, she would make a bowl of soup, relax, then go off to bed until the next day.

For a break from the routine, she would head home on one of the slowest trains in France, the Michelin, which chugged along at a snail's pace to Écueillé. The signature yellow and red train heaved its passengers between the smallest of villages. It was a bumpy ride and watching the passengers jostling around in their seats like they were dancing to and fro, then side to side amused Yvette on each trip. Once in Écueillé, it was a quick jaunt to her mother's new house across from the train station. Between the pay from her job in the shirt factory and the pension from the government, her mother made ends meet.

Écueillé was emerging from its ashes. The second bakery had reopened, and they had repaired the girl in the fountain, with water cascading around her feet once again. Businesses began flourishing around the town square with a renewed influx of people. Familiar faces greeted each other, stopping to catch up on small-town gossip like before the war. Plus, children were being born by the dozens, filling the streets with strollers and sounds of laughter again.

"Marie had her baby last week—it's a boy! They're naming him Jean, after Jean Moulin, the great resistance fighter," a neighbor said.

Yvette was overjoyed to see life return to her village and especially loved seeing the twinkle in her mother's eyes when children came to visit.

"Look what I found in an old box in the cellar. It belonged to your grandmother."

Yvette admired the crystal blue bowl brimming over with hard candies.

"This way, I have something to offer the children when they stop by."

It didn't take long for word to spread about the treats and children ran in and out like bees to their hive. Nothing made her mother happier.

"Children are the joy of life with all their energy, plus you always get an honest opinion from a child," her mother said.

Unions began to take shape as the French demanded for better work conditions and pay. Women had the right to vote, the government implemented a social security plan covering most medical costs and many companies were being nationalized. But inflation was running rampant. The average citizen had little money, food, and few prospects for employment. Life was hard for the French with a government in transition.

After the liberation of France, they dissolved the Vichy government and replaced it with General Charles de Gaulle's Provisional Government. He had gained recognition and respect for his leadership during the war.

In August 1944, it was de Gaulle who marched down the Champs-Élysées to celebrate the ousting of the Nazi soldiers. Heard by all of France, his speech at the Hotel de Ville resonated with pride.

"Paris! Paris outraged! Paris broken! Paris martyred! But Paris liberated! Liberated by itself, liberated by its people with the help of the French armies, with the support and the help of all France, of the France that fights, of the only France, of the real France, of the eternal France!"

Yvette noticed the lack of mention of the Allied Armies' role in the liberation of France. What about the British support of the Resistance? The Allied invasion of Normandy and the American's successful combat against the Germans in the Ardennes? The speech was passionate but seemed one-sided. Maybe de Gaulle believed the French needed to hear that after such a long battle. Or perhaps he feared the Allies would try to control the new government in France. Being a proud Frenchman and allowing another nation to rule over *his* France would have been unconscionable.

General de Gaulle became head of the provisional government, attempting to return order to a country in disrepair. He resigned in January 1946, unable to accept the direction the politicians were choosing. The Fourth Republic gave the National Assembly more power than the President, but De Gaulle had wanted the inverse. The Assembly of Communists, Socialists, and Republicans had so many opinions it was challenging to reach a consensus. It was like attempting to get a group of Frenchmen to agree on the best wine to drink with the meal.

On top of all this, the country was experiencing an exorbitant rise in the cost of living, with the most severe impact on the lower and middle classes. People were becoming more disgruntled with the incompetence of this new government.

"Have you seen the price of coffee? After drinking barley coffee for the past five years, the least we could have is coffee we can afford."

"That's nothing compared to the cost of fabric. I need to make my husband pants if he's to look for a job, but we can't even buy muslin."

Yvette overheard many discussions such as these while shopping at the local marketplace.

It was a difficult time for the Fourth Republic of the French Government.

Under this government, France was rebuilding fast and furious. The United States was funding reparations with what they called the Marshall Plan. Starting in 1948, the U.S. gave several million dollars in grants to Europe, including France. The support helped pull countries out of the state of poverty and starvation left after the war. The U.S. being the one nation saved from attacks on its homeland, was hoping to help its Allies. Once allied with Russia during the war, the U.S. was now at odds on how to govern the newly freed European nations. Russia was controlling with a firm hand, enforcing communism in the Eastern countries of Europe. The U.S. couldn't let Eastern Germany on the other side of the "Iron Curtain" prosper better than Western Germany. A democratic government had to be successful, but communists made up a significant part of the new government. Under the American "get-tough-with-Russia" policy, they moved the communists out. France joined with the other Western countries, forming a more centrist government.

The money from the Marshall Plan was a great aid but added to the inflated cost of living. Coming out of the darkness of war was full of challenges.

26

BACK HOME TO SEATTLE
SEPTEMBER 1950

Art spent ten grueling months studying the art of being a mortician at the Cincinnati school. Getting back into academics was an arduous task. The topics ranged from human anatomy, restorative and embalming techniques, grief counseling, how to run a funeral service, and ethics surrounding grief. He buried himself in his books, hoping to glean everything he needed to be the best funeral director ever.

Much to his relief, he hadn't lost his study skills and was scoring among the top of the class. After the hard start following his return from the war, he had a renewed sense of purpose in finding the right path for his life.

"Wow, Art. Cutting on these cadavers doesn't seem to bother you."

"It's a matter of concentrating on the task at hand. And be respectful of the person you're working on. I saw much worse things in the battles in Europe. You don't know how lucky you are, having avoided the war."

He feared ridicule, so he kept his beliefs about the deceased to himself. The belief that the soul continued their activities after death, and the spirit lingered for weeks to months. This gave him solace, thinking the person wasn't gone yet. If he quieted himself, he could sense their presence hovering and watching.

The letters from Kimi had dwindled from every few days to weekly, then trickled down to one every three weeks. Her last letter struck the final blow. It was the equivalent of a Dear John letter. Their relationship was only beginning, but it still hit hard. His plans to build something with her after his return to Seattle — vanished. Now he was alone again.

The day to return home had arrived but it brought both relief and anxiety to Art. He was unsure what awaited him. He had a career so why did he still feel empty? His spirits lifted seeing Tosh waiting at the train station. They drove by the familiar haunts and seeing things hadn't changed much during his absence, buoyed him. Tosh stopped in at the Imperial bowling lanes to meet up with the rest of the gang.

"Welcome home, Art! We've missed you—guess what's new? Tosh and Toshi are engaged."

"We waited for you to come home. We want you to be our best man. How about it?" Tosh asked. He hugged Toshi close to him, who vigorously nodded her head in agreement.

"Yes, oh yes! You know I'd do anything for you two. What a wonderful homecoming." Art was happy for his friends, yet felt a twinge of jealousy.

"Bring a round of beers over here. Let's celebrate," Tosh said.

Art looked around at his friends, who shared a unique bond, having seen the worst and the best of times over the last ten years. The gnawing empty spot in his heart left by Frank and the others was still strong, and he knew everyone around him had similar spots for those they had lost in Europe. Studying amongst the Buddhist priests helped put some of these losses into perspective. He didn't want to forget, but tucked the memories away to bring out when he was alone or in the right company. There was a profound connection between them all, the ones alive as well as the ones left behind.

"Tell me about Kimi. Do you know why she ended things with me?"

"It's tough, she started to go around with Sam about a month ago. You're better off without her. There'll be another gal before you know it."

Art was skeptical. It seemed everyone was pairing up, and he was the last man out.

Once Art settled back in, he contacted Jim, a fellow graduate from the Cincinnati College. He was the manager at the well-known funeral home, Butterworth. Established in 1903, it was the first mortuary in Seattle, occupying a grand building with everything under one roof. Maybe there would be enough room for him to put his newfound skills to work. He hoped to entice the owner with his draw on the Japanese community. Butterworth's was in an ideal location, close to Japantown and the Buddhist church. Jim confirmed he'd landed an interview.

On the big day, Art donned his only suit, noticing the tattered hem. His mother had tacked it up here and there, but because the fabric was thin and worn, it hung off-kilter. There weren't any obvious holes, so he hoped no one would notice. It had belonged to his father and was a bit dated, but it fit and his mother was proud to see him in it.

"You look so handsome," his mother said, stepping back to admire her son.

Art jumped on a bus from Renton to travel the thirty minutes to downtown Seattle, hiking up Pine Street. At his destination, he stood in awe, taken aback by the sheer elegance of the building. It had a hushed ambiance of calm and sophistication, with impressive stairs leading to the entrance. Stately columns flanked either side of the door, reminding him of some buildings in Europe. Jim was waiting and greeted him at the door.

"Follow me," he said. He turned right to enter the office where Mr. Butterworth was waiting. Art felt dwarfed, reaching up to shake the man's hand.

"Let me take you for a tour of the place."

The mortuary was more than Art could have imagined. The funeral home had a chapel, three visiting rooms, an embalming area, a garage with two hearses, caretaker apartments, and an elevator. Art had never been in an elevator before. Mr. Butterworth pulled open the glass door, then slid the black grill to the side for them to enter the small lift. As he pushed the button marked '2', the contraption groaned, then creaked into motion. It was very impressive to Art, and he hoped, in turn, to make enough of an impression to get a job offer.

Mr. Butterworth returned with him to the office, where the two sat to discuss the job prospect. His face was pensive as he listened to Art's offer to bring in Buddhist funerals and Japanese clientele. It was hard to tell what he was thinking. Would he face another rejection based on race?

"Hmm, that could be a new niche for us to explore. I say we give it a try for a year. We'd like you to join our team, but you'll need to set up an office at a different location. I hate to say this, but I doubt our union will let you join and practice in downtown Seattle. Don't take it personally, you know, but being Japanese and all."

Overjoyed by the offer, Art was speechless. To imagine he would work in such a grand facility, he barely noted the suggestion of having his office off-premise. He thought back on a recent discussion with the other

442nd soldiers.

"I tried to join the local vet's group, but they gave me an explicit *no*."

"Me too. I was told it was against the rules. They said, 'No Japs in our association.' Makes you wonder what's changed since the war. Fighting for our country doesn't seem to have helped us to be seen as Americans."

"Let's not dwell on those bigots. I say we start up our own."

It was 1947. Art swelled with pride as they broke ground at 12th and King Street to start their own association, proudly named the Nisei Veterans Committee.

Realizing he had drifted off, he looked at Mr. Butterworth, whose expression was a little perplexed about the silence. "Gosh, that's not a problem. I'm thrilled to accept the job."

"Thanks for being so agreeable. I've got another great idea for you. My son, Bert was in the Air Force during the war and has joined their reserves. It's a sweet deal, only takes one weekend a month and you get a nice stipend."

"I could do that, thanks for the suggestion." Art was excited about all these offers. Things were looking promising. He would get established, make a little money, and settle down to start that family. With a good job and future, he would have something more concrete to offer a future wife.

Art flung the door open to the small apartment he shared with his mother and two sisters. His mother ran out to welcome him, searching his stony face for clues to how the interview went. Not able to hold back, he let out a beaming glow and she clapped her hands in joy.

"We'll have a celebration tonight! I had a good feeling, so I made your favorite—steak and rice."

The job started without a hitch. He found a small

office on Jackson Street on the edge of *Nihonmachi,* or Japantown. After running a few ads in local Japanese newspapers, the phone began to ring. A deep satisfaction filled him, as he cared for his community during their time of need. From the one-room office, he took calls, met with families, and arranged details with the Buddhist priests. The rest of the work he did at the main building of Butterworth's with services held at the Buddhist church. He had found his place and things were going his way. It wouldn't be long until he found that someone special to share his new life.

A letter from the Air Force arrived. He opened it, expecting further instructions on where and when to meet for the first weekend of training. It was anything but. He sat down and stared at the page in disbelief.

"Oh Mama, I'm being sent back to France."

Art commiserated with his mother's shocked face. *This must be a mistake.* But the letter was clear. His reserve unit was being activated.

He wondered if his life would keep doing this. Just when things started going his way, *bam,* something would happen to derail him. Why did he join up with the Reserves? He would have been fine on the salary from the funeral home. Why wouldn't lady luck shower a little on him? It was like she was determined to keep him from ever achieving his dreams. Tosh was settling down and Tom had met a girl at his school in Wisconsin. How would he find anyone at this rate? And he wasn't getting any younger.

So, with bags packed, Art said his goodbyes to family and friends. The destination sounded dreary and dull, somewhere in central France at an old military installation. He tried to figure a way out, but since he had enlisted in the Reserves, he had little choice. Besides, his father had taught him never to back out on his obligations.

"There's nothing more important than your word. When you say you will do something, always follow through with it." Art heard his father's words echo in his head.

After a long flight to France, Art climbed aboard the last train in a series of trains from Paris to his destination. The train rattled into the station and he gazed out his sleepy eyes to read the sign, Chateauroux—population 30,000. He groaned. It looked like this place was going to be a real drag, being so small. What was he going to do here? Lifting his weary body from the shabby bench, he exited the train, slipping down the metal steps to land on the wet platform.

He followed other reservists to a military shuttle headed to La Martinerie, the old French airfield, which housed the actual base he was to call home for the next eighteen months. The skies were dark gray and rain was pelting down. It was drearier than any dreary he could have imagined.

Art looked around at puddles the size of small swimming pools surrounded by mud everywhere. Rain never bothered him, being from Seattle, but this time he felt his emotions sinking with the rain, drowning in the bottom of the muddy puddles. To add to the misery, the housing was a Quonset hut he would share with nine other men. With a sigh of defeat, he picked up his duffle sac and headed to the headquarters for further instructions. What was in store for him? In France once again.

The divide between Russia and the Allies had widened since the end of WWII. During the war, everyone had the same goal to eradicate Hitler's regime. Once that was achieved, any similarities between them crumbled. Russia wanted communism, while the U.S. wanted democracy and capitalism.

Since Russia had suffered extreme losses at the hands of the Nazis, they were demanding reparations. They seized control of German factories and their agricultural products, shipping the goods back to Russia. Stalin began to force communism across the Soviet-occupied nations with the intent to spread it across Europe.

Making matters worse, the Soviets refused to take part in the U.S.-sponsored Marshall Plan and wouldn't allow any of the countries under their control to participate either. This widened the economic gap between the East and West, angering the Soviets further. On June 24, 1948, the Soviets began a blockade of electricity, coal, and other essential supplies to West Berlin, hoping to force the people to flee to East Berlin. There was only one thing to do and one way to do it. The U.S. and Britain transported by air the needed supplies for the next fifteen months, an extreme undertaking, but it succeeded and West Berlin survived.

On arrival at the Martinerie base, the first order of business was to brief the reservists. "No one wants another war, but something needs to be done to support Europe's defense and security. As you know, nine West European countries, the U.S. and Canada, formed the North American Treaty Organization—NATO—in April of '49. The Cold War's here. Thankfully, the French offered this base to serve as the depot for the air forces of NATO. The job of you recruits is to rebuild the old airfields and warehouses, and to store up supplies in case the day arrives none of us want to see— WWIII."

A chill filled the room at the thought of another war on the heels of the last. Murmurs drowned out the speaker.

"Quiet men, we have two missions here. The first, our commitment to the NATO pact against Russian aggression. And second, to cement good relations with the Europeans, particularly the French. That's it for now. Everyone report at 0800 tomorrow."

The men left quietly, reflecting on the thought of being in the center of the Cold War.

Upon his arrival to their country, Art noticed the French had lost considerable fight since his last tour. It was hard not to blame them after everything they had suffered. How could they want to arm themselves for yet another war? And the positive feelings he received after the immediate liberation of France had cooled to a chilly frost. This became more apparent during the next week on his first trip into town.

"I was walking to the bookstore when I noticed an older man heading in my direction. He was glowering at me. I should have crossed the street. He wadded up a ball of spit in his mouth then he hocked a loogie, right on my freshly polished shoes." Art complained to some fellow soldiers back at base.

"Yeah, I've seen graffiti, 'U.S. Out' and 'Yankee Go Home.'" another soldier added.

"Those are from the French Communists—they didn't want the Nazis in France and now they don't want the Americans."

"Funny, only seven years ago, these same French welcomed us with open arms," Art said.

"We were fighting a fascist dictator then. Now there's a thirty percent Communist population here and a general distrust of politicians."

With a large percentage of Communists in France, it was fertile ground for the Soviets. They had to be stopped before they spread their government system throughout Europe.

"Being here is important, after all we fought for. We don't want to see democracy lose. We'll prove our way is the best," Art said. *They discriminated against me in the U.S. for* being Japanese, and now I'm discriminated against here for being American. I can't seem to win.

Art settled in at the Martinerie, also known as the Chateauroux Air Depot, or CHAD for short. His responsibility was cataloging materials arriving at the base. It was simple work, and he searched for ways to stay entertained. He missed his friends and eating his familiar foods. There weren't any other Japanese or even Chinese here. Potatoes were the order of the day and he had to go out of his way to find rice.

He worried about his community back home. Was he letting them down? He had covered the specific funeral procedures with Mr. Butterworth and made the introductions to the Buddhist priests. But the priests were the older generation and spoke little English. Leaving was a terrible burden on all involved. He could only hope for the best.

The Air Force provided bus service between CHAD and the center of Chateauroux, which was about five miles due west of the base. There wasn't much to do in town—two nightclubs, the Tivoli and the Lido, plus a sprinkling of cafés and restaurants. The clubs became inundated with U.S. servicemen after 5 pm every night. They drank and caroused, which wasn't helping to earn respect from the locals. The only ones who seemed pleased were the bar owners and the female clientele. Some servicemen had cars, big American cars that didn't fit on the narrow French country roads. Combine that with the heavy drinking and accidents started to happen. Signposts and fences got knocked over, but worse, bicyclists were being run off the road and sometimes hit. Their second mission to build rapport with the French was failing from the get-go. Art feared something was going to come to a head.

Art liked to visit the town on market days, giving him a chance to practice his limited French. He noticed more anti-American signs but now knew better than to wear any clothing suggestive of affiliation with the U.S. military. The rules had loosened, allowing the servicemen to wear casual clothes.

On market day, the two main squares burst with activity. Farmers and vendors brought in everything from clothes, furniture, and food to sell. It was a colorful sight—tomatoes, lettuce, strawberries bulging over the tops of their containers, and flowers of every type. Art found it was inefficient for anyone to bring a truckload in for only one day. Why would they want to drag all those things in and back out again? It seemed more sensible to combine all the wares into a large store like back at home. One-stop shopping. Who doesn't love that? There was so much to teach these people.

27

CHATEAUROUX
1950

Yvette was looking forward to spending the weekend in Écueillé. It had been a few weeks, and she missed relaxing at home with her mother, but Odette had other ideas.

"Please, I've been dying to go dancing. I can't go alone. What would that look like?" Odette pleaded.

"I'm tired of meeting those American GIs. They're more interested in groping and kissing than dancing."

"It's not *that* bad. I'll stay by your side." Odette didn't seem to mind the raucous behavior and lack of respect the GIs displayed around them. "It's just a fun evening of dancing."

"They seldom stop at just dancing and their attitude that they've 'saved' France is getting old. Sure, they helped end the war, but what about all the thousands who perished before they finally committed to help?" But Yvette caved to the whining of Odette.

She did love to dance and as the years passed; it was becoming easier to enjoy herself again. It was hard to say no to Odette, who was her best friend since they were five years old. They hadn't seen much of each other during the war and needed to make up for lost time.

Life was taking shape for the citizens of France again. Yvette had settled well into the rhythm of work, alternating between visiting her mother or staying in Chateauroux with her friends. The U.S. had installed a government facility near the town. Along with it came many American soldiers flooding the small town of Chateauroux, more than tripling the town's population. This concerned many French, since these newcomers didn't or wouldn't speak French, drove monstrous cars too fast on their roads, and complained about the local facilities. They were quite condescending about her country and its offerings. They loved to bellow out complaints:

"These restaurants are old and dingy!"

"These are holes in the ground, not toilets! And what kind of toilet paper is this? It feels like construction paper."

"What's a dog doing in *our* restaurant?"

The insensitivity of these people amazed the French. After all, they were still pulling themselves out from not just one, but two wars. How could they be so graceless and behave with such entitlement?

Yvette didn't like the change as the American soldiers started invading the dance halls. She had wondered what an American would be like, but wasn't sure she thought much of what she saw. Being accustomed to the usual French group, the change was dramatic to her. Though most of the Frenchmen with any drive had moved on to bigger cities where there were job opportunities or a chance to get an education. So there were few men of interest, and she still struggled with thoughts of Didier and their plans. Plus something else held her back. She wasn't sure what it was or if it was even real. However, she never ignored a powerful instinct.

Yvette searched her small armoire, wishing something new would appear. But no, there were two lonely blouses, one dress fraying on the edge—*I must fix that next week,* she thought—and one even more pitiful skirt. She stepped into the skirt, buttoned up the blouse, then got busy drawing lines up the back of her legs with a black pencil to mimic the seam of stockings. The hand-drawn lines were a sad replacement, but stockings were a rare commodity since silk was at a premium. She stepped back to look at herself in the small mirror hanging above her wash basin. Scrunching up clumps of hair, she was pleased to see that the rags she had rolled it up in the night before had done their job; her locks falling in gentle waves atop her shoulders.

Odette was calling from the street, Yvette ran to the window.

"*J'arrive!*"

Heading down the street, Yvette had trouble keeping up with Odette's brisk march. When that woman had something on her mind, she was galvanized. Her drive was one thing Yvette loved about her since she was more of a follower.

She and Odette had been at the dance hall for over an hour. Yvette danced a few waltzes with awkward American soldiers who found keeping their hands to themselves a challenge.

"*Non, non,*" she said, moving their wandering hands back to her waist.

She had had enough. She glanced at Odette who was half dancing/half kissing a tall GI. Trying to make eye contact without success, Yvette sighed, wondering what to do next.

Suspecting Odette wouldn't miss her, she decided to head home. Just then she noticed a man looking her way, someone completely different from the other Americans. He had a shorter stature yet was well-muscled, with broad shoulders and thick, black hair surrounding a square-jawed face. His dark eyes were masked behind round, metal-framed glasses, and his gaze was more curious than lustful. He didn't seem interested in the other women that were displaying their "feathers" trying to entice him. Realizing he was walking towards her, she felt an unusual knot in her stomach, something she hadn't felt for years. All she could do was smile and nod when he asked her for a dance. Before she knew it, they were twirling across the dance floor, his hand firmly against her back, almost lifting her as they did a quick-paced fox trot. She couldn't help but laugh out loud and heard him laughing as well.

After a few dances, he stopped and asked if she would like to go outside to cool down. Or at least that's what she thought he had asked. That too, charmed her as he stumbled over his French words. Would a step outdoors be the end of his gentlemanly ways? But what did she have to lose? Somehow, she felt safe with him and agreed. Her young man took her by the hand, leading her outdoors. The fresh air was a refreshing treat as the hall was now steamy as well as smoky.

They walked around the corner of Rue du Tivoli while he continued to fumble with his French. He paused often, searching for the right words, occasionally throwing in an English word. His arms waved about, performing pantomime.

"*C'est une* very *jolie* night, *n'est pas?*" as he swept his hand across the sky. "*Voulez- vous* a cigarette?" displaying a packet of Marlboro. "*Je m'appelle* Art, and *vous?*" pointing from his face to hers.

"*Je m'appelle Yvette.*"

"Vevette?"

Yvette smiled. "*Oui.*" Close enough, she thought.

Yvette found it easy and relaxing to communicate with him. It charmed her how he tried to speak, searching for words, his steady jaw and determined look combined with a gentle nature. She smiled to herself, *I'm glad Odette insisted.*

They stayed outside through the band break. When the music started back up, he escorted her back in and she crossed her fingers, hoping to continue dancing with him. It wouldn't be the first time such an adept dancer would head off in search of a new partner. Instead, he led her to a table offering to buy her a drink.

"*Voulez -vous une whiskey?*"

She cringed. A whiskey sounded horrible. A glass of wine more suited her, but in the steamy bar, she thought a beer would be cold and refreshing.

"*Peut-etre une biere, si'il vous plait?*"

He smiled and returned with two whiskeys.

Maybe he didn't quite understand? Yvette smiled and accepted the glass. It was neither cold nor refreshing, but somehow she didn't care.

The night ended without any surprises. Yvette was pleased her new dance partner spent the rest of the evening with her, even walking her back to her apartment. After saying good night in the traditional French manner—a kiss on each cheek—he turned and left.

Odette was pounding on her door the next morning.

"I saw you dancing all night with that interesting man. Is he Oriental or something?"

"I'm not sure. I know he's American, but I've never met anyone like him. I think I'm falling for him already."

"He's a great dancer—it looked so effortless as you two swept across the dance floor, like two birds circling each other in the air." Odette wrapped her arms around herself and waltzed around the small room.

Yvette couldn't hold back a laugh—a profound, happy laugh, one she hadn't had in years. Yes, she hoped she would see him again, but had promised her mother she'd go home the next weekend.

"You're the only one who can peel the peaches correctly. Your other sisters leave chunks attached," her mother had said.

She crossed her fingers that another wouldn't snatch her new beau.

The next few weeks crawled by slower than an escargot. Yvette's usual tricks of rolling the cigarettes as if they were soldiers didn't keep her occupied. Her mind kept wandering over to dancing, moving the cigarettes in rhythm to waltz or fox trot music, one-two-three and one-two-three. It was near impossible for her to concentrate on anything else, humming and rolling the cigarettes as if they too, were dancing. A quick glare from her supervisor convinced Yvette it was time to focus on the task at hand.

As Friday approached, she became both excited and nervous. What did she have to wear? Maybe her cousin Fernande would loan her a different skirt. They were the same size, and Fernande had a few more items in her armoire.

Saturday morning, bright and early, Yvette jumped on her bicycle. Fernande was outside, tending to the flower baskets by the door.

"Your geraniums are beautiful."

"Thanks, I use a small amount of milk in the water to get more blooms."

Yvette smiled, there was always a trick she learned from her family about gardening or cooking.

"I'm planning to go to the Tivoli tonight, but have nothing to wear. Do you think I could borrow your blue skirt?"

"Of course, it looks better on you anyway. Let's go in for a coffee and fetch it."

"Will you join us? Odette and I are going around nine."

"Sure, it's been a while since I've gone there. Lately, I've been spending time with my brother in his favorite bar, but there's no dancing. You know he isn't fond of American GIs. It will be nice to see some new faces."

Yvette knew the bar, popular with the Communists in the town to which Fernande's brother belonged. They continued chatting over coffee, then wandered to admire her flowers in the back courtyard.

She prepared for the evening, surprised at her nervousness, her hand shaking as she drew the line up the back of her leg. Just relax, she thought. It's only a dance, he may not even be there.

Odette and Fernande arrived at 9 pm sharp, perfect timing—late enough for a small crowd to have gathered, but not too crowded. They entered the bar, and Yvette's heart sank. There was no sign of him.

The three of them find a small table and Odette began tapping her foot in beat to the music, beaming around the room.

"Looks like a good crowd tonight. Lots of gents, not too many women."

"Yes, I see a few acceptable prospects," Fernande said, tipping her head towards two men smiling in their direction.

"Hmph." They didn't impress Yvette.

"Ignore her, she wants the one from the other week. And I think I see him now!"

Yvette's eyes raced towards the door. Sure enough, there he was, coming their way. Her hands suddenly clammy and her stomach a flutter.

Art was glad he had dressed in his street clothes. The dark color and cut of the trousers made him look taller among the other GIs who stood at least a half foot above him. He saw her right away when he entered the dance hall. Had he imagined it or had her face lit up when she saw him?

"*Bonsoir.* I'm pleased you're here tonight."

He hadn't felt this way about seeing someone in a long time, and his French was improving since he had hired Martine for private lessons. Between the reading exercises and verb drills, he was gaining significant ground in the language. Martine was a skilled teacher, patient and always quick with a smile while he fumbled to find the right word. He had signed up for her intensive French, hoping to improve his chances of getting to know Yvette. He hadn't thought of anything beyond that.

Yvette smiled, feeling clumsy, not knowing what to say without looking overanxious.

"*Moi aussi.*" *Me too,* she squeaked out.

"May I get you a drink?"

"Certainly, *merci.*" As he left, she glanced at her companions, who were smirking from ear to ear.

"We're moving over to the other table across the way. Let us know if you need anything."

He returned with two whiskies again. Yvette wondered if she could change that selection someday, smiling as she accepted it. *This will probably last me all night.*

The one-man band started her favorite song by Edith Piaf—*Je ne Regrette Rien,* perfect for a fox trot. Art extended his hand. She accepted, and off they went, dancing in perfect unison. Humming along, she couldn't remember ever having a better dance partner.

The evening flew by until closing. Arm in arm they walked back to her apartment building, her feet and legs aching a joyful pain she didn't mind in the least. He paused at the door, pulling her close to kiss her. It had been so long since she had kissed a man or heard words like *beautiful, fun,* and the name he called her, *Vevette.* She didn't want to correct him, preferring this special name between them.

Should I invite him upstairs? What would he think?

Before she said anything, he interrupted her thoughts.

"*Merci.* It was a wonderful evening. Can I see you tomorrow?"

"I'd like that."

"Good, I'll come by around 1 pm—we'll get lunch and go for a drive." He turned on his heel and headed back towards the club.

Yvette climbed the stairs to her first-floor room, collapsing on her bed while kicking off her shoes. She was exhausted, but hadn't been this happy in years. Tomorrow couldn't come soon enough.

Art arrived exactly at 1 pm. She invited him in as he handed her a small package. Inside were a box of chocolates and a pair of silk stockings.

"Oh, my goodness. I've never had a pair of these." Shocked he had offered such a wonderful gift, she slid the stockings between her fingers, letting the silk caress each digit.

"I hope you like them. I know they're hard to get here. We have them at our base exchange along with sweets too. But let's go. I've picked out a little place on the other side of town."

He led her out to a car parked in front, opening the door for her before getting into the driver's side. Yvette hadn't been in a car for a few years either, so the entire day was turning into quite a treat.

The restaurant was a small bistro, full of French customers, not an American to be found. Art seemed as comfortable as anyone else, nodding at the patrons as he passed each table. *That is so French to greet each person, I wonder how he knew that?*

When the server came to their table, Art ordered the steak with fries. He hesitated when asked about the doneness of the meat, flashing a desperate look her way.

"*A point, s'il vous plait,*" she said.

She hoped rare would be fine, since most steaks came that way, regardless. A steak prepared more than rare ruined a prime piece of meat according to French chefs. So, rare was how it was served, no matter how one may have asked for it.

She watched with trepidation as he cut into the steak, the red juices seeping across the plate.

"This is perfect," he said, much to Yvette's relief. She had heard Americans liked their meat well done. He was full of pleasant surprises, this one.

Savoring their meals with a couple of glasses of red wine, she noticed a crimson red hue develop over his complexion. He seemed fine otherwise. *Should I ask him if he's okay?*

Art felt the warmth spread a red glow over his face and neck, a familiar event whenever he drank alcohol. Something about the Japanese missing an enzyme to break down alcohol. He never felt conspicuous around his friends, since most of them had the same response. He worried when he noticed a strange look creep over her face. *Should I say something? No, maybe it's not that noticeable.*

The meal finished without a hitch. Afterward, he drove them to the countryside, pointing out a small grassy area under a canopy of trees.

"Vevette, let's stop here. It's nice under these trees and we can visit." Even after he learned the correct pronunciation, he continued to say Vevette, claiming it would be his secret name for her.

He laid a blanket down and then sprawled back on his elbows. It wasn't long before he had dozed off. She snuggled by his side and slipped into a dream-like state. *Today couldn't have been more perfect.*

28

Yvette hurried to tidy her room, made her bed, and pushed it against the wall. She sat at the small table which served as a vanity, as well as her place to eat. Arranging her few lotions and the jar of make-up pencils, she removed the rouge and filled in her thin lips, pressing them together. If only they were fuller, like the movie stars seen in the magazines. She pushed the wash basin underneath with her foot and stood to look around. Everything was neat and clean. Art had hinted he had a surprise for her. He kept her stocked with chocolates and stockings, but this time he sounded different. She wondered what he had planned.

They were spending much of their free time together, sharing their love of dancing and music. He even favored her favorite singer, Edith Piaf. As usual, he arrived on time, at 3 pm bearing what looked like a small suitcase.

"Now we can listen to music in your room. Look, it opens to reveal a turntable. Ta-da!"

Being the first time to see such a device, she was duly impressed. He placed a vinyl disc on the rotating plate and Edith Piaf belted out *Padam Padam*, captivating her. He swept her up and twirled her around the room, which was so tiny, they tumbled onto the bed, falling in a heap. His face changed to a serious look, one she had seen on Didier, taking her thoughts back in time. Though things had been amorous with Didier, they never had the chance to be intimate. It was hard for them to find time alone together. Then the war stole many men of her age. Not only were they killed, but countless were left broken and destroyed. She too, had to find herself and work through the effects of the war. There wasn't a clear path to follow. She needed to figure things out on her own before bringing a companion into her life.

When she met Art, the confusion melted away—like a camembert sitting out all day. In fact, the first time he had ordered some, he agreed the best way to eat the cheese was soft and runny. They both dove in with their chunks of bread, wiping it up from the plate, laughing as the cheese dripped off the bread and down their arms.

Now alone, she succumbed to her desires, apprehensive at first, but he was gentle and took things slow. In the background, she heard the music stop, replaced with a repetitive scratching sound to which he seemed oblivious.

The night was more passionate and satisfying than she imagined possible for her first time. Emotions exploded out of her like a Bastille Day celebration. Surprising herself, tears streamed down her face, releasing years of tensions she had locked up inside. Her body sank into a serene state and she slept deeper than she had in years.

The next morning, she awoke to his arms wrapped around her. "Oh Vevette, you are so warm and soft. What a lovely way to start the day," he said, nuzzling her neck, sending tingles down her spine.

She wasn't sure she was up to more lovemaking just yet. A rest would do her more good at this point. Her face flushed, wondering what to say if he suggested recommencing.

"Let's go get coffee and croissants. I hope they have apricot jam, that's my favorite," he added, much to her relief.

As they walked down the street, she strode with a new confidence. No longer searching for her place in the world, she had found it. They settled in the nearby bar for a traditional French breakfast, sitting at their regular table by the front window. The waiter approached, looking debonair in his black slacks and white apron. He flashed a coy grin, as if he knew what Yvette had experienced the previous night. She blushed, but no, there wasn't any way he could know, was there?

Art made it a habit to mention how he wanted a side of bacon with sunny-side-up eggs and toast to the waiter, who rolled his eyes in his usual manner. In France, one was lucky to get jam with croissants or baguettes. She agreed that eating a larger breakfast started the day off on the right foot, but it had always been this way. If someone wanted anything more, they would have to wait until lunch.

"How about visiting a chateau today? I hear Valençay is beautiful and not far from here," Art said, slathering butter on his baguette.

The mention of that name brought back memories of driving with Thomas on their mission to collect arms for the Resistance. It was near Valençay where Pauline, the British agent, had been stationed. Flashbacks of the Nazis pulling them over in the pouring rain entered her mind. Goosebumps started forming down her back and arms. She broke out in a sweat, thinking of what would have happened if their stash of supplies had been found.

"Uh oh, did I say something wrong? Isn't it a nice castle?"

Yvette snapped back to the present, relieved it was all

behind her. "No, it's fine. It reminded me of a woman who lived near there during the war. She worked with the Resistance. I'm sad to say, I don't know what's happened to her. Anyway, Georges Sand, my favorite writer, called Valençay one of the most beautiful castles she knew. I'd love to visit it."

It was a sunny day, perfect for a drive. Yvette gazed at fields of wheat, separated by hedgerows where Nazi soldiers had hidden only a few years back. It was amazing how serenity had engulfed the devastated countryside, leaving no apparent scars on the land. But if one looked close beneath the greenery, they could see gouges cut deep into the landscape. The evidence of where bombs had exploded and blood had covered the ground. Life continued though the scars remained, leaving people to heal the buried wounds with time, love, and hope. She settled closer on the seat next to Art, drawing relief and comfort from him. Somehow, he helped her find strength, giving her a new lease on life.

They passed through small towns, coming close to Écueillé. The landscape grew familiar to her—each tree around each bend was like an old friend welcoming her back. It had been years since she had ridden her bicycle down these roads, enjoying the shade provided by the trees lining either side. Peaceful and content, she decided it would be a good time to mention her family.

"We're close to my hometown of Écueillé. My mother still lives there, as well as my brother and many cousins."

"You've never told me you were raised so close to Chateauroux."

"I guess it never came up. Someday it would be nice for you to meet them."

"Hmm, yeah," Art said in a distant voice. He seemed perplexed about the idea. Maybe he wasn't interested in pursuing the relationship that far.

As they turned the corner, Chateau Valençay appeared before them in all its grandeur. She gasped at the sight. None of her previous trips to the area had come close to the castle. As they made their approach, sweeping gardens as far as the eye could see ran along both sides of the road. The castle's domed turrets at either end were covered with black slate tiles, causing a dramatic contrast with the white stone body of the building.

They parked near the castle and wandered around the grounds, admiring the towering building from below. A few of the rooms were accessible to visit, allowing a glimpse of how the royalty lived during the Renaissance period. Entering the first room, it appeared to be a sitting area of sorts. They admired the intricately carved oak and walnut legs that supported the tables and chairs.

"Think about having to dust all those nooks and crannies while crawling on your hands and knees," Yvette said, entering the next room. "And look at these embroidered spreads on the beds and the tapestries on the walls. They must have kept the cold away from those stone walls."

"Such privacy with velvet curtains wrapping around the beds. Do you see the length of them? Royalty were even shorter than us," Art said.

"This is my first visit to an actual castle. It's magnificent," Yvette said.

"And how, I had no idea it would be so elaborate. Look at the beautiful china over there," Art pointed to the adjacent room where a dining table was covered in blue flowered dinnerware and crystal glasses.

A woman stopped them on their way out, peering over her half glasses. "Did you enjoy your visit? Were you wondering how this chateau survived the war unscathed?"

"Yes, actually I did. I was here fighting with the Americans. The destruction was brutal. We tried not to destroy buildings, but it was impossible with the Nazis holing up in them. They had to be flushed out somehow," Art said.

"Well, at the time, the Duke of Valençay was neutral and had some connections to the Prussian House of Lords. They considered this a "safe house" making it ideal to hide treasures from the Louvre. There's another local chateau, Chambord, where many more works of art were safeguarded, including the Mona Lisa and Venus de Milo." She studied their faces for recognition.

"Wow! *The* Mona Lisa *and* Venus de Milo—that's really something," Art exclaimed.

"Yes, they transported thousands of treasures from the Louvre in 1939 as fear grew about the invasion. Fortunately, both chateaux escaped any damage. They saved the art and returned it all to Paris."

It was an exciting visit for both of them as neither had been in a castle, especially one so grand. Georges Sand didn't disappoint.

Yvette had found her best friend and lover in Art. The sight of him still caused her heart to skip a beat and butterflies to flutter in her stomach before a date. Yet there was comfort and safety found in his arms. It was time for him to meet her family. She was apprehensive about mentioning it, to take their relationship to this next level. American soldiers were told to be cautious of women eyeing for a way to the U.S. This might sound like the first step to a commitment. Until now, the most profound conversation they'd had was choosing what to have for dinner or whether to sit out the next dance. She had tried to lead one of their chats toward a more heartfelt direction, but always veered away out of fear.

She gathered her courage. *Yes, I will ask him tonight*

at dinner.

The time had come. Seated in their favorite bistro, it was the perfect place to bring up the delicate matter. Before she had a chance, Art cleared his voice and said he wanted to disclose a few things about himself.

"My mother is old-school from Japan. She doesn't speak much English and is set in traditional ways. I'm not sure you know, but when Japan attacked the U.S. they sent all the Japanese Americans to a type of concentration camp."

Yvette shook her head. She had never heard this. Why did the U.S. put them in camps?

"It was devastating, we lost everything. After I returned from the war, I did a lot of soul-searching, trying to figure out what to do with my life. I hit rock bottom. I couldn't find anything I was good at doing," Art confessed.

Yvette reached for his hand, he was so somber. What had changed him into the confident man sitting across from her today?

"When my father died, I discovered my niche to become a funeral director. But then I enlisted in the Air Force Reserve for a bit of financial help and instead of a weekend a month service, they shipped me over here. So you see, this stint's temporary. I should be back home within the year."

Yvette frowned, was this all a charade? Was he only buying time until he went back to his "real" life? Was she just a good time to wile away his "stint" of being assigned here? She had imagined he was in the Air Force as a career. Would she even be a part of his life, and what would a Japanese family think of her?

She was sure he cared for her—his regard suggested this, maybe even love. He wasn't one to express his sentiments, not being the type to wear his heart on his sleeve, as they say. That irresistible beam where his entire face lit up and his eyes twinkled. Was she wrong to imagine it was something special between them? How she purposely would make silly comments or perform an amusing antic to coax out one of those expressions?

He never murmured any words of commitment, nor was she much for expressing her feelings, making the situation doubly unsure. So they continued, growing closer each day without verbalizing any actual sentiments. It was superficial on one level, yet impassioned on another. How would she bridge these two?

She didn't say much after his discourse, nodded and agreed. Being sent to France was a terrible stroke of luck, especially after everything he and his family had experienced. He seemed content with the response and the evening went on without any further mention.

Whether there was a future for them or not went unanswered.

Yvette dropped the subject and tried to enjoy the time they were having together. She pushed all thoughts of a long-term relationship out of her head, but projections of the future kept including him. She needed to get the courage to ask what was to become of them when his assignment was over. Shouldn't he be wondering the same thing?

Adding more concern, her monthly cycles had stopped, despite the precautions they had taken. Aware some women used this tactic to hook a man, she feared he would think her pregnancy was intentional. Yvette overheard women discussing the idea at work.

"I'm going to land myself one of these soldiers. If he won't commit, then I'll get pregnant and guilt him into it. Anything to get to the U.S.," a colleague had said.

Yvette wasn't looking for that, ensuring they take care, but apparently not enough. Neither of them had discussed the possibility of her becoming pregnant, leaving her no choice. She would return home, knowing her family wouldn't shame her. She couldn't ask him to sacrifice his future for her. The only choice was to leave him, then he could go back to the life he had started before coming here.

She sat down to write a letter.

Dear Art,

This isn't easy for me to do, but I don't see a future for us. You'll be leaving for your home soon and I have my home and family here in France. I've grown very fond of you over the past year, but I know now we can't continue. Please don't try to find me. Let's keep the wonderful memories we had together as just that.

Je t'embrasse,
Yvette

She posted it to his address at La Martinerie, packed her bag, and went home on a month's leave from work. If only she didn't feel so sick about it. Maybe it was the pregnancy and hormones. It felt like her world was caving in and there wasn't anything she could do about it. She had never felt so alone in her life.

Was she prepared to handle a baby on her own?

Yvette returned to Écueillé on the premise of helping her mother in the home and with errands. She kept to herself the first week, surrounded by visions of what to do and where to go from here. And to lose the memories of Art which were causing so much strife within her. The sadness kept building until she thought her heart would collapse under the crush of her sorrow. She would catch herself bursting into tears over the silliest things. The sight of a daffodil reminded her of the first bouquet he had brought her or when her mother asked where she got the chocolate bar. It was even greater than when she had lost Didier, which she hadn't thought was possible.

Her mother didn't say anything but looked concerned with the sudden arrival of her daughter. Had she noticed the slight bump around her belly? Yvette would tell her tonight at dinner. She needed to describe Art and portray him in the manner he deserved.

Her mother poured them glasses of red table wine her cousin made from his own vineyards down the street. It wasn't a potent wine. It had a watered-down flavor compared to the wines she drank with Art in the restaurants. She took a sip, gazing across the table at her mother, finding comfort in her presence.

"Mama, I've something to tell you. For the past few months, I've been seeing an American soldier. He's a kind man but doesn't have any intention of staying here. He'll be leaving within the year, and I don't think we have a future together."

"That's fine, *ma cherie*. But why have you come home? Has he done something to hurt you?"

"Oh no, *au contraire!*" She hesitated, then shared, "I'm carrying his child and I don't think he wants to settle down." Yvette frowned. "It would look like I had tried to trick him."

"How can you say this? If he's a kind man, as you say, he'll want to know. He has a right to know."

"I don't think you understand, Mama. He hasn't said anything about a future together. I think he's only passing time while here."

Her mother looked pensive, circling her fingers around the rim of her wine glass. "I don't know this man and must trust your judgment. It's your choice, and I'll respect whatever you decide."

Yvette took a deep breath. This wasn't what she had

wanted to hear. Instead, she'd had a twinge of hope her mother might insist she tell Art about the baby. She hated the thought of losing him, but didn't want to keep him this way. Why had she let herself get pregnant? And why hadn't he ever brought up the subject? He knew just as well that it was a possibility.

They finished their dinner, discussing other topics. What were her cousins, Fernande and Fernand, doing? How was work? Her mother filled her in on her siblings and their activities the past few months. She tried to push any further thoughts of Art out of her head. It would be her and the baby from now on. With the support of her mother and family, what else did she need? She had a good job with maternity leave. Everything would work out fine. Then why did she feel so empty and hollow?

29

It was the start of another work week. Art finished his breakfast of eggs, bacon, and toast in the mess hall. At least the base served proper breakfasts. It was a wonder to him how the French made it all morning, having only bread and coffee. On his way to the main office, he stopped by to get his mail. There was the usual collection of letters for work, but one stood out. He examined the envelope, clearly a woman's handwriting with no return address, postmarked Chateauroux. As he opened it, an uneasy sensation crept over his body. He had tried to find Yvette all weekend. Her neighbors didn't know where she was and she didn't answer the door both days he had stopped by. Why hadn't he pinned her down for a day to see each other? How silly to assume there was an unspoken agreement to spend each weekend together. Had he been presumptuous in believing this? He regretted not discussing their future and had run the words through his mind, but never found the right time. They had a good thing going, and he didn't want to ruin it with serious talk.

As he read the letter, his head started to reel, and he had to sit down. He read it over and over. Maybe he wasn't understanding the French, but it wasn't complicated. It was clear as day. She was ending their relationship when it was going so well. How could she have made such a decision? *Well, okay then. If that's what she wants. I'll be fine on my own. It won't be long before I head home. Back to Seattle, to my friends and family. Where I can speak English and eat good ol' American food. Especially good ol' Japanese American food.* He stomped around the room, sure this was the only way, yes, the best way, for him to wrap up his time in France. He would go home, start his new job, and settle down to raise that family he kept dreaming about.

He buried himself in his work and even went to the dance hall a few times, but his heart wasn't in it. He danced a few waltzes but didn't find anyone who could hold a candle to Yvette.

Art convinced himself she wasn't important, that he was better off without her. The race difference was enormous—his mother and friends would find it easier to accept a Japanese girl. What would they say about a blonde from France who didn't speak English, much less Japanese? No, forget those thoughts of bringing her to the States with him. What a silly idea that had been. So why was he becoming more despondent by the day?

He should have talked to her, but it was hard to say the right words—his French being limited. They had a communication on a different level, one he'd never experienced before with a woman. They shared their feelings without words, or at least he thought they did. Now it was too late. Before long, he'd be back stateside and this would be all behind him. But that's not what he wanted.

He missed her smile and the playful way she would glance over her shoulder, which always made him laugh. And he even missed those unsatisfying breakfasts they shared. He should have broached the subject of marriage when he had the chance. Was it too late? No, he still had time to find her and learn the truth behind her decision. There was too much to lose to give up this easily.

It was only Monday, which left the entire week to stay on base. *Tonight I'll go find Fernande, she'll know where I can find her—I hope.*

As soon as his duties were done, he hopped in his car and sped over to Fernande's. He was glad to see she was home, bringing in laundry from the outside line.

"*Salut*, Fernande! I'm sorry to bother you, but I'm worried about Yvette. She's left without a word. Do you know anything about that?"

"Oh Art, please come in."

Fernande hooked the laundry basket under her arm and motioned for him to follow her through the back door. She pulled out a chair at the kitchen table and smoothed the plastic cover protecting her blue and yellow tablecloth.

"May I offer you a glass of wine?"

"Yes, that's very kind of you. Have you any news about her?" Art was quick to ask, not able to wait any longer for an answer.

"No, she didn't say much, except she was taking some time off from work. Maybe her mother isn't well? I haven't heard anything from Écueillé lately."

"I must go there this weekend. It's impossible to stay here, not knowing why she left—without an explanation."

"I understand, you two seemed to be hitting it off so well. I've never seen her this happy and can't understand why she left without a word."

Art drank his glass of wine, not noticing if it was red or white. It tasted bland and dull, just like he felt.

The rest of the workweek crawled by. Saturday seemed five weeks away, instead of only five days. When the day came, Art was ready. The car's tank was full, and he had studied the map for the best route to Écueillé. It wasn't far, but he had learned the hard way about French roads. He would arrive at a fork with signs pointing in opposite directions for the same destination which had sent him in circles more than once.

"It depends on which road you want to take. There are bigger, faster ones or meandering, sometimes dirt ones that will take you all around the area. You may end up where you want, or not," Yvette had said and seemed quite pleased with this explanation. Art found it confounding. One time, he had ended up right back at the original sign. This time, he was sure he had figured out the best route.

First thing Saturday morning, he tucked the directions in his pocket and headed to the outskirts of Chateauroux. Arriving at the first fork, he was pretty sure he wanted to continue on the main road and not take the left. Next was the sign for a town, *Pellevoisin*, which, according to his plan, was the correct direction until he saw a sign for *Heugnes*. Wasn't that the town Yvette had said was close to Écueillé? Should he take it? Miles passed with no further signs or indications he was on the right road. He began to second guess himself and was about to turn around when he spotted the sign, Écueillé.

Winding around the village, he wondered what would be his next step. How would he find her and what would she say when she saw him? Would she be upset, or was she missing him as much as he was missing her?

He stopped at the train station—someone there should know her family.

"*Les Gauvains?*" The man pushed his beret back, shading his eyes to get a good look at this strange man visiting their small village. "Yes, of course. Madame Juliette lives right across the street, in the left half of that house," he said, waving his arm towards a white house with lime green shutters.

"Merci beaucoup."

Would he be able to follow through with his plan? Actually, his plan had only gone as far as finding Yvette. He hadn't an idea what to do next.

30

A knock at the door interrupted Yvette in the middle of cutting potatoes.

"Mama, can you get that? I suppose it's Mr. LeGrand dropping off some eggs or perhaps your friend, Brigitte, with the most recent town gossip."

She went back to the potatoes, pretending not to have a care in the world, humming an Edith Piaf tune. That only flooded her mind with memories of him and the phonograph player. She felt his arms come from behind, encircling her waist, to swoop her around the apartment. A smile crept across her lips, followed by a tear she quickly wiped away with the back of her hand.

A familiar voice spoke to her mother at the door in a stilted, hesitant French. It had that characteristic American accent, sending a spark up her spine. She had tried to quell any hopes he would come to find her, protecting herself from the disappointment. But here he was. Wiping her hands off on her apron, she hurried towards the door.

His face lit up when she approached and she spotted that wry smile she loved. Looking down at her feet, unsure what to say, her mother broke the silence.

"It's so nice to meet you. Let me fix you both something to drink. Take him out back, honey. It's a lovely afternoon."

Yvette parted the multicolored plastic slats separating the kitchen from the garden. She led him past the beds where her mother's favorite flowers, begonias, and impatiens would soon emerge, over to a sunny spot in the back of the garden. Sitting on the bench surrounded by bunches of strawberry plants was reminiscent of the last day with Didier on a similar park bench. Would this turn out to be the last time she would see Art? Dread filled the long moments of awkward silence until, finally, he turned on his hip to face her.

"I was dumbstruck by your letter. Did I do something wrong? Was I mistaken to think things were going well?"

"I don't know. I didn't want you to feel trapped."

"Trapped? Why would I feel trapped? Your letter said we were over." Art looked perplexed at her comment.

"I didn't know where we were going or if we had a future together. I've been afraid to bring it up and put you on the spot." Yvette dropped her head down and began fussing with her skirt. *Should I tell him I'm pregnant? And how? What if he runs out?*

"It's my fault, I should have said something. I guess I was afraid to scare you off. We're quite the pair, aren't we?"

They both laughed a nervous chuckle, which was followed by another awkward pause as each waited for the other to say something.

She was relieved to see her mother coming with a tray.

"I made some fresh lemonade and here are a few crackers to nibble. The weather's perfect today, isn't it?"

"Yes. And you have a beautiful garden." Art stood to take the tray, placing it down next to Yvette.

"It's nothing compared to the large place my husband and I had before the war. I couldn't afford the rent after he died."

She said it matter-of-factly. Yvette knew she felt fortunate her children had survived and were living close to one another. What would her mother do if she moved away? It was amazing how she had raised five children on her own, never complaining. Even after ten years, she still donned the traditional widow's attire of a dark dress, black stockings, and flat black canvas shoes. The only splash of color came from a muted purple and gray apron. Widows in France dressed in somber colors for the rest of their lives, as if mourning was required until the end of their time.

"I'm making beefsteak for dinner. You'll be staying, won't you?"

"*Oui, oui.* That's perfect, thank you." Art looked at Yvette and she nodded.

After her mother left, Art sat back down, close to Yvette, and took her hands, his face resolute as he stared into her eyes. "I realized some time ago I was falling in love with you."

Yvette's heart skipped a beat, swallowing to quell the sensation back down. "You've never said that to me. I didn't know... I—I didn't think."

"Shhh." He pressed his finger to her lips and continued. "Vevette, it's my fault. I've been wanting to say something for a while, but I was too stupid to ask. I want to spend the rest of my life with you if you'll have me."

"Yes, oh my yes. We both do."

"Both?"

"Hmm, yes... I'm going to have your child." *There, she had said it.*

"Oh my gosh!" he exclaimed, jumping up.

He paced up and down the garden until he walked back to her and knelt by her feet, placing his hands on her knees. "That's good. It's okay, we'll figure this out. We'll get married here and you'll come home with me to the U.S."

"I was unsure what you'd think, what you'd want. That's why I ran off. It was silly, I know. This is such a big step. Me, to leave my home to start our family in the U.S."

"Oh, boy." Art stood back up and started pacing again in front of her. "Yes, this is big, big news. My mother will be excited and I'm not sure in a good way. It's okay, you'll see. She'll love you—after a while. I wasn't sure how to tell you about my family. Falling in love with you, I needed you to understand my background. I didn't know if you'd want to leave your home." Art's French was choppy, but she understood his sentiment.

Yvette was worried about his family and friends. There were rumors of what people thought about "war" brides. She wasn't like that, wouldn't they see? Was she ready for such a big step? And with a child? She didn't speak English. And to leave her mother, the woman who was her anchor, her foundation.

"It's settled then. Let's go tell your mother. I can't wait to get to know her and the rest of your family." Art stood and took her hand.

Yvette had no doubts everyone would love him. Now if only she was that confident about his side. Their child would be a mix. How would Americans accept that? What did he mean when he said his mother would be excited, but not in a good way?

They went back into the kitchen to tell her mother, who was delighted, just as Yvette thought.

"We must celebrate!" She ran down to the cellar, returning with her arms full of bottles. First, they started with a sparkling Vouvray to toast, followed by a red to complement the dinner. Afterward, they topped it off with her cousin's famous *eau de vie*. Art was looking pretty rosy again, but her mother didn't seem to notice. She took Yvette aside and whispered in her ear.

"Your crow has returned for you. This is a lucky omen."

"What do you mean, Mama?" Yvette glanced across the room to Art, who was admiring the plates of Loire Valley castles mounted on the wall.

"Why, look at his sleek, black hair—and his name is Arthur! Remember your crow you nursed during the war? He has come back. It can't be a coincidence, it's fate. How perfect! Tomorrow, we'll go see your brother and sisters. The whole town will know by the afternoon, I'm sure," her mother said.

Yvette smiled. She hadn't made the connection to her beloved crow all those years ago, but leave it to the superstitions of the older generation. Who knows, maybe it was a sign. He *had* come back for her.

Their relatives made up most of the town, Renée and Pierre, with their four children, plus what seemed to be an endless number of cousins settled in and around Écueillé. News traveled fast in this little town. It frightened her to leave the only home she knew. She loved her family, this Berrichon region, and the country she had fought so hard to protect. She wasn't sure if the churning in her gut was excitement, remorse, or the baby. To go to such a foreign place, completely dependent on Art. What would it be like in Seattle?

31

FEBRUARY 1952

A rt's mind flooded with thoughts of having a wife and
baby. How complicated his life had suddenly become. He
had entered the weekend a happy-go-lucky *(well, okay, not so
happy)* single bachelor, to a man with the responsibility of a
wife and child.

Foremost, how to break the news to his mother? What
was she going to say? He should have warned her a few
months ago, mentioning he was seeing a French woman, to
break her in slowly to the idea. Instead, he would announce
the upcoming marriage and instant grandchild. He could stay
in France, but no, that was a silly idea. He had a good job
waiting for him and he loved Seattle and the close-knit
Japanese community. The history they shared from the
eviction and incarceration, the service in the 442nd, and the
struggles upon their return home. It had forged a relationship
unlike any other. There was no other option than to return to
Seattle.

What were the logistics to bring a wife into the U.S.?
There must be hundreds of things to do. Nothing in his life had
prepared him for such an endeavor. Getting married was
supposed to be a delight, but being alone in a foreign country
complicated everything one thousandfold. He would make a

list. That always put things in perspective for him.

First stop, the Air Force administration office—they would know what steps to take, so on Monday morning he swung into the office on base.

"You're taking the plunge," the man behind the desk said. Art stared at his bulbous nose, wondering if French wine was the source of this distention. The veins spreading across his cheeks formed an interesting map, all the roads meeting on the mountain of a nose in the center of his face. There were even creeks of sweat trickling down his forehead, which he kept wiping with a handkerchief.

"Ahem," the man cleared his throat to get Art's attention.

"Oh, right. Ha ha, I guess so."

"Well, first off, you will need to complete form AFR 37-11 in triplicate."

The man used his feet to slide his metal chair with a difficulty that amused Art. The portly man refused to stand, forcing the wooden wheels to squeak over to a gray file cabinet. Pulling open the third drawer, he flipped through the files, pulling out a folder marked 'Marriage.'

"You'll need certified copies of both parties' birth certificates, medical exams to prove you both are of sound mind and body, proof your fiancée has never been charged with a crime, a sworn affidavit by each of you regarding birth, nationality, prior marriages, and the purpose of the marriage. Plus, you need to prove you have lawful employment, what the salary will be, and if it's a temporary or permanent position. If you still want to marry after completing all these forms—remember, in triplicate—then you're a better man than me."

"That doesn't sound so bad." Art was relieved the military had everything laid out. If there was anything he could do, it was follow orders, especially when they were in tidy lists like these. He had more concerns about getting the Catholic Church to bless this union. When he told Yvette's mother he was Protestant, he saw an expression of concern creep across her face.

"Oh dear. You'll need permission from the Pope in Rome to allow the marriage in the church. And you must be married in a Catholic church," Yvette's mother said.

"Yes, definitely in the church." Yvette nodded.

Art didn't have an opinion either way, but it was apparent Yvette and her family did. They also agreed that time was of the essence.

"We should pick a date," Art said.

"I think within the next month or so."

"How about March 15th?" *That's tax day so I'll never forget my anniversary!* Art thought he was being clever.

So Art worked on the military end of the marriage, and Yvette set out to discuss matters with the local priest in Chateauroux.

His next step was to write to Mrs. Gilner, the secretary at Butterworths, asking her to put together the needed documentation.

Dear Mrs. Gilner,

It's been awhile since I have written. And here's the happy reason. Next month, bachelor Art signs a contract for life with Yvette (photo enclosed).

I need to complete the multitudinous papers necessary to prove that I was born, that Yvette was born, that we are married, that we have a place to go and that I can support her after we get there.

In this last item, I shall need your help. On my form, I-133, for the American Embassy, it requests a notarized certificate from my employer showing:

    1)   Nature of employment

    2)   Salary paid

    3)   How long employed

    4)   Whether the position is temporary or *permanent*

    NOTE: In duplicate

    It will be a tough haul, I know, but the harder one works for anything, the more you appreciate it. That's the way I look at it—I am open to advice and comments.

    You'll all meet her when we get home later this year.

    That's "30." Regards to the gang.

                Love,

                Art

With that, he sent his first letter announcing his engagement. It was a breeze to send a couple more to his buddies back home, Tosh and Tom. So much for the easy part. Now how to tell his mother? She had the firm belief of keeping the Japanese race pure, which was ironic since Caucasians had similar judgements. Hadn't people realized that one's merit should be based on their actions and character and not on race alone? Humans had much more in common than not and he had met the best of the best and the worst of the worse across all races. Having had the U.S. Caucasians judge them severely, it was unfair for the Japanese to turn the tables and judge Yvette. But it was unlikely his mother would agree with that logic. If there was anything he had learned, it was racism had deep-set roots.

Art thought it might be best to send it via a telegram, short and quick and to the point.

Mom(stop) I'm getting married March 15 (stop) Can't wait for you to meet her (stop)

That sounded terrible. Plus, telegrams almost always delivered bad news. And this may, no, it *would* be bad news to her. He had better figure out a way to wrap the news up in such a stunning manner that anyone would be thrilled. He thought back to his English teacher, Mrs. McKenzie. How would she put these words on paper?

Dear Mother,

My time here in France has been difficult. I've missed home and your wonderful cooking. The days have dragged on. Work fills many hours, but the evenings are lonely. You know how much I love to dance, so I did find solace in a small hall in town. And there, I met a lovely young woman. We are to be married and I hope for your blessing.

I know you will worry about me. How can I think of being with someone not Japanese? What about the culture, the food, the customs, and most importantly, if we have children? Please don't concern yourself with these things. I know what I'm doing.

I am very fond of her. I am sure you will love her too.

Your son,

Art

That wasn't such a tough task. The harder part was placing it in an envelope and sending it off in the post. Once that was done, all he could do was sit down with his head in his hands.

32

Classified as a mixed marriage, the Catholic church did not favor it. Again, Art faced prejudice, this time because of his religion and not his race. Discrimination was threatening to prevent their union. Though it was refreshing that it had nothing to do with his race.

The Catholic church wanted to ensure that Yvette was free to practice her religion and that any offspring was baptized and educated in the Catholic faith. Art had to promise not to cause any obstacles to this mandate. That seemed simple enough, Yvette would take care of that end of the business. There were Catholic churches in Seattle for her to attend, even if he'd never actually seen her go to church.

"I wasn't sure you were a particular religion. Don't Catholics need to go to church?" Art had asked. Maybe he was naive but was certain weekly attendance at Mass was recommended if not required, at least in the U.S.

"Why yes, I'm Catholic. We aren't strict about going to church here. I attend the important events, you know—Easter, Christmas, funerals, and of course, weddings." She flashed her coy smile his way, making him grin.

They convinced the priest they were serious. Next, he needed to write the Pope in Rome for authorization of the marriage. It would take four to six weeks to get the approval from the Pope. With the date set, they hoped the blessing would come in time.

Only a week was left—they were under the wire. Even the priest seemed anxious.

"Has anything arrived from Rome?" Art asked on one of his daily visits.

"I've been checking the mail twice a day for the letter from the Vatican," the priest said. "Nothing so far. We may need to postpone or cancel the wedding if he denies the request."

With the announcement placed in the local paper, *The Nouvelle Republique,* and the invitations sent, they were down to the wire. Everyone was getting nervous. A church marriage couldn't take place without final authorization from the highest voice.

"At least we can have the civil wedding, right?" Art asked Yvette.

"I suppose, but it won't be the same. I've always dreamed of a church wedding." Yvette's voice was deflated.

"We still have a week. I'm sure we'll get the approval."

As the week passed, a few congratulatory cards came from Art's buddies, but nothing from his home. This was an extra worry for Art. How was his mother taking the news? He hoped his sisters had consoled her. It would be a blow for her only son to marry without her consent. He was certain she was upset. If only someone else had done this before, broken the mold, so to speak. He was the first in his circle of friends, if not all of Seattle, to marry outside of their race. These obstacles kept interfering in the joining of him and Yvette— his race, her race, his not being Catholic—what else would try to block this marriage? He wouldn't allow the challenges to bring him down, deciding to focus on something more uplifting, like where they would spend their honeymoon.

Art had fond memories of Nice and the French Riviera. The hotel that his battalion had frequented during the war would be perfect. He remembered how wonderful the family who owned the hotel had treated him and the enjoyable memories of their little daughter, Jeannette. He smiled, recalling the afternoons spent along the beach practicing French with her. The way they teased back and forth while alternating between his French and her English. She must be grown up now. He looked forward to introducing them to Yvette.

Since he had to write the letter in French, he would need help. Writing in a foreign language was more problematic than speaking to him. His letter had to be polite and succinct. How to request a room for them to spend their first few days as newlyweds, without seeming as if he was asking for any favors. There wasn't anywhere more perfect than the beaches along the Mediterranean for their honeymoon—and to catch up with old friends. He would engage the help of Martine in their next class to ensure the letter was perfect.

The week ended on a high note. The priest had received final approval from the Pope and not a moment too soon. Everyone breathed a sigh of relief. Yvette would get her church wedding after all.

Art was on cloud nine. Everything was falling into place. Now for the letter to his long-time friends in Nice. He showed up at 6 pm for his French session with Martine. Before he had the chance to discuss the letter, she had a generous proposition for him.

"You'll need a family to represent you at the marriage. I spoke to my parents and it would be their honor to stand in as your parents."

"I hadn't thought of that. What a touching offer. Please tell them yes and thank them."

Art had forgotten about witnesses and sponsors. He had visited Martine's home a few times and met her parents. They would be perfect. He had found a sense of home here in Chateauroux. Now if only news would come from his mother. What could she be thinking, and why hadn't he heard anything from her or his sisters?

33

MARCH 15TH, 1952

The day of the wedding didn't actually dawn—it was a grey, misty morning with intermittent showers predicted.

"In France, they have a saying, a rainy wedding day means a sunny marriage," Yvette said while peering out her apartment window.

Art propped himself on his elbows, still laying in bed, deep in thought about his mother back home. He'd always tried to be the dutiful son, supporting the family in every way possible to weather the challenges they'd faced over the years. She would have to understand this decision he had made. Looking at Yvette, he couldn't imagine a person less like the image his mother would want him to marry. He had to think of the big picture and how things happen for a reason. Finding his bride here in France must be part of the grand plan. For the moment, he was concerned if this was going to turn out well. Envisioning the treatment they both would receive kept gnawing at him.

First, Yvette wouldn't have a stellar reception from his family or friends. No one ever dated, much less married outside of their Japanese community. He hadn't known how to prepare her for this. Instead, he had avoided the topic, afraid it might scare her away. It seemed better to meet it head-on once in Seattle. The second issue was the acceptance of the Japanese by the Caucasians. Racist feelings against them were still laced through the community. The influence was more subtle, from refusal of service in certain businesses to housing covenants restricting them to living in only a few neighborhoods. It was going to be a double whammy for her. Thank goodness she was a strong woman. They would worry about those issues when and if necessary.

She throws one of her coquettish smiles over her shoulder, drawing him back to the present and he focuses on the upcoming events. Nothing would ruin today for either of them. They each had two weeks off of their respective jobs and a great post wedding trip planned.

"The weather will be sunny and warm in Nice," Art said, stretching his arms overhead as he stood up. "I'll be ready in a jiffy, my suit's laid out and my shoes are shined."

Yvette stood before him in a new navy blue suit. She had borrowed a white hat and gloves, both old. The superstition of something old, something new, something borrowed, and something blue was satisfied. He realized as they headed to the hired cab; he had forgotten to put the penny in her shoe. *Wonder what punishment that forecasts?* Guilt about his mother crept over him. He tried to push it out of his mind.

They mounted into the back seat of the cab Art had rented for the day. The driver looked dapper in his cap, which he had cocked off to one side of his head. His thick mustache curled up on the ends as he smiled while holding the door open for them.

"You've picked a perfect day for a marriage. The rain will wash away the sad times of your past and bring the good fortune of many children," the driver said.

We're off to a good start with one on the way already.

Art winked at Yvette, but she was too busy smoothing out her skirt to pay any attention.

"You're handsome in your black suit. Here, let me fix your tie." Yvette reached over the seat to fuss with his tie and lapel.

The car jostled them around in the back seat as it traveled over the old cobblestone roads. They held each other's hand and laughed, bouncing against the old seat springs that had lost its protective padding years ago. The driver, oblivious to the bumpy journey, continued to fly down the road. Out the window, Art noted the familiar sites where he had courted Yvette.

"Look, there's the Tivoli bar where we had our first dance," he said.

The car dashed down the street and swerved around the corner.

"There's the café. We've had lots of good meals there," Yvette added.

"And see Fernande's house? Thank goodness she encouraged me to find you in Écueillé after you disappeared."

Deep in reflection, he admired his soon to be wife, wondering what the future had in store for them and whether their marriage could survive the upcoming stormy seas.

Martine, her parents, and Yvette's mother were waiting for them at the city hall for the civil ceremony. It was a simple process of signing a few papers and then onward to St. André. The cab screeched up to the church, sending them both tumbling forward. Art helped reattach Yvette's hat while the driver ran from side to side, opening doors, gallantly bowing while they exited.

As Art stepped out of the car, the beautiful church took his breath away. It was a stunning example of Gothic architecture, reminding him of a smaller version of the Notre

Dame in Paris. Similar to its larger cousin, St. André had a rosette of stained glass above the main door, and on either side were two towering steeples that seemed to reach toward the heavens.

As he followed Yvette up the stairs to the grand doors, a powerful sensation stopped him in his tracks. It was like someone was holding him back. He looked around. It felt so real, but there wasn't a soul. Could it be the guilt built up from his shame? After all, his mother and sisters should be sharing this monumental day with him. They had suffered through so many things together as a family over the years. They should be part of this important day as well. Everything had happened so fast, a whirlwind of changes since he'd arrived in France.

Yvette was looking back at him, a perplexed look on her face. Nodding at her, he tried to shake the worry and release the pressure on his chest. He shrugged and dropped his shoulders. He stumbled up the first step, took a deep breath, and continued.

Glancing above the church door was a statue of Jesus, with angels on either side. They seemed to smile down, as if to say, *Don't worry*. The clouds had parted, and the sun was peeking through, causing the raindrops to sparkle on the stone facade of the church walls. Art wasn't a religious man, but he felt a surge of warmth and a trust that everything was going to be fine. Confident in his actions, he climbed the few remaining stairs to join Yvette.

She wasn't sure what he was thinking, why he had hesitated. Maybe they shared the same worries. The day was getting brighter, but she still had underlying concerns festering deep inside. Her love for him was sincere and strong, like no other she had known. Would it be enough to survive their vast differences? Leaving her home to go to a foreign land was frightening, though everyone had told her how lucky she was.

"The roads are paved in gold and opportunities are endless," said one woman at the tobacco factory.

"Maybe not paved in gold, but at least not old cobblestone, bumpy ones like ours. And I hear they have indoor plumbing with hot water even," another one added.

"Sure, but it's another country, far from my family and friends." Yvette was concerned, thinking of the distance and difficulties of being halfway across the world.

"It's the chance of a lifetime. Grab and run with it, I say," they said almost in unison.

"I suppose you're right," she surmised, not totally convinced. Her wish to see another land and travel outside of her small enclave was materializing. She hoped it would work out.

"Of course we are. You'll see."

There was no turning back now. Art joined her on the top step. Any appearance of previous doubt was gone from his face, replaced with a warm glow. This filled her with a sense of assurance. She held her head high, knowing that yes, their love would get them through anything. Together, they entered the church, side by side, both walking with certitude. They turned briefly for photographs by the news reporter. Their marriage was the first to occur between a CHAD serviceman and a local French girl. It was the talk of the town.

Art relaxed once alongside Yvette. The sun shone through the stained glass, illuminating the attendees seated in the pews. On one side of the aisle were fellow members of Art's squadron and on the other, Yvette's family. In addition, there was a spattering of French locals, curious to see a wedding between a French girl and an average American Joe. Art sensed the absence of his family and friends. They would have filled well over half the church. There was no time to dwell on his misgivings and he turned to face the priest, a gentle, soft-spoken man who seemed satisfied with their union. Art wasn't sure if the priest knew Yvette was carrying his child, though he had seemed eager to help them set the date as early as possible.

The priest ushered them past the main altar into the vestry, where the marriage was to take place. Yet another complication of Art being Protestant and not Catholic. They couldn't marry in the sanctuary directly in front of the main altar. This didn't upset Yvette or her family. It seemed enough that it was by a priest and at least under the roof of a Catholic church. They stood before the priest, Yvette's mother by her side and Martine's mother alongside Art, standing in for his mother. The ceremony was brief and all in French. He followed most of it, saying *"Oui, je le veux,"* Yes, I do, at the appropriate times.

Kissing his new bride, he gazed into the emerald eyes that had lured him in on their first encounter. They locked arms and headed down the aisle to the reception line, where they were met with well wishes, a barrage of cheek kisses and handshakes. Even the locals that neither Art nor Yvette knew joined in on the congratulatory line. The bells of the church were ringing a splendid melodious chorus to declare the marriage to the entire town. It was impossible not to feel elated at this moment. Art's worries floated away with the resounding harmonies playing up to the heavens.

Yvette's cousin announced the continuation of festivities at Rosy's Restaurant and Bar. There would be champagne, hors-d'oeuvres, and the traditional *piece montée,* the equivalent of a French wedding cake. It was more like a towering pile of cream puffs stacked into a cone, but did have a tasty type of caramel syrup swirled over it. Art thought sushi would have been perfect if he could have found some. Nothing of the sort to be found in this small town, so a typical French wedding it was.

Following the reception, they had tickets to board the train southbound to Nice, taking most of the night with a few changes of trains. Once they arrived, it would be rest and relaxation on the Riviera.

Art and Yvette stood at the top of the church stairs with arms entwined, ready to close the chapter on his return to France. Rice showered down over them as they headed down the church stairs. Their taxi awaited to sweep them off to Rosy's. Before entering the cab, Yvette turned and flung the bouquet. Odette, standing front center, giggled and leapt sideways to catch the flowers. Yvette shook her hat as Art picked rice out of her hair.

The cab drove a precarious route to the bar, giving the newlyweds time to reflect on their future. By the time they arrived, everyone had started in the festivities. Dancing had commenced to the tunes of the accordion player. When they walked in the door, the crowd parted and clapped their hands for the couple to lead in a dance. The one-man band began a fox trot.

Art lifted Yvette's right hand and swept his other hand around her petite waist. There was that familiar connection he recalled from their first dance, their bodies moving together in perfect unison. He knew they would face missteps and run into obstacles, but together, they were entering the dance of their lifetime.

EPILOGUE

Seated at the head of the table, Art leaned back in his chair, relishing this moment with his family. Sitting to the left was his sister Grace, who Art rarely called Chibi any longer, her three children, and their families. To the right sat Yvette, their two daughters, and spouses. Grace's husband had passed away many years before, as well as Art's other sister and parents. Grace's daughter, Noreen, had taken over the tradition of inviting family for the New Year's Day celebration. His mouth watered in anticipation of the array of sweets that lay before him. Would he start with the chocolate mousse cake or the cream puffs?

It filled him with satisfaction and gratitude, realizing how far the Japanese American community had come. Life had turned out much better than he ever imagined possible when he was a young man. The outward discrimination against them had receded over the years, though there was still an underlying prejudice. Nothing as blatant as before or right after the war, but he still caught a scowling glance or overheard a racial slur muttered under the breath. He had worried his girls would suffer, as they were a mixed race of Japanese and Caucasian, but that hadn't occurred to his knowledge. Isn't this why his generation had fought so fervently during WWII? That everyone would look upon them as Americans and not divide them into different classes. It had been hard, but as his parents had been Buddhist, there was never a complaint.

"Accept everything as it comes. It's important to live in this moment and not dwell on what could or should have been," his father would remind him. So when Yvette suffered a brain aneurysm five years ago, Art took it with stride. He was grateful it hadn't happened when she was younger and the children were small. There was always a silver lining if one looked hard enough.

The stroke had taken away her ability to speak and robbed her of coordination between her thoughts and movements—something the doctors called apraxia. In addition, she had lost partial use of her right side. Nothing was wrong with her mind, allowing them to still share many good times. She understood everything, and her memory was stellar, which complimented his slightly diminishing recollections. There wasn't anything wrong with his memory. It was just becoming short, sometimes very short.

Art did notice one positive change in Yvette. She had developed an appreciation for a favorite of his past times— watching golf. Now they spent long afternoons planted in front of the TV, exclaiming admiration as Tiger Woods hit another birdie. She never would have done that prior to the aneurysm. *"I've too many things to do than sit around, watching people chase little white balls around lawns."*

Now the extent of her communication was yes, no, and I don't know. This left him the chore of asking question after question until he determined what she was trying to say. Many people spoke of how unfair this was to happen to them but he made the best of it. If there was anything he was keenly aware of, it was that life was not fair.

Noreen had picked a fine choice of traditional Hawaiian music to play on the stereo for him, which was the icing on the cake. Vivid memories of fighting alongside the 100th Battalion during WWII flooded his mind. It wasn't often he thought of his service in the 442nd Regiment. He closed his eyes, allowing the music to bring back visions of the soldiers playing their ukuleles and singing to break the tension between battles. It had taken some time for the "mainlanders" to learn the pidgin English the Hawaiians of the 100th spoke, and to adapt to their casual ways. Once they had bonded, there was no breaking the kinship and their fighting record reflected the strength of the regiment.

After finishing his plethora of desserts, his daughter drove them home to West Seattle. "I'll be back on Wednesday." She kissed each of them on their cheeks, a French tradition her mother had passed on to her.

The next day, Art was still craving more sweets. That was his downfall, making it near impossible to keep his blood sugar regulated, though the pills the doctor prescribed helped. He headed down to Krispy Kreme for a few donuts to go with his coffee.

Later that evening, he heard a commotion in the garage. *Darn, I bet those raccoons are back eating the cat food.*

He tiptoed downstairs to avoid awakening Yvette. Sure enough, a raccoon was gorging on the kibble as fast as it could. Looking up at him, its eyes peeked out from behind its black mask, like a bandit, waiting to dash off with all the cat's food.

Art grabbed a broom and tried to chase the animal toward the pet door. He ran around the car a few times, swinging the broom to no avail. A deep pull in his chest froze him in space and he fell against the car, his arms limp as he slid down to the cold ground, darkness penetrating his vision.

He wasn't sure how long he had laid there, but enough time had passed to worry Yvette. Somehow she had descended the stairs into the garage and was rubbing his shoulder, murmuring to him in her limited manner.

"Yes, yes. Oh my, no!" she whispered. He was glad to see she was wearing her coat, as the garage was cold. It was clear to Art he had suffered a heart attack. It wasn't his first, but he felt this was his last. His legs were limp and motionless, like when he got hit with the shrapnel in Italy, but tonight his arms wouldn't move either. Trying to lift his head, nothing responded. He wasn't sure how he knew he was dying, but he was certain of it. He was slipping away and there was nothing left to do.

"Stay with me, don't go."

Yvette knelt, using her left arm to bring herself alongside his motionless body. Art became weaker and didn't have the strength to speak. He thought back over his life, how this woman had brought his dreams to reality. She had left her country to be with a man and a culture unfamiliar to her. At first, the Japanese community didn't welcome her, being Caucasian. Little by little, his friends and family brought her into their close-knit group. She never seemed to stand out to him with her beautiful blond curls. He saw past her race, as he had wanted others to look beyond his. It had been a long journey for the two of them. He was fading and tried to reach out to her one last time, but his body was motionless. Then he felt a sudden release as if he were floating, free of physical limitations, free to reach out to her.

Yvette lay against her husband, aware her worst nightmare was happening. She was losing him—her rock, her everything. He had found her struggling in post-war France when she had nothing left but her pride. He had rescued her and brought her to the United States. Their love had held them together through the difficulties. The racism they met was overwhelming. Not only did the Japanese dislike her, but the Caucasians looked down on their mixed marriage. Even after his service in the U.S. Army, he couldn't buy a house in West Seattle. No, the housing covenants restricted them to living in a few areas in Central Seattle, which came as a shock to Yvette. Prejudice like this didn't exist in her small village in France. In spite of it, they built a home and life on Beacon Hill near many wonderful people and she had found a good job in a school lunchroom. How she loved working with those adolescent kids, a mixed bag of races as well, making it a perfect place for herself and their daughters.

After retirement, the restricted housing covenants had all but disappeared and they returned to within a few miles of Art's birthplace. By the 1980s, Americans were pleased to have "Japs" living next door. That word still cut into her.

Yes, with Art, she lived a life she never would have, had she remained in France. They returned often to visit her family there, yet her life was more fulfilled in America. Everything changed after her aneurysm. At first confused, she didn't understand why her body wouldn't move when she commanded it. And when she opened her mouth, volumes of conversation should have spewed out but instead, only a few yes's and no's were uttered. He stayed by her side, never complaining about their newfound lifestyle, caring for her, unlike anything she could have imagined. He cooked for her, massaged her paralyzed arm and hand, caressing each finger to relieve the painful restrictions, and took her out for many visits with friends. The worst part was when she soiled herself. It was exasperating and embarrassing since she had always been so clean. But he would wash her without a complaint. It shouldn't have surprised her. He was a man of his word, of true moral character.

What will I do without him? He's been my world, and now he's getting cold, fading away. The cement floor of the garage was unforgiving as she curled up, as best she could against his body, not wanting to leave him. She lay there until the morning, speaking without words, hoping his spirit was listening.

I can feel you with me, your hand caressing against my cheek, and your lips murmuring, "Vevette, je t'aime, mon amour."

She smiled as tears fell down her cheeks.

AUTHOR'S NOTE

My parents' early lives were the motivation to write this historical fiction. My father wrote memoirs at the beginning of WWII, but neither finished nor spoke of them. I found the writings after his death. The letters from Butch were tucked in these notes, and I added them to the novel without making any changes. Unfortunately, I could not follow up on their relationship, but she was clearly a significant presence for him during the war.

My mother didn't talk much about the war years either. Her family did speak of her father, Maurice's, involvement in the French Resistance and how they harbored the Jewish couple, the Wolffs. The town dedicated a road in honor of his heroism near the site where he was killed by the Nazis. Sadly, the Wolffs never reunited with their daughter.

As I grew older, I wanted to understand the experiences that defined both of my parents. This novel is the result of my research.

The events in this book are based on actual people and events, though I changed many elements and added fictional characters to support the story line. I spent years delving into old letters and military books, traveled to areas in France to interview relatives and to visit battle areas of my father's regiment.

My mother Yvette was too young to be involved in the Resistance, but I added a few years to her age to highlight the essential role of women fighting in the war. And the romance with Didier was invented to document the tragedy at l'Oradour. I also created a few soldiers basing their characters on actual soldiers. However, some names of soldiers were retained to honor their actions during the war (Capt. Robert Shorey, Pfc. William K. Nakamura, Cpl. Yosh Aoyama, T/Sgt. Uetaro Sanmonji, Col. Miller, Col. Pursall, and Pfc. Sadao Munemori).

But a relative of Yvette did deliver supplies on her bicycle to the Maquis hiding in a camp near Heugnes and Yvette rescued a crow she named Arthur during the war. When she met my father, with his sleek black hair and sharing the same name, her family was convinced her crow had returned.

Cecile Pearl Witherington (Alias Pauline) who was stationed near Valençay, played an important role in the war. France awarded her the Legion of Honor and parachute flight wings for her brave service to their country.

After the war, the story follows the lives of Art and Yvette closely. Her best friend Odette and her cousins Fernande and Fernand lived in Chateauroux. Yvette worked in a tobacco factory and met Art at the Tivoli. Dancing was an important part of their lives. I added minor events I imagined could have happened, to complete a story only known to them.

I hope this story will help bring to light the importance of treating everyone with kindness and equanimity.

I used many books over the years to complete this novel. I've listed them in case anyone has an interest in pursuing these topics further.

Bodin, Léon. *Les Journées Tragiques d'Ecueillé.* Arrault et Cie. Tours, 1948.

Cornioley, Pearl Witherington. *Code Name Pauline.* Chicago Review Press, 2015.

Hosokawa, Chester. *NISEI — The Quiet Americans.* William Morrow and Co, Inc. 1969.

Ito, Kazuo. Translated by Shinichiro Nakamura and Jean S. Gerard. *ISSEI — A history of Japanese Immigrants in North America.* Japan Publications, Inc. 1973.

Kanazawa, Tooru Joe. *Close Support — A History of the Cannon Company of the 442nd Regimental Combat Team.* Cannon Company, 442nd RCT, 1993.

Moulin, Pierre. *U.S. Samurais in Bruyeres.* Editions Gérard Louis, Vagney, France, 1988.

Multiple Military Handbooks: *The Story of the 442nd Combat Team, The Story of the 34th Infantry Division, With the 92nd Infantry Division.* Information and Education Section, Mtousa, unknown publication dates.

Nicault, Maurice. *Resistance et Liberation de l'Indre, les insurgés.* Royer, C.C.B. 2003.

Ousby, Ian. *Occupation — The Ordeal of France 1940-1944.* St. Martin's Press, 1998.

Pauchou, Guy and Dr. Pierre Masfrand. *Oradour-sur-Glane Vision D'Épouvante*. Charles-Lavauzelle et Cie, 1970.

Schrager, Adam. *The Principled Politician - Governor Ralph Carr*. Fulcrum Publishing, 2009.

Shirey, Orville C. *Americans The Story of the 442nd Combat Team*. Infantry Journal Press, 1946.

Steidl, Franz. *Lost Battalions: Going for Broke in the Vosges*. Presidio Press, 1997.

Tanaka, Chester. *Go For Broke: a pictorial history of the 100th/442nd Regimental Combat Team*. Presidio Press, 1982.

CHRISTINE SUSUMI is a Seattle native and is Art and Yvette's youngest daughter. Susumi still lives in the Seattle area with her husband and a multitude of pets. She is a graduate of Washington State University School of Veterinary Medicine. This is her first novel.

Printed in the USA
CPSIA information can be obtained
at www.ICGtesting.com
CBHW052158201024
16153CB00013B/962